When I'm With YOU

A Hope Town novel

HARPER SLOAN

When I'm With You
Copyright © 2016 by E.S. Harper

ISBN 13 – 978-1530728602
ISBN 10 - 1530728606

Cover Design : Sommer Stein with Perfect Pear Creative Covers
Cover Photography : Perrywinkle Photography
Editing : Jenny Sims with www.editing4indies.com &
Ellie with Lovenbooks.com
Formatting by Champagne Formats

To Contact Harper:

Email: Authorharpersloan@gmail.com

Website: www.authorharpersloan.com

Facebook: www.facebook.com/harpersloanbooks

Other Books by Harper Sloan:

Corps Security Series:

Axel

Cage

Beck

Uncaged

Cooper

Locke

Hope Town Series:

Unexpected Fate

Bleeding Love

Standalones:

Perfectly Imperfect

Disclaimer:

This book is not suitable for younger readers. There is strong language and adult situations.

Playlist:

"Hollow" by Tori Kelly

"In Case You Didn't Know" by Brett Young

"Hold Back the River" by James Bay

"Ride" by SoMo

"Reverse Cowgirl" by T-Pain

"Sleep without You" by Brett Young

"Oh, Tonight" by Josh Abbott Band

"Talking Body" by Tove Lo

"Stitches" by Shawn Mendes

"T-Shirt" by Thomas Rhett

"PILLOWTALK" by Zayn

"Pony" by Ginuwine

"Wasn't That Drunk" by Josh Abbott Band

"Anywhere" by 112

"SexyBack" by Justin Timberlake

"Rock Your Body" by Justin Timberlake

"Lollipop" by Framing Henley

"Turn Down for What" by DJ Snake

"History" by One Direction

To follow the *When I'm with You* playlist: https://open.spo-tify.com/user/1293550968/playlist/1Cca7XUYvNUWxoeK-29n7Aj

Dedication

To Felicia Lynn.

Everyone should have a weird best friend like you in his or her lives.

Well, not *you* because you are mine and I don't share.

They should also have the right to refuse cuddles when said best friend breaks the 5.2 second skin contact rule and/or that best friend has proven themselves to be quite handsie when sleeping.

(Spoiler alert : I'm talking about you, Felicia!)

I'm pretty sure no one will ever love me as fiercely as you do or support me as brilliantly as you do. I've been one hell of a lucky chick to have you by my side day in and day out.

Plus, no one could spend hours and hours sitting together writing, never speaking a word, and even a writing session feeling as if we had just spent every second of those hours talking about any and every thing.

Best friend. Best writing partner. Best don't-touch-me sleeping buddy.

Best YOU.

I love your weird ass.

Also…Nate Reid is yours.

Prologue

Ember

GRADUATION NIGHT

"I LOVE YOU," I WHISPER, MY voice coming out in a weak wheeze.

Holy crap, I can't believe I just said that. It has to be the beer. Or as my best friend, Nikki, calls it—liquid courage.

I force my hands to stop twisting the bottom of my sundress and look up at the man before me. Not a boy, no … he is all man.

His green eyes, the ones that always make me think of sunrises and dew-covered grass, are wide with shock. The thick lips I've spent way too much time dreaming about are parted in shock.

In all the time I've put into thinking about this moment, I never thought that shock would be present. I've built this moment up to be perfect in my head. Nothing but innocent dreams and naïve wishes clouded this moment because of course shock is what I should have expected. But no, all I've longed to hear when it came to me admitting my feelings for him are much deeper than 'just friends' is him repeating those three words right back to me.

Oh, God ... what have I done? He doesn't feel the same. I mean I was so sure ... so stupidly sure that he felt the same. That he saw me as more than a friend.

Thick panic fills me, and I know before my mouth even starts moving that I'm about to nervously ramble a string of verbal vomit that I'm powerless to stop. It never fails when I'm uncomfortable; the words come and come until I'm stopped or I slam a hand over my mouth.

Sure enough, the words rush past my dry lips as I silently scream inside my head for the earth to open up and swallow me whole. You know when the voice in your head takes over so loudly that you can't even hear the crazy nonsense that is coming out of your mouth anymore.

"I mean ... I'm in love with you. You know I love you, of course, you're like one of my best friends, but I'm *in* love with *you.* I wasn't going to say anything; in fact, maybe I shouldn't have. I didn't ... I mean I don't want this to mess things up between us. I would probably die if that happened. Well, not die, die ... but I would probably feel close to death emotionally. I just wanted you ... no, I needed you to know how I feel." I finally get my mouth to stop moving long enough to take a deep breath. I feel my heart speed up and force myself to continue to hold his gaze. "Please say I didn't just screw up big time?"

"Em," he starts before clearing his throat. His voice is thick and deeper than normal. The plangent tones vibrating from his chest wrap around my senses, and I shiver. "Ember, where is this coming from?"

I blink. Actually, I'm pretty sure if there were such a thing as slow-motion blinking, I would be doing that right now.

How could I have been so wrong?

"It's just … I'm making a huge mess of things, aren't I? God, I'm so stupid."

I'm not normally a crier. Then again, I'm also not normally a drinker. I've had a few mixed drinks with Nikki this past summer, but for some reason, I decided I needed to take up the art of drinking for courage. Of course, with my luck, I would end up being one of those people who get overemotional when drinking. My sister, Maddi, warned me about those annoying girls when she brought the beer over tonight.

My nose prickles with what feels like a thousand needles being pushed through the bridge. I can feel that thick bubble of emotion crawling and scraping up my throat, and I know I'm just seconds away from my eyes tearing up. I take a huge gulp of air, and it rushes out in a wobbled wave of emotion.

His normally carefree expression is nowhere to be seen. His eyes look troubled and his mouth pursed, making his lips look like two thin lines. When he moves from where he had been leaning against the porch railing, my gaze follows him closely as he takes a seat next to me on the swing. He lifts his arm and places it on my shoulders, pulling me into his stronghold. I go willingly, but I stiffen when my body encounters the heat of his.

The hardness of his muscles starts a slow burn in my gut. I

couldn't explain the feeling, but I've felt it for the last four months.

It started with a crush from afar. Then my crush turned into a pact with Nikki to try to get him to notice me. It was time. So I did what I needed to do, and for the last few months, he's been helping me get my stupid calculus grade up.

We've always been 'friends.' With a makeshift family like we have, it would have been impossible not to be. But I've always been the baby of the group and getting the man I've crushed on to notice me always seemed impossible. That is until he started coming around twice a week, every week, for the last few months. During that time, our friendship grew stronger, naturally, because we had more time with just the two of us. Well, I guess we were never alone since we could always hear my parents from where we studied in the basement.

Many people don't take Nate seriously. Mainly due to his carefree, jokester persona, but also because he has never flaunted the fact he's insanely smart. Which he probably should—maybe then I wouldn't have had to convince my dad he was the best person to help me get my grades up.

Regardless of how it happened, my crush bloomed like a well-watered flower. During my tutoring, we shared lots of laughter and teasing moments. A few times, I even caught him just looking at me in silence. Little things added up in my head until I was sure this moment was worth the leap.

Clearly, I was mistaken. I thought things would be different, that this would be different, for us. But this *something different* is nothing like I had dreamed it would be.

"Em," he says softly, breaking me from my thoughts. "You

know I love you, but I don't love you like that. We've known each other forever, and you know I would do anything for you, but I love you as a friend. What you're saying, suggesting, would change a lot more than our friendship."

Oh, God. There it is.

"I'm sorry." I sigh, feeling every second of those mistaken dreams about some big love between us crumble around me.

"There's no need to be sorry, firecracker." I close my eyes when he says the nickname he had given me. "We've spent a lot of time together lately; it's normal to get some wires crossed when you're around someone so often. Maybe when you're a little older, you'll understand better."

My eyes pop open, and I turn sharply. My body jerks, and I'm seconds away from jumping from the bench seat and pacing. His arm falls off my shoulders and hits the back of the swing. "When I'm a little older?"

His brow furrows; clearly, my Jekyll and Hyde move has confused him. I went from sullen to pissed off in two point five seconds. Like a firecracker. He always said my temper would light up and take off like an out of control firecracker, thus the reason for the nickname.

"Uh … yeah?"

"I'm eighteen. I'm not a two-year-old who doesn't know right from wrong."

He nods. "I know how old you are, Emberlyn."

"I'm old enough to know my own feelings, Nathaniel." He's never liked being called his full name—but neither have I—something we both are clearly using against each other in the heat of the moment.

"Jesus," he mumbles.

His eyes leave mine when he stands and starts to pace in front of me on the porch. The music I hadn't even noticed being so loud before vibrates through the wall of my parents' house, but thankfully, the large group of my friends and other random kids from our graduating class have stayed inside during this conversation.

I force myself to watch him. His large body moves in choppy agitation and annoyed steps, so different from his normal fluid movements. He's always moved in a way that looked almost like he floated. His large body always moves with a graceful silence that reminded me of a ballet dancer. Which in turn would cause me to giggle uncontrollably because just thinking of the manly man in front of me in tights is too much to imagine.

"You *just* turned eighteen, Em. Just. Turned. You might not understand what I'm saying, but dammit, you don't even understand what you're saying. It's a crush. That's it. All I'm saying is that you're going to be able to make sense of that better when you're older. Not to mention, I'm six years older than you are. Six years is a huge deal. Not just to everyone else, but our families would shit themselves. Not to mention, what your dad would do? Do you even have any idea what people would say?"

"I'm not a baby," I snap, at a loss of what else to say, as I ease back down onto the swing's seat.

He stops his pacing and turns to face me. One hand pushes through his thick dark hair in frustration. I watch in fascination as his overly long hair moves in a thick wave before falling back into the mess it's always been since he decided to start growing it out. When he stops, his hand rests at the base of his skull and the end of his hair falls over a few fingers.

Finally, his words reach my lust-filled brain and a new burst of anger fills me. Making me feel even more the fool.

"I'm not a baby!" I repeat on a yell into the still night, my voice shrill, and I cringe at the emotional hit his words cause me.

"I didn't say you were. You just don't understand what you're saying."

"I assure you, I do."

He shakes his head, his hand still resting on the back of his neck. I notice briefly that his grip has tightened to the point of his fingertips turning white. When he starts to move forward, closing the distance from where he's standing and where I'm perched at the edge of the swing's seat, I jerk back, making the chains holding the swing up rattle loudly. He narrows his eyes and lets out a long breath. Dropping to his knees in front of me, he pulls my hands from their death grip on the wood next to my bare thighs. He doesn't speak for the longest time, and I foolishly let that flicker of hope light, thinking he must have realized he's wrong.

"I'm sorry, Em, but I don't feel that way toward you. I don't want to hurt you or lose your friendship. You might hate me for it, but we just can't be what you're saying. You loving me would do nothing but cause your heart ruin."

"You're wrong." I force the words past that damned lump in my throat.

"I'm not," he says softly, a sad smile ghosting over his lips, gone just as quickly as it appeared. "We're friends and always will be. One day, you'll see that."

Pulling my hands from his, I instantly miss the warmth of his skin as I stand and move around him. He doesn't move from his crouched position, nor does he turn to look when I move around him.

"I know what I feel, and you're going to be the one who has some grand understanding one day when you realize what you're denying. Sure, I might be young, but I'm not a baby and I know what I feel. I also know that you're using our families as an excuse. Especially my father because he also knows that I'm smart enough to know my own feelings and follow my heart. I thought you were someone different, Nate, I really did. I ..." I sigh deeply, the one sound full of so much emotion. "You know what? Just forget I even said anything. We can chalk it up to me having some foolish, *childish*, drunk admission. After all, I'm just a kid ... what do I know?"

It takes every ounce of strength I can muster to turn and walk away from him. Leaving pieces of my heart smashed on the deck at his feet while he just sits there and lets me go. The tiny sliver of my heart that had held on praying he would change his mind and stop me dies and joins the rest of the pieces on the ground.

Unfortunately for me, I'm so lost in my own pity party that I miss it. I walk away without knowing that the second my back was turned, he had silently moved, jumping to his feet. One arm started to reach out to me, only to drop heavily at his side after I moved out of his reach. I was so blinded by my own heart breaking that I missed the visible pain on his face as he felt the same pain with each step I took away from him.

Had I looked back, even stopped for just one second, maybe I would have heard his whisper, but instead, his words just floated away with my dying hope.

"I love you, too, Ember."

Chapter 1

Nate

I PRESS MY FOREHEAD AGAINST THE wall, ignoring the bite against my fevered skin. My lips dance across the shoulder held captive between the hard surface and my body, as my head spins faster from the amount of alcohol I consumed tonight. With each pass my hands make over the silky smooth skin underneath my fingertips, I trail more wet kisses and bites across her neck. The rasped breath that escapes from the mouth pressed close to my ear only fuels the desire raging through my body.

Fuck. Have I ever been this powerless against the need to take someone?

Blindly moving my hands down the slim torso, my fingers dig in when I hit her hips, giving her a firm squeeze in warning before I pull her body closer to mine. Her legs wrap around my hips easily as her dress rides up and my dick instantly finds a home. Or the warm home he wants to go inside of, that is.

Fuck. I can feel how wet she is, the thin barrier of her underwear doing nothing to shield that from me.

I'm drunk enough to know I should stop, but even though the rational thought keeps crossing over the intoxicated waves rolling in my head, I would never be able to step away from this feeling. I justify that decision with the mental reminder that I'm not *that* drunk.

Drunk or not, even I have a few reservations about taking her when I don't even know her name. I might have been fucking my way through life the last few years, but even I have some morals.

The smell, taste, and *feel* of her are like nothing I've ever felt before. If I weren't already flying on a beer high, I would swear it was this little firecracker doing it to me.

Firecracker.

Even with another woman warm and willingly wrapped around my body, the vision of Emberlyn Locke hits me hard with just that one word. It's been years, years of fantasies and forbidden desire, and it never changes. I try my hardest to shake the image that is holding my mind hostage, using my body's desires for the willing woman in my arms to try to replace it as I move against her.

"Take me," she whispers on a moan when I thrust my hips harder against her pliant body.

I know from experience that now that I see *her* in my mind, I'll never be able to see the reality in front of me, so I'm not sure why I'm even trying so hard. This chick is just another faceless woman who will wear the mask of Ember's face. Like many before her have.

I push my cock rougher against her while reaching behind me for my wallet, hoping I remembered to stuff a condom in there earlier. She loosens her grip on my hips as I struggle to free the damn thing, and I feel one of her legs drop from my body. The sounds of music and people enjoying themselves float in the air around us, reminding me that I need to hurry this along before someone finds us. The last thing I need to get caught doing at my sister's wedding reception is fucking some chick.

Her hands roam all over my body as I make quick work of protecting myself, touching every inch she can reach. I go to lift my mouth from her neck, but she just tightens her grip on my neck, not allowing me to leave the spot I've been feasting on for the last ten minutes. If she's so dead set on me not looking at her, that's all the green light I need to hurry this along.

Finally, I grab the leg that dropped from me with a firm hold against her smooth thigh while pushing her back against the wall a little harder in order to stabilize our bodies. With one of her legs tight around my back, the other being held in my hand, I reach my free hand between us and curl my fingers into the crotch of her lace panties. In one powerful jerk, they're on the ground at our feet.

Turning my mouth from her neck, I bite the skin under her ear before lifting my rock hard cock from her body, feeling like my balls are about to fall off they're so tight. "Going to fuck you now. Fuck you so goddamn hard, babe."

"Oh, God," I hear, just barely, over the heavy panting coming from the two of us. Her voice so low I almost miss her next word.

"Finally."

I laugh, the sound coming out more animalistic now that I have her wet heat kissing the tip of my cock. "Yeah, babe … finally. I wish I could wait to get you somewhere more accommodating, but I'll make it worth it." Remembering my earlier thoughts, I rush out the next words in a hiss as I start to push inside her. "Tell me your name, babe," I ask, moaning loudly when the tip of my cock enters her and is surrounded by the tight, scorching wet heat of her cunt. I might be an ass, but I'll, at least, let her think I care about who I'm fucking by recalling to ask her what her fucking name is.

Her legs lock and her body goes from soft and pliable to rock hard instantly. Confusion makes me pause in my movements, not pushing any farther into her tight as fuck little body. I can feel sweat beading on my forehead. I've never fucked a woman who felt this good around me, and I'm only an inch inside her snug pussy. The painful gasp that comes from her makes me jerk my head up from where I had been nibbling from the back of her ear down to her shoulder. I knew I should have waited until I could get her off this wall before fucking her.

With a gasp, I open my eyes for the first time. Confusion holds me in its grip for a beat before I realize I had been dreaming. *What the fuck?* The same one had haunted my dreams for longer than I care to admit and it never fails. I wake up with my cock hard, seconds away from coming, but never getting past that one fucking moment.

I search through the darkness of my room as I try to grab hold of the dredges of the dream that I never get to see the end of. No matter how hard I try, I never see her. I never get anything past that breathy gasp. Well, that's a lie ... I did get a bed of my own come once when I decided just the thought of that tight cunt was worth letting a load out.

"Goddamn," I bark, the sound echoing off the empty room around me.

Lifting off the mattress, I toss back the covers and move to stand. My whole body is alive with the dream that never seems to leave. The location changes, as it always has over the years, but lately, it's been the same.

Me taking a woman I mask as Ember in some drunken haze fuck against the side of my parents' house during my sister's wedding reception. The hell if I can remember when it turned into that, though. I only recently started picturing and hearing the sounds of everyone partying around us.

The dreams started shortly after her graduation party, but they have never, not once, felt this real. Reaching down as I walk, I wrap my hand around my balls, feeling for the wetness that had been falling from her body in my dream, only to come up empty. Well, not fucking empty since I can feel just how real my mind thought that dream was.

Walking through my bedroom, I keep my hand on my balls as the discomfort from each step I take seems to hit me right between the legs. A painful reminder my cock needs attention now.

As I walk past my open bedroom door, I'm thankful that I live alone now. Not bothering with the light, I walk into the bathroom, opening the glass door of the shower, and turn the water on. I don't wait for the water to heat; I don't even feel the cold blast when I step in and under the spray. I'm too busy still trying to continue the dream.

With a sigh of resignation, I realize it's a fruitless endeavor even to try. Might as well give me a memory I would love to have had a chance at making a reality. My hand goes for the body wash as my mind brings up the most recent picture of Ember in my mind. Squeezing blindly, I fill my palm before soaping up my body, trailing my hand down my abs before moving back to my balls. I give them a little attention before my fist wraps around my painfully hard cock, stroking slowly as the vision fills my mind like a motion picture.

She hasn't changed much in almost three years. Her small body, big tits, and face that would tempt a saint have only matured. She was beautiful at eighteen, but now, just shy of twenty-one, she's breathtaking.

The last time I saw her feels like a lifetime ago, but it was maybe six or so months ago standing outside my parents' house during one of the monthly dinners we all have. Our parents have been a tight-knit group of friends since way before we were all born, and ever since they started adding kids to the group, monthly dinners have become a must for all to attend.

Everyone was there that night since it was her father's birthday. Thinking back, that was probably the only reason she was there, since she's made it a point to make herself scarce. Even before that night, she hadn't come but every other or so month.

The vision of her fills my mind, and I moan deep in my throat when the hand not busy with my cock rubs over my hard nipples; twisting the metal piercing through them causes the hard cock in my hand to jerk.

She'd pulled her dark auburn hair back in a high ponytail that day, highlighting her long neck. I remember wondering what it would be like to wrap her thick, long hair around my fist as I took her from behind with just that hold on her hair. She never took off her sunglasses, which, at the time, pissed me off because I could always tell what she was thinking with one look in those dark brown eyes. She kept herself distant from me, which also pissed me the fuck off, but I remember a breeze bringing the intoxicating scent of her to my nostrils.

Lemon and wildflowers.

Licking my lips, I stroke myself a little faster and let my mind continue with the thoughts of her.

I watched her all night; the vision in my mind as clear as it was that day. Every step she took highlighted every tan inch of her bare legs in her cut-off shorts as she walked around the back-yard. Her legs, long and toned despite the fact that she's so short, moved gracefully with each step. But that's when I stop thinking about that night. Instead, I use that vision of her as a mold to place her in the dream that had woke me up. Now, in my dream, she's wrapping those legs around my body as I finally feel what the reality of fucking her is like.

I have to reach out to stabilize myself at the thought and I place one palm against the cool tile in front of me before dropping my head and feeling the water run down my back. My breathing speeds up until grunts of pleasure start to fall from my open mouth. I tighten my fist and work the straining flesh with a renewed fervor as thoughts of me taking Ember overwhelm me.

"Ah, fuuuuck," I moan, moving quickly so that my back takes the place of where my palm had just rested against the tile. The bite of the cold against my skin doesn't even register because the second my body is stable and braced against the wall, I bring my other hand down to join the one frantically pumping the top half of my cock. I squeeze my balls before moving up to fist the bottom of my cock as I tighten the hold I have over the tip, using both hands as I begin to fuck my tightly clamped fists, pretending with each thrust that I'm taking her.

My arms burn as I continue to fuck myself, my cock getting even harder under my wet hands until my orgasm rips through me. The thick jets of my come shoot forward, falling with the steady stream of the shower, as I ride out my pleasure.

My legs start to shake with the force of my orgasm, and I almost lose my footing. Releasing the firm hold I have on myself, my cock falls, still heavy with leftover desire, against my body.

I hate this feeling. No matter how great the pleasure my body gets from picturing her, I always feel empty after. A big giant reminder I'll never know what having her feels like. Like it or not, this is all I'll ever have. A hollow pit inside me that I've only ever felt was filling up when her smiles came at me without pause. A pit that's taken up residence inside me since the night she admitted to having the same feelings I've been feeling for a long time. Fighting with myself, I evaded the magnitude of fear those feelings brought with them.

"Fuck, it's going to be a long day," I say to the emptiness around me, stopping myself from continuing the depressing thoughts rolling through my mind.

I finish showering before I get out and start to get ready for the day, unable to shake the feeling of loneliness that I've had plaguing me lately.

Chapter 2

Nate

AFTER MY MIDDLE OF THE night shower, I had given up any hopes of returning to sleep. If I was honest with myself, it was more about self-preservation than actually not being able to sleep. I worried I would be haunted with more thoughts of Ember in my arms, and I just don't have the energy to deal with that shit right now.

Three hours later, just when the clock in my truck's dash turns over to seven in the morning, I'm pulling into the parking lot of the security business my dad owns with some of his old Marine buddies. No matter who you ask, they all say Corps Security was what brought all of our families together. I think after the parents of our group started having us kids, there was always a hope that we would all, in some way, join the business. Unfortunately, like our parents, we had our own dreams and many of them didn't include anything CS related.

Cohen Cage, my best friend and brother-in-law, started working here after he left the Marines himself, right before he married my sister, Dani. He followed his own father's footsteps into the 'family business,' which was probably the catalysis for my dad's desire to get me here.

Cohen's dad, Greg, was one of the men my dad had served with before they both joined the two security businesses they separately owned to form CS. My dad brought along John 'Beck' Beckett and Zeke Cooper when he moved to Georgia from California. Uncle Zeke passed away a few years later, but now, his brother, Asher, works for CS. Ember's dad, Maddox Locke, was also part of their brotherhood and the man I currently work side by side with.

I respect the hell out of my dad and the men who work here, but I'll never be the man he wants me to be. I've been here for about a year and a half, but it wasn't until six months ago when I finally put my foot down and told them it wasn't for me. It only took one long-as-fuck stakeout with him before I realized watching cheating spouses will never be something I want for my future. Sure, they do a lot of other shit, but none of the cloak-and-dagger shit will ever be for me. Nah, not me. I've just been biding my time until I could do what I really wanted.

The second my dad realized how much I hated just about every aspect of CS, he decided to put my computer knowledge to work, and I've been doing the IT shit that no one but Maddox has ever been able to do since. Of course, when you can hack into just about anything, even Maddox couldn't keep up with me. It's never been more than a hobby out of boredom, or stinginess to get free porn. No matter how much fun I find the challenge of a good hack, the last thing I want is to spend my hours locked inside some dark room staring at computer screens. The plus side, though, is that the pay is ridiculous, and because of my time here, I was finally able to save enough to start living my own dream. So for the last six months that I've been working here, I've gone down to part time. Eventually, I'll be too busy for even that and only come in when they need my skills for a special case.

Unlocking the front door, I walk through the doors of CS. I look over at the picture of my Uncle Coop front and center when you walk in before moving to disarm the security system. The lights flick on after I punch the codes into the high-tech monitor. It takes a few seconds of my fingers flying over the screen to re-arm the system and make sure the screen registers me as 'in,' so the alarms don't start blaring the second I move farther into the building. With a sigh, I walk around the empty reception desk to the thick closed door that separates the lobby from the offices. I press my thumb on the panel, waiting for the multiple locks to disengage as they recognize me before pushing the heavy door open. I repeat the same process when I get to my 'office' door; only, this time, I tip my head up and look into the camera above the door as it registers my facial imprint before disengaging the door lock and allowing me to walk into the dungeon. Or IT central, rather, but dungeon fits.

Not a single window exists in here and they painted the walls black for a reason I will never fucking understand. Being that it houses about twenty computers and enough technical crap to give the biggest nerd a wet dream, the air in here is kept cold as shit to prevent anything from overheating.

We monitor numerous residential and business properties around the clock, so this room is always humming, but since we don't currently have any active cases that require constant monitoring, things have been quiet in here. I hate when we get those cases. Maddox and I tend to switch off duty with a few other guys since it becomes tedious to stare at that shit for hours on end.

I move around the hub in the middle of the room that houses the bulk of our monitors and slide into my chair. My desk is pushed up against Maddox's, forming a square of sorts in the back corner of the room. It's easier this way, and our own personal computer monitors are designed so that, when we need to, we are able to swing them around to face the other person when another eye is needed. It's easy enough for me to get lost in my coding, surfing the dark corners of the internet looking for all the things that people think they've hidden forever. However, when he's sitting in his chair, I always feel like he's studying me more than he's studying his own monitors.

Secretly, I don't mind his dark looks or attitude since his frustration usually warrants it. I'm usually easily fifteen steps ahead of him on cases he's been stumbling through for days. Normally, anyone at the receiving end of his death glares would probably shit themselves but not me. No, I love it because while he focuses on being pissed at me, I can focus on things he doesn't need to notice me taking in. Sitting on the left side of his desk, butted up to the wall and turned slightly so I have it perfectly in my line of sight when I jot something down, is a picture of his girls.

Maddi and Ember.

But I only have eyes for Ember.

I do my best to ignore the taunting frame to my right as I quickly power on the computer. I grab the file I had been working on yesterday before I closed up, and it doesn't take long before I lose track of the things around me. I'm finally able to let go of the tense feelings I've been carrying around all morning.

I had been working steady for an hour or so when I hear the steady beep of the security system, alerting me to someone else showing up for the day, but I've been so close to closing this case that I don't budge. They'll see me show up on the security panel when they shut that shit off. I designed that brilliant system, knocking the old shit Maddox had installed out of the water. The iPad-size panel I had fiddled with when I came in the doors this morning not only works for the boring alarm functions of arming and disarming, but this one also keeps a running tally of the bodies in the whole office.

After an incident that ended with the death of Uncle Coop, they had installed some safeguards. But none of them had made this place as secure as my program. Now, you need to go through a few steps just to get in the front door when no one is manning the desk, but also, thumbprint and facial recognition is needed once you get deeper into the bowels of the building.

Which brought me to my favorite feature of the system. The second you step foot in the front door, the system recognizes you by a series of body and facial scans, leaving a small icon of your face on the bottom of the screen. It's helpful for everyone at CS to know who is in the building at all times. New clients sometimes act like they have a giant stick up their ass when we require them to be put into the system, but it beats the alarm going off all day during consultations because it doesn't recognize someone who's been past the main lobby longer than the registered safe period, which it's designed to do for our well-being.

"Son." I hear in the way of a greeting from the front of the dungeon.

"Morning to you, too, old man," I reply. I don't look away from the monitor, nor do I stop the rapid speed in which my fingers are dancing over the keys in front of me.

"Yeah, Nate, mornin'. Want to tell me why you're here, again, hours before any other of these sorry bastards even got out of bed?"

I let out a laugh. "You know you're not just talking about yourself since I beat you here, but also the golden boy who shares a bed with your little princess?"

I don't need to look to know my dad has a scowl on his face. He still can't handle the fact that his little girl is grown up and married with two kids of her own. It's way too much fun to remind him just how his grandsons got here.

Just the thought of Owen and Evan is enough to lighten a little of the dark mood that has followed me around since the dream that woke me up way too fucking early this morning.

"Don't be a punk, Nate."

I laugh, making sure to write down where I was in my coding before I drop the pen next to my log sheet and turn to where my father is now sulking.

"What's up?"

"Not what's up with me, Nate. What's up with you?"

"Yeah, not following you. Old age making you go nuts already?" I lift my hand and point at the top of my head. "A lot more gray in there these days. You're starting to lose the whole salt and pepper look and become more salt only."

He shakes his head, not falling for my taunt, and pushes off where he had been leaning against one of the large floor-to-ceiling columns that hold our storage drive systems, or what I like to call 'mother ships.' He might ignore it, but I watch as he rubs a hand over his head while pulling one of the chairs around the hub monitors. I bite back the laugh as the few streaks of gray shine in the light of my computer screen when he pulls his seat toward my desk, settling his six-foot-six frame down with a grunt. I have to force my silence when the urge to take a jab at his struggled grunt when he sat hits my mind.

"Your mother is worried. When she's worried, she isn't happy. And, Nate, I hate it when she isn't happy."

And … there went the playful mood.

"Why do you automatically assume that I'm the reason she is worried?"

"Because she's been like this since she found out you've been working yourself to the ground here, showing up before the sun, and then staying at that club until who knows when at night."

At the mention of *that club,* I feel my temper rise. It doesn't help that he still can't seem to mask his disapproval when it comes up. It's been a constant fight between my father and me since I bought *that club*.

"I'm fine. It's taking longer to finish the renovations, which is the only reason I'm there late. I don't know why she's worried.

I'm a grown man, Dad."

He laughs, his deep booming chuckles breaking through the silence harshly. "Grown in age, maybe."

I flip him off, brushing off how annoyed I get when people assume that I'm not mature simply because I enjoy joking around. Especially since I've done nothing to substantiate that assumption. Sure, I like having fun and living the kind of life where laughter comes easy, but that doesn't mean I don't have a brain in my head.

He slaps my hand away, still laughing. "She won't ever stop worrying about you, son, and a mother knows when her kids are hurting."

Not liking how serious this little chat has turned, I can feel my hackles rising. "Well, this kid is just fine. Just stressed with getting everything finished over at *that club*," I snap.

"Nathaniel," he starts, and I take a deep breath so I don't blow up on him. One thing I've learned the hard way is no one blows up on Axel Reid without being burned in the process.

"Honestly, Dad, I'm fine. Stressed a little, but that's normal since I'm in the middle of trying to get shit finished with Dirty Dog, you know *that club,* and keep up with shit here. I promised you when I bought the place that I would stay on here so you wouldn't feel the weight of my absence. I'm allowed to feel stretched a little thin."

"You wouldn't feel that way if you wouldn't have bought that place."

"With all due respect, I'm trying really hard to remember you're my parent and that you're coming from a good place. I'm old enough to know what I want with my life. Too old to sit on my ass and not go after what I want, and what I want doesn't involve me sitting in this room for the rest of my life."

He's silent, his green eyes bright, while he processes his words. Finally, he lets out a long breath. "I'm sorry, Nate. It's just hard for me not to be concerned that you're throwing away a fuck load of money on that place. Club Carnal's been closed for a long time and that place needed a lot more work than what it's worth. I just hate to think that you're setting yourself up for failure."

"Well, shit. Once again, thanks for the vote of confidence."

"I don't mean it like that, Nate. I'm just worried. You've been so closemouthed about this whole club thing. This is new for us, and we're allowed to be concerned. Your sister always had a clear path, no guessing games, so we're just trying to figure it out with you."

"Did you think that maybe that's because I've been looking forward to showing it off a little? Fuck! This is getting so old; the constant assumption that I'm going to fuck it all up because I'm not as driven as Dani."

"That's not what I mean, and you know it."

I do, which sucks, but I can't help but get pissed that we always seem to have this fight. "I'm sorry. What can I tell you so that you can stop worrying that I'm going to go off the deep end and end up homeless?"

"Don't be a smartass."

Throwing my hands up, I lean back in my chair and scowl at him, measuring my words so that maybe, hopefully, he will get it. "How's this," I start. "I've saved up enough money to buy the old club outright as well as the two units that were on either side. I've been able to get all of the renovations finished on the budget that I set, without having to get a loan, and I did that by being hands-on and doing most of the work myself. My business plan is solid. Regardless of the fact that I didn't actually finish school to get my degree, I did remember the shit I learned. I've already hired a complete staff as well as worked out a plan to ensure that if I don't start turning an immediate profit, I'll be fine. I have entertainment booked so far in advance I could sit on my ass and drink at the bar instead of actually work once I open. All permits and licenses are in my possession and the interest for opening night was so heavy that I've had to sell tickets, and those sold out in four minutes and sixteen seconds. You think that's enough to stop worrying about me? I'm already in the black on Dirty Dog and the doors aren't even open."

I know I've shocked him because, by the time I finish talking, his mouth is wide open. Yeah, guess there wasn't too much faith in his little boy, after all.

"You're in the black?"

Taking another calming breath, I relax in my seat. "I've saved every dime I've ever gotten or made for almost twenty-eight years. Aside from buying my truck and the house, I haven't touched a dime. Further, when my trust was released, I didn't touch that either. Instead, I invested all of that and it grew. It grew a lot. Everything I've ever had or made has been building for this, Dad. Just because I didn't talk about my future dreams like Dani didn't mean I didn't have them."

He doesn't speak, but I can see the pride in his eyes. As good as it is to finally see, it's annoying that I had to prove myself in order to have it.

"I'm not sure what to say, son."

"How about start with I'm sorry and end with how you're going to let Mom know she can stop losing sleep."

"Smartass." He laughs, easing some of the tension in the room. "I'm sorry, Nate. I worry about you just as your mom does, and that's never going to change. We don't compare you to your sister, but it's hard for us not to have concerns when you two are traveling on completely different roads."

"One of these days, you're going to realize that I like being on my own road."

He laughs again. "You always have, son, always have."

Chapter 3

Nate

AFTER MY TALK WITH MY dad, I finished what I needed to on the case I was working there. It's a simple, well … not-so-simple hack and monitor of a large corporation out of Atlanta that suspects one of their chief financial operators to be laundering money. Tedious but easy, since the owner had given me full access to their secure network, camera systems, as well as the cameras in the CFO's penthouse paid for by the company. It's taken me spending two months deep in cyberspace, but I've finally uncovered almost all of the fucker's dirty secrets.

Maddox hadn't come in by the time I finished up, and I needed to get over to Dirty Dog, so I saved my shit and left. I avoided stopping by my dad's office. Instead, I pulled out my phone to call Shane—my soon-to-be club manager—in order to be too busy to talk to anyone I passed.

"Headed to Dirty, want to meet me there?" I ask when he picks up.

"Already there." And he disconnects.

I laugh to myself and toss my phone over on the passenger seat of my truck before pulling myself in.

Shane's been a damn good friend since we met during my short attendance at the University of Georgia. I say short because I was more interested in partying than I was going to class. How we met was unconventional, at best, but he's been around for almost a decade and proven his loyalty to me more than once.

By the time I make the half-hour drive to what used to be Club Carnal, I'm about to come out of my skin with excitement about today. When I told my dad I had enough entertainment booked, I wasn't kidding, but a large part of that is because about seventy-five percent of that entertainment is in-house.

Dirty Dog is, in a sense, my play on Coyote Ugly. Only, because I know where the money is from experience, we won't have smoking hot chicks dancing on the bar. We've split the old club into two sections, which is the main reason I bought both surrounding units and knocked down some walls.

The entrance is on the side now, going into the first building on the side of the old club. When you walk in, there is now a large 'holding area.' Our hope is that we're so popular that there will always be a line, but by creating the holding area, no one will ever have to stand in the elements. It was a bitch getting that set up with fire codes and all, but we eventually decided that unit would stay intact with just a single black door added inside to lead to Dirty Dog. Our way of saying fuck you to building code and the fire marshal's rules; even if we're the most popular club in the southeast, the holding area will never fuck with the club's max out capacity since it's a large area in its own right.

Once through the door separating the two, you hit the sanctuary. In the center of the room is a large square bar with a thick wooden finish built to withhold the heavy bodies spotlighted throughout the night.

When I first decided to play off Coyote Ugly, Shane was the first to jump on board. All I told him was that we would have dudes dancing and not chicks. That was enough for him. When I told Cohen about it, his first assumption was that Shane was gay, but he couldn't be further from the truth.

It's simple really. Girls flock to clubs. Girls love seeing men who know how to work their bodies. When the girls get one look at the talent at Dirty, it won't be long until they're going to be rushing us. Any man with a brain would be able to look past anything when you basically guarantee massive amounts of horny women. Which, if everything goes as planned, will be the reason that we don't just succeed in having a successful club but we fly through the top of all the popular ones around.

I shouldn't have been shocked with Cohen's concerns about Dirty. Unlike my dad, he didn't voice them because he doubted me; he just couldn't see the big picture like I could. To him, he thought we would turn into a gay club with little success because we aren't exactly a town with a need for one. I wasn't going to let him know the reason why I was so sure we had this.

The idea for this place came to me back in college when it became crystal clear that sex, men dancing, and booze were all you needed to build an empire on a party life. No one knows about the six months I worked at a strip club out of pure boredom and a sex drive that was borderline sex addiction levels bad. Pussy just fell in my lap when I danced at the club in Athens.

Since Shane had spent the last five years stripping, continuing well after I left town, he knew more than anyone the untapped market I was about to break into. Women loved men. Plain and simple. They went stupid over half-naked ones, and when you threw in some carefully placed hip thrusts, well … you might as well be a fucking god.

And that's where Dirty Dog turned from just a small, fleeting dream to what is already turning out to be the next best thing to hit the South.

I pull up behind the bar and park next to Shane's BMW. The smile on my face grows as I walk from my truck and through the back of the building. I really should stop calling it a bar because this place is a monster too big for such a small word. We're so much more than just a bar. We're a nightclub formed with the bar atmosphere in mind. I guess the reason I always fall back on calling it 'the bar' is because each of the five bars that fill up the vast space work to form the whole basis to our appeal.

The old converted warehouse used to be on its last leg, but almost a year after buying it, the transformation is like night and day. The hallway that the back door feeds into leads to our storage units, coolers, and locker rooms for staff, as well as the large break room for some downtime between shifts. I even went as far as to add a gym so that the guys wouldn't have to keep paying for memberships elsewhere. After all, our bodies are the main attraction here.

The center of the main room for Dirty holds the central and biggest bar. Each side of the building has two smaller, but no less impressive, ones with a huge open area between all of them for dancing. One back corner holds the DJ booth, stage, and electrical area for all the music. Then you have the second-level VIP area that runs the whole length above the holding area. Two staircases lead to that level with ten separate VIP areas.

My office takes up the other side building, running half the length, and the other half houses the gym. The only thing you can see from where I'm standing in the main room is a wall of black windows that runs from each side flanked by stairs like on the VIP end. Under that area, we have one more bar in the center surrounded by multiple booths and such.

After taking in all that is Dirty Dog, I walk farther into the main room to find Shane talking to six of the bartenders I had hired. I give a nod to Travis and Garrett, the Hanks brothers who used to dance with Shane. Brent, Logan, and Matt are standing behind them, and I get the same greeting back from them.

Denton, the sixth to round out our main bartenders, is already on top of the bar with his shirt off, showing them what he wants them to do. He's taken on the role of resident dance coordinator, a job both Shane and myself were happy to pass on to him.

We lucked out picking up Denton. Not only does he have the look that will guarantee him being a crowd favorite with his background in modeling, but he also recently tried out for the show *So You Think You Can Dance*. He didn't make it to the very end, but he got far enough to be our own little celebrity here at Dirty.

"You plan on just standing there, Dent? Or are you going to show us how it's done?" I deadpan, only to laugh when he flips me off.

"Have you decided how you want the first showcase to go?" Shane asks when I drop down onto one of the barstools he had pulled over from one of the tables scattered around the room. I look the few feet that separate us from where Denton is now standing with his hands on his hips.

"Fuck yeah, I did," I say with a smile. Just thinking about the ingenious idea I had around not only the first spotlight, but also what will be the signature drink. "How do you feel about lollipops, gentlemen?" I ask.

"What the hell are you talking about, Nate?" Denton calls down before bending at the waist and sitting on the edge of the wooden bar top.

"Lollipops, how do you like them?" I ask, again.

Seven sets of eyes just blink at me, clearly not following my train of thought. Nothing new there.

"Fine." I sigh with fake exasperation. "How about I show you what I'm talking about?"

"Might be a good idea since you lost us when you started talking about candy," Shane jokes, earning a laugh from the others.

"Where is everyone else?" I ask, getting up and walking across the large open space toward the platform in the corner where the DJ booth and sound system are set up.

"All the girls are in the holding room finishing up their uniform fittings with Hilary. She was finishing up the last I went in there, though, so you should be good."

I give Shane a nod while looking through the extensive list of songs we have on our playlist software—another program I created. Finding the song I need, I set the timer before turning up the volume, making sure to engage all the speakers and subwoofers before making my way behind the main bar.

"Do me a favor, Trav, and go get the girls. Get off my bar, Dent."

I look up and see Shane's mouth form a smile knowing where I'm going with this. None of these guys, besides him, have ever seen me dance. I don't give a shit how big of a dancer Denton is, either. He's about to learn just how to make a girl melt in seconds.

Making sure I have what I need: coconut rum, clear apple juice, and one of the thousands of cotton candy flavor lollipops I ordered in bulk, it takes me no time to get the drink measured out, sugar around the rim, and the lollipop wrapper off. I check my watch to see how much time I have left before the song will start then drop the candy into the glass so just the stick is popping out and push it forward.

The girls start walking in just as I rest my hands on the bar top. A few of them are new faces that I haven't gotten to know as well as the others. I look over and let my gaze hit all twenty faces of our floor girls, stopping when I see the one that will work for what I need.

"Come here, Julie," I demand. One blond brow goes up, but she doesn't miss a beat, and just when she steps up to the bar, the first notes of Framing Henley's "Lollipop" blasts through the room. Some of the girls jump but not Julie. She takes the glass sitting on the bar, then pulls out the lollipop and lifts it to her red stained lips.

The second she finishes the last drop and places the lollipop into her mouth, I use both hands still resting on the bar to push my body up and leap onto the sleek wooden surface.

Then I get the reaction I want.

I have only a second to appreciate the way the uniform of choice—black shorts that might as well be a pair of those sexy boy short underwear chicks wear and a black corset—fits her body before looking around her to make sure I have everyone else's attention.

My eyes settle back on Julie just in time to see her own widen as she steps back slightly, wobbling on her tall-as-fuck blood-red heels, another Dirty Dog requirement.

I grab the bar that hangs down from the ceiling above the bar, parallel with each length of wood and pull myself up, using one of the rotating hooks to spin myself in a quick but powerful circle before slamming my feet back down on the wood.

She stands there as I lean down and take the stick from her red lips. Holding the stem to my crotch, I pull her from behind the neck until her lips are touching the wet candy. She gasps when I run the wet candy over her open mouth by thrusting and rolling my hips before I release her head and stick the lollipop back in her mouth. I give her a wink before I finish moving on top of the bar. Continuing to move my body with the heavy thumps of the music, I run my hands up my tee shirt, starting at the hem, and pull the fabric up until it's over my head and tossed to the floor at her feet.

I don't put my all into the dance, but regardless, before the song is over, there's no question in anyone's mind that had there been a woman up there with me, I would have been fucking her right there on the bar.

"Wow," she pants when the song ends and silence once again fills the room around our group.

"Thanks, ladies. What do you think of our spotlight dance and the new signature drink here at Dirty Dog?" I ask the room before jumping off the bar and letting my heart rate settle back to normal. They all give different variations of the same nod and breathy praise.

Just what I was hoping for.

"Well, I guess that's one way of doing it." Denton laughs.

"Someone's been practicing," Shane grunts, slapping me on my sweaty shoulder. "And here I thought you would have lost some of those moves over the years."

"Do you see this," I ask him while gesturing down my body. "No need to practice when you're working with perfection."

He rolls his eyes. I open my mouth to say something to the guys but stop when Julie walks into my space.

Rolling onto her toes so that she can get closer to my ear, she says, "Call me later?" She drops back down so that her heels are back against the concrete floor before giving me a devious smile. I should have known it was a mistake to bring her on; we hooked up once, a long fucking time ago, but now that she's working for me, it won't happen again.

I don't respond. Instead, I pick up my shirt and pull it back over my head.

"Opening night is Friday," I tell the room, instantly feeling the energy go from aroused to electric with excitement. "Has everyone got their schedules for the next month?"

"Went over those before they had their fitting with Hilary. We're set, no issues, and we've already gone over the girls' responsibilities for working the floor." Shane grabs a clipboard from behind the bar. "We've got these three ugly bastards working opening night and the next three nights after." He points at Travis, Garrett, and Denton before looking back at his paperwork. "After that, it's a rotation between them. Some nights all six, though, especially weekends, working the main bar. Then we have the other guys working the three other bars, but they won't be in until tomorrow."

I nod. I know without adding that he's made a note to have Denton fill them in on "Lollipop" before looking over to where the girls are standing. "You ladies ready for opening night?" They all smile and nod. "Things might be a little intense, but you're all aware of where the bouncers are stationed and there won't be a second when you girls aren't covered. But if you don't feel safe, find one of them or us and let it be known."

"And let's not forget that we're expecting close to five hundred bodies opening night. That's just ticket holders, so I'm sure we're going to have our share in the holding room. For those who aren't assigned the VIP area, don't forget to make the rounds out there, too. None of the VIP assigned girls should be handling anything but the people in your area up there. Everyone else remember—just because they're not in the hot zone and stuck out in the holding room doesn't mean they shouldn't have fun. Plus, allowing them to drink in there means they're going to be ready to party once they get in the door. They're carded before they even get that far, so no worries there." Shane looks over at me when he's done talking and we both get the same giddy-as-fuck smile on our faces.

"Most importantly, have fucking fun and remember we're the best of the fucking best," I boom. Everyone laughs, and with the excitement of opening night giving us all one hell of a high, I walk around the bar and start making enough of my go-to drinks for everyone. "Grab yourself a drink and let's toast to Dirty Dog!"

Chapter 4

Ember

"FAMILY DINNER," I HEAR MY sister bark through my phone, and I pull it away from my ear with her sharp tone. Bam, my five-year-old English mastiff, looks up from his bed in the corner but loses interest quickly. With a huff, he drops his big head back down. "That means the whole damn family, Em. What part of that is confusing to you? You've skipped the last eight! Eight months you haven't been there and don't think that hasn't gone unnoticed."

Dropping my brush into the water next to my canvas, I walk over to the couch in the corner and look out the window of my back room. When I moved out on my own, this room sold me on the small house. Huge picture windows cover every inch of the back wall, giving me a breathtaking view of the woods that surround my property. I've been here a year now, and I still get chills when I'm in my painting room.

"I'm busy," I tell her, which isn't a lie, just not the full truth. "And it wasn't eight. I came a few months back." Six actually, but who's counting.

"You're *always* busy. I know for a fact that you finished up the last piece you had to do for your exhibition next month, so don't give me that busy shit."

I sigh. "Just because I finished all of that doesn't mean I don't have other pieces that need my attention."

Maddi's humorless laugh comes through the line. "You could knock out any of your beautiful paintings in no time. What is going on with you? You've been like this for a while now."

I watch a bird fly around one of my birdfeeders before leaning back on the couch. "I'm just busy, Maddi." Bam's head settles on my leg, and I move my hand to scratch him behind his ears like he loves.

"Dad said if you aren't there, he's going to come toss you over his shoulder and force your ass to—and I quote—make time for your goddamn family."

"No doubt he will too." I laugh.

"Don't you know it," she responds, her tone less heated than just moments before.

"I'll be there, okay?"

"Perfect. Don't forget we have plans this weekend too!"

My brow furrows, and I try to remember what plans we could possibly have.

"What plans?"

"I swear, Emberlyn Locke! You're the only girl I know who couldn't care less that her twenty-first birthday is coming up. We have plans! All the girls. Even Dani's in. Her parents are watching the boys, and you had better believe she's ready to turn it up now that Evan's finally off the tit."

"You're so crass," I interrupt.

"No, I'm not. She's the one who said it. The second he hit six months and tried to take off her nip with his tooth, she was done. Off the tit, she said. Time to party, she threatened. So Cohen is all-in for a girls' night out getting his wife drunk off her ass because he says he will reap the benefits when she gets home."

"That should be interesting," I comment, not really listening to her.

"You bet your ass. She hasn't had a lick to drink since right after the honeymoon when she found out he knocked her up again. She might just be all the entertainment of the evening we need."

"Who else is coming? And what are we doing?" I ask, picking at some of the dog hair and lint on my leggings.

"Everyone," she responds but doesn't elaborate and doesn't answer my other question. That could mean so many things, but since I sadly don't have many friends outside of Nikki and the close-knit group of kids that make up our 'family,' I figure everyone isn't that big of a bunch. I know it's pointless to try to get my stubborn sister to spill the beans when she clearly doesn't want me to know the plans, so I just let it go.

"Sounds like a blast." I dryly sigh.

"Yup. I also heard from Dani that Nate's new club is opening this weekend. I can't wait to check it out! He hasn't said much, but just by the hype he's gaining on social media alone, it's supposed to be a club like no other."

At the mention of Nate, my throat closes and I forget about the lint picking.

Of course, she doesn't understand that Nate is the main reason I've been skipping our monthly family dinners at the Reid house, a tradition started before I was even born. No one knows that he's the reason I've backed away and now spend so much time focusing on my paintings that I eat, sleep, and breathe brushstrokes.

And humiliatingly enough, not even Nate seems to know what he did to cause me to pull back.

"We aren't going there? Right?" I ask.

"I'm not telling you what we have planned. Plus, I heard it's sold out, tickets only, for opening weekend. Oh! I already talked to Nikki, and she's also in. I think that *friend* of yours is coming too since Seth is going."

I don't even waste my breath to respond. My sister had made no bones about letting me know she didn't approve of the man I've been seeing for the last two months. She loves Nikki, even gets along with her boyfriend, Seth, but Levi ... no, she hated him on the spot. It's been a constant bone of contention between us. She does nothing to hide the fact that she doesn't like him—even to his face—while I'm helplessly stuck trying to keep the both of them happy.

Of course, Levi only gets frustrated when Maddi starts her crap, so it's made me pull back from her more to keep him happy; another thing that hasn't escaped her notice.

Just another reason I've felt like breaking things off with Levi is the best move. I hate that I've even let him come between my sister and me.

"No worries about Levi; he's working this weekend. Please drop it, Maddi. I don't have the patience to deal with it right now. I'll be there tonight, okay? We can talk more about this stupid birthday celebration then."

We make small talk for a minute before I drop the phone on the couch next to me and look back over at the portrait I had been working on. One of the many I have of the very man who's caused me more pain than I thought possible. No matter how many times it happens, I'm still shocked when I see a picture-perfect likeness of Nate Reid filling a once-blank canvas. What's sad is I don't even realize I'm doing it. I just zone out and hours later … there he is.

Leaving everything where it is and ignoring the huge canvas of Nate, I walk from the back room and through the house so I can start getting ready for tonight. Bam's nails click on the hardwood behind me as he follows. It's been childish for me to skip these monthly dinners, I know that, but that doesn't matter. The hurt he caused me years ago holds nothing on the pain he inflicted more recently. He was right that night I professed my true feelings for him when he said he would ruin me, but stupidly, I was too naïve to believe him then.

Pushing back the same hurt that ruin caused, I do what I have been doing for the last year and pretend it never happened.

When I pull up to the Reid's house later that night, I curse myself for procrastinating leaving my house for so long. I spend so much time lost in my head that I'm almost always late, but since Maddi made such a big deal about me showing up tonight, I can only imagine that they've assumed I wasn't coming again.

I park my car behind the many others that line their driveway and groan when I see my dad leaning against his truck. True to Maddi's word, it looks like he was prepared to follow through with his threat.

Turning off the ignition, I fiddle with my phone and shoot Nikki a quick text to let her know I'm at a family dinner and I'll call her later. We've made a habit recently by turning Wednesdays into our wine night, so if I don't let her know I'm not home, she's going to freak out. I'm always home, so it would be about as abnormal as it gets for me.

The second I reach the handle to open my door, it's swung open and I let out a startled scream. My phone clatters to the driveway with a sickening sound that has me saying a prayer I didn't just crack the screen.

"Cutting it close," my dad says, bending over to pick up my phone and handing it over before stepping back so I can get out.

"Sorry," I say with a shrug and lean up to give him a hug. He bends, meeting me halfway, and I instantly feel settled when he wraps his arms around me. Just like coming home. "I lost track of time. You know how it goes when I'm working."

He leans back, giving me a kiss on my temple, and I get one of the rare smiles that he reserves just for 'his girls.' Eyes so like my own crinkle at the corners, and he just shakes his head.

"I'm here?" I continue, hoping to get off the hook from what I'm sure would end up being the third degree of questioning if he had his way.

"Yeah, sweetheart, you are. I've missed you," he says, and I instantly feel guilty for not being around. It's not his fault this is the last place I want to be.

"I missed you too, Dad."

He turns, favoring his bad leg, and I frown. He just shakes his head. "Don't even start, Emberlyn. Your mom's already been on my ass for overdoing it this weekend."

"Then maybe you should start listening to her before your ass is on the ground."

"Sass," he warns. "Just like your mom. Just like your sister. I'm surrounded by fucking sass."

"Whatever." I laugh, wrapping my arm around his waist as he pulls me to his side with one arm over my shoulders. "What did you do this time?"

"And still she sasses me."

I look over and up, way up, and stick my tongue out at him. His soft laughter vibrates against me, and I smile at him.

God, I love my dad.

"Went head to head with Asher at Crossfit the other day. Little shit still can't handle the fact that I can kick his ass with one leg."

"I swear you two act like kids sometimes," I joke.

We walk the rest of the way together, and I selfishly soak up the comfort his nearness brings me before we walk into the madness of family dinner night. As usual, the Reid's house is full to bursting and the echoes of two dozen or so voices carry from the back deck. When we round the corner to where their back family room is, I stop short at the sight in front of me.

"I think the little fucker has some cross-dressing tendencies if you ask me," I hear and take my eyes off the scene in front of me to look over and meet Cohen's laughing eyes.

"I'm starting to agree," my dad jokes, releasing me and walking through the open patio door that leads to where the rest of our huge family is.

"Molly!" I look up when Megan walks in from the porch and give her a smile.

"Yes, Mommy," Molly sings from her spot in the middle of the living room.

"Would you leave Nate alone and come on out?"

"I can't. He isn't a princess yet," she continues with her singsong voice, the smile in her tone matching the huge toothless one on her face.

"Yeah, definitely has some cross-dressing tendencies," Cohen repeats, taking a huge pull from his beer. "Hey, Em," he says and walks over from the kitchen island to give me a hug.

"Hey," I softly respond, looking back at Nate.

"The girls are asking about you. They're down at the dock acting like little schoolgirls. All you hear is giggles coming every few minutes. They've been like that for the last half hour, ever since Dani got out of time-out."

"Time-out?" I laugh, my eyes moving back to Nate again.

He looks up after Molly stops brushing the god-awful electric blue shadow on his lids and gives me a smile. My stupid body starts to burn with just that little bit of attention from him, and I hate myself for it. Why can't I get over him? Even now, when he is as far from appealing as it gets, I crave him.

His shoulder-length hair is pulled in every direction with little butterfly clips of every color of the rainbow. Aside from the eye shadow, he has bright pink lipstick on, what I'm assuming is blush making huge circles on his cheeks, and as if that wasn't enough, he has a bright pink tutu on.

And still, he's the most beautiful man I've ever laid eyes on.

If anything, the horrendous makeup just accentuates the hard chiseled lines of his face. He looks just like Cohen said, like a cross-dresser, only a cross-dressing Adonis.

"She needs to learn to listen. She tried to tell my Molly-Wolly that blue wasn't my color, so she had to go to time-out until she thought about her actions. Right, Molly-Wolly?" Nate answers my question with a smile.

I ignore his smile and turn my back to him, just as I've done every time I've seen him over the past year. I can feel his eyes on me as I make my way out back. Maybe a year ago, I would have laughed with him and asked him why he continues to put the women in his life in time-out, but not now.

Cohen continues down the steps when I pause at the railing and look around at everyone spread out over the large backyard. Megan is walking away from her husband, smile on her face, and heading down toward the dock. Lee, her husband, is standing with Cohen's brothers, Cam and Colt, following his wife's retreating back. That is until Cohen steps up and gives him a good-natured shove. Zac, Jaxon, and their dad, Asher, are tossing the football around with Beck and Greg. Axel and my dad are standing around the grill while Izzy, Dee, and Chelcie move around the huge farm table that takes up one side of their outdoor dining area.

Spotting my mom with Melissa, Sway, and his partner, Davey, I make my way to where they're playing with Dani's boys. I stop to give my mom a hug, saying hello to everyone else I pass as I make my way down to the dock.

Just as Cohen said, all the girls are there. All six of them indeed giggling in their little makeshift huddle. My sister looks up when my feet hit the wooden planks and gives me what I couldn't mistake as anything but a relieved smile.

Being the baby of the girl side of our group—hell, the baby of the whole group—I don't spend as much time with them as she does, but it doesn't mean our bond isn't strong. All of our parents have been friends for so long that even though I only share blood with one of them, we are very much a family.

Dani breaks away and gives me a hug before pulling me forward. Megan smiles and gives me a hug as I walk by, and then Stella, Lyn, and Lila are next before my sister gives me one of her bear hugs that I swear cracks a rib every time.

"About time you got here!" she yells after backing away.

"Don't start. Dad was in the driveway when I pulled up."

She laughs, and the others follow suit. "I told you. Over the shoulder threats are never made lightly by him."

"Yeah, yeah … what did I miss?"

"Oh, nothing," she says sweetly, a little too sweetly.

"We're planning Saturday night," Dani says, earning a scowl from my sister.

"And that would be the party I didn't ask for?"

She nods, and I see the others' smiles grow. Shit … this can't be good.

"Would anyone care to fill me in?"

Each of them barks out a 'no' at the same time, and I narrow my eyes. No one moves to speak, but Stella starts laughing so hard that I worry she might fall into the lake.

"I'm not sure I like the way this is going right now," I admit, feeling even more uneasy about the weekend plans I don't want.

"Well, you don't even need to worry about a thing. We've got it covered from your makeup and hair, all the way down to what underwear you're wearing under the dress we've already bought. All you have to do is show up at Dani's house to get ready around dinnertime Saturday."

I narrow my eyes at my sister, but before I can speak, Axel bellows out that it's time to eat. "This conversation isn't done," I threaten, but they all wave me off as they start to walk up to where the food is being set out on one of the custom-made buffet-style bars that line the Reid's outdoor kitchen of sorts.

I do my best to ignore the huge six-foot-four man wearing a tutu as I fix my plate and wedge myself between Cam and Colt at the large table. I swear this thing is big enough to fit a whole football team, but even with all that space, I feel like nowhere is far enough away with Nate here.

My eyes never leave my plate, but I see him sit down across from me next to his sister and Cohen. I can see him out of the corner of my eye bend down to kiss his nephew, Owen, before looking back in my direction.

Conversation flows easily when we're all together. Typical

catching up on what everyone has been doing. When Melissa, Greg's wife and Cohen's mom, asks about my art exhibition coming up, I finally look up.

"It's already looking to be pretty big. From what the owner of the gallery has said, there are already whispers of a few pieces that she anticipates will sell quickly."

"That's wonderful, Ember!" she praises. "You know we're all going to be there."

"Hell yeah, we are," my sister yells from the other end of the long table.

"Maddisyn Locke," I hear my mom scold. "Children at the table."

I watch Maddi raise one perfect brow at her, and I know she's about to throw some of what my dad calls sass. "Need I point out that these children have heard much worse from every person in attendance, especially all you elders?"

I hear a grumbled 'sass' from the end my father is sitting at, and my mother just laughs.

"Nate, how are things going at the club?" Asher's wife, Chelcie, asks.

I look back at my plate but listen for his answer. Truth be told, I've been curious about this new project of his. But not enough to ask anyone openly about it. I've followed the news on social media, which it seems like you see something everywhere. Every local radio station is plugging the opening of Dirty Dog, but no one knows much besides it being billed as the biggest thing to happen to the Atlanta area club scene in decades. All everyone sees are the pictures of the old Club Carnal, what used to be a popular club years and years ago, transformed into a huge and breathtaking mix of class and rustic flair. Everything on the outside has been pictured everywhere. The huge warehouse covered in brick is now painted black with steel accents. When the Dirty Dog logo went up, in all its bright red glory, it popped so brightly it demanded attention.

"Sold out every weekend for the next three months. We didn't do tickets for the weekday nights, but I'm pretty confident that it will be crowded. Or hopeful, at least."

"Well, isn't that lovely," she says, looking over at where Nate's mom, Izzy, is sitting across from her. I don't miss the look that passes between them, but it shocks me to see the worry on his mother's face.

Worry? Anyone with eyes and ears can see the hype surrounding his grand opening is going to carry for a damn long time. If I let myself, I would feel so much pride for him.

"Yeah, I guess."

"You going to dress up like a fairy on opening night too, little princess?" His sister laughs at him but snaps her mouth shut when he turns slowly to face her.

Cohen, not ever one to miss anything, takes his son from Dani's arms just as Nate stands from the table. He bends his tutu-covered waist and pulls his sister from the table before tossing her over his shoulder.

"You big jerk! Let me down, Nate! Daddy, tell Nate to leave me alone!"

"Nate, leave your sister alone." He complies, stuffing another piece of steak in his mouth and not even looking in their direction.

Dani continues to smack his back and kick her feet, but he just walks over to the back corner of the covered dining area and drops her to her feet. He silently spins her so that she's facing the corner and points at the stone covered wall in front of her.

"Two-minute time-out for insulting the princess," he tells her, then silently walks back the way he just came. He stops to give Molly's beaming face a kiss on the cheek before taking his seat and picking up his fork.

"Maybe we'll check it out," I hear his father say, continuing like nothing happened as his daughter stomps back to the table, shocking me enough that my eyes automatically shoot from Nate's face to his before looking back at Nate.

He looks ridiculous, but he puts his fork back down and turns to look at his dad, the makeup on his face making him look anything but serious. "Afraid you're going to be out of luck there, old man. Unless you get lucky and find a scalper out front, we're sold out."

"Nathaniel." His mom gasps on a laugh. "Not even for your parents?"

I watch him shake his head at her before looking over and meeting my eyes, holding them captive with the intensity brewing in his emerald gaze. With my heart in my throat, I look down at my plate and busy myself with moving some food around while listening intently to his words.

"I'm not sure it's your scene, Ma. Definitely not something for the faint of heart, and to be honest, I'm not really sure I want my parents to see me in action."

"In action?" I hear someone ask from the end of the table.

"Ha!" Cohen burst out laughing. "Trust me on this, Izzy, the last thing you want to do is see your boy here in action."

"You make it sound like he's running a brothel," someone else jokes making Cohen laugh even harder.

What in the world?

"Well, I'm going, and you can't stop me. Even if I have to buy a ticket because my own son won't let me in."

"We've got ten!" I hear my sister yell, making Cohen laugh even harder.

"Ten? What the hell," Nate calls her way.

"Oh yeah, we've got *bigggg* plans this weekend, don't we, girls?"

Shit, kill me now. They're taking me to Nate's place? No … no way.

"Would you stop laughing," Dani tells her husband, only causing him to start a new wave of hilarity.

"Uh … big plans for what?" Nate continues, ignoring his sister and brother-in-law.

"It's Ember's big twenty-first. What better way to celebrate than doing it Dirty style, right Nate-*Dog*?"

At that point, Cohen is laughing so hard I fear he might break something. The only thing I can do at this point is to pray this is all a joke, but when I look up and meet Nate's eyes again, I know if it is, then the joke's on me.

His lips are tipped up in what can only be described as a shit-eating grin sinful enough to melt panties, pink lips and all. I don't even try to figure out what he's thinking because all I can focus on is trying not to throw up.

Chapter 5

Nate

EMBER'S TAN SKIN HAS HELD a blush on her cheeks for the last two hours. Dinner continued as normal after the announcement of the big plans for her birthday, but other than that moment when she looked at me in shock, she hasn't given me those eyes once more. I've tried because I can't understand for the life of me why there was pain dancing in them when she found out she would be spending her birthday at my club.

How have things gotten so strained between us?

Sure, we had a moment when things were awkward years ago, but we had settled into our friendship easy enough after some time passed. Things were never the same— fuck, far from it— after she admitted her feelings toward me. Feelings I had been fighting for her for a damn long time surfaced and obviously haven't gone away, but they have never put this kind of tension on our friendship.

It's been bothering me for months, but I still can't figure out what I fucking did to make her look at me like she wishes she had a knife to stab into my back. Hell, up until Dani and Cohen got married a year and a half ago, things had been fine. Then she started skipping out anytime everyone was together. When she did show, she avoided me like I had the plague. I can't even remember the last time we had a conversation, let alone a time that I was on the receiving end of a genuine smile from her.

Plates pushed aside, everyone continues to talk and catch up. I look back across the table as Evan pulls on my hair, ignoring the pain in my scalp as he tries to pull my hair from my head, and kick my leg out in her direction. She jumps but doesn't move her attention from Cohen's brother, Cam. She listens to whatever the fuck he's carrying on about and ignores me as usual.

Fuck this shit.

"Ember, mind giving me a hand getting this shit off my face?" I ask, knowing she has too good of manners to ignore me when I've spoken directly to her. Especially as I did it loudly enough that those around us look over and laugh at what Molly did to me earlier.

I watch her take a deep breath before looking away from Cam and fucking finally giving me those eyes.

"I'm pretty sure you can handle it," she says softly, and once again, I see that pain just below the surface.

"Might be so, still asking for your help."

One way or another, I'm getting to the bottom of this shit. I finally have everything in my life going on the right track, full speed ahead, and I want my little firecracker along for the ride with me.

Her lips thin for just a second before she catches herself. Right when she's about to open her mouth, I assume to give me another line of bullshit, my mom interrupts her. "You can use my bathroom, honey. Ember, the makeup remover is in the second drawer on the left."

I raise one of my eyebrows at Ember, daring her to fucking say no now. Panic briefly crosses her face, so fleeting I question if that's what I saw, before she stands from the table and starts to walk up the deck stairs and into the house. Not even saying a word.

"Come here, little prince," my sister coos and takes her youngest from my arms. "Be nice," she whispers at me when I move to stand. I look at her with confusion, but she just gives me a sad smile.

What in the fucking hell? I swear all the women in my life are insane.

I unsnap the tutu I had made for myself when Molly told me she wished I had one just like hers as I walk up the deck stairs, dropping it on the couch when I enter the house. The silence around me is so thick I want to knock something off the wall just to ease the trepidation it's creating. Shaking off the ridiculous feelings, I walk through the house, up the stairs, and into my parents' bedroom at the end of the hall. I find Ember in their bathroom pulling out some girly shit, and I stop in the doorway to wait for her to acknowledge that I'm there.

"How long are you planning to stand there?" she asks a minute later, not looking away from what she's doing.

"Depends. How long are you planning to ignore me, babe?" I shoot back, my confusion growing when her shoulders pull tight.

"Don't call me that," she seethes, only pausing briefly in her task.

"What the fuck, Em?"

"Just don't. Do not call me babe. I'm not your fucking *babe*," she says with so much hate in that one word I'm struck dumb.

"Right," I stutter, finding my feet and walking into the room. Maybe it's her lady time? I sit on the chair in front of my mom's vanity and look up at her. Her eyes are pinched tight and her chest is moving rapidly with her rushed breaths. "It's just a word, Em. I didn't realize it was offensive."

Her eyes snap open, and she looks down at me, the pain not even masked in the slightest.

"What's going on here?" I cluelessly question.

She picks up one of the square cotton looking things in one hand and a bottle in the other, back to ignoring me, but her face is saying enough. I search my mind trying to figure out what's happening right now, but fuck if I have a single light bulb going off.

I close my eyes out of instinct when she moves toward my face with that shit, her movements angry as she roughly wipes my face.

"Keep your head still," she snaps.

"Kind of hard to do that when you're dead set on removing a layer of skin, babe."

She stops instantly, and I curse myself.

"Do *not* call me *that*!" she screams.

I open my eyes, blinking when whatever the fuck she had been wiping on me gets in my eyes and burns. I stand quickly, knocking over the chair and stick my head down, turning on the water in the sink and grabbing the towel off the hook. I scrub quickly before standing and looking down at her. She hasn't moved an inch, but now, her hands are gripping the counter so hard, it's as if it's the only thing keeping her standing.

The water falling from my face is soaking my shirt, but I turn and look in the mirror to make sure I got all that damn makeup off, and frown at the clips still in my hair. I pull at them angrily, throwing them down onto the floor. When my hair is free, I pull it up in a knot on the top of my head and bring my attention back to Ember.

"Tell me what is going on, Em. What have I done?"

She's silent but turns to look at me.

"What did I do to get this kind of reaction from you?" I continue.

Still nothing.

"Fucking tell me, Emberlyn! What made you look at me with hate in those beautiful eyes? I can't stand it anymore."

She jerks back with so much force that I know there is no way she didn't feel the snap all the way down her spine.

"What did you do?" she weakly questions.

I nod. "Yeah, what did I do because, for the fucking life of me, I can't figure it out."

"What did you *do*?" she repeats, her tone getting harsh.

I don't say a damn thing. Growing up with a sister, I know when a woman is on the edge of crazy.

"You really have no fucking clue, do you?"

I shake my head, but clearly, even that was the wrong move because she again jerks but this time with her whole body.

"You're unbelievable, Nate."

The silence continues after that, more because I'm afraid if I so much as breathe, she is going to stab me with my mom's cuticle scissors.

Just when I think it's safe, her eyes narrow and she leans up. Because I have a foot plus on her, that doesn't do much, but still, I don't move. Even pissed as hell, she's still beautiful.

"What's your name, *babe*?" she oddly asks, before walking around me and slamming the bathroom door in her wake.

I look around the large bathroom, trying to figure out what just happened before looking at my reflection. "What in the fuck just happened in here?" I ask my reflection, stupidly wishing it could throw me a bone here.

I hear another door slam, and I throw the door open and move to the window in my parents' room just in time to see Ember running to her car and jumping in. It's gotten darker out, but her dome light is illuminating her, and the second I see her swipe at her eyes, I kick my own ass.

If I could just get her to talk to me, without it turning into whatever just happened in the bathroom, I could fix this. We could go back to the way things were. With my mind made up, I rush out of the room and down the stairs, taking them two at a time. I open the front door just as she turns the engine over.

"Ember!" I yell and race down the driveway.

Before I can reach her car, she's backing out so fast that her tires protest against the speed.

"Ember!" I bellow, running down the driveway trying to catch her. A feeling of pure helplessness starts to crawl up my throat when she looks over at me with tear-filled eyes before gunning the gas and taking off. "Em," I whisper, pleading with her taillights for what, I have no idea.

"Figure it out yet?" I hear behind me but don't look until the glow of her taillights is completely gone.

When I turn, Maddox is standing at the end of the driveway, arms crossed over his chest, stoic mask in place.

"Not even a little," I tell him honestly, hoping that he's going to be more of a voice of reason and not a pissed off father right now.

"You aren't a stupid man, Nathaniel, so it really shouldn't be this hard. I'll help you out because I love my little girl and her happiness means more to me than kicking your fucking ass right now, but you best believe that moment is coming and I'll be nice enough to give you time to prepare for it."

A normal man would probably shit himself right now, but I match Maddox in size, and if anything, I'm bigger than he is, so if I'm looking at a beating to come, I'm fairly sure I could hold my own. I think.

"You know I respect the hell out of you, Maddox, but I'm not sure what I've done to earn that anger from you."

"You aren't now, but you will be and I suspect that you'll come willingly when I tell you it's time for that fight."

Cryptic motherfucker.

"My little girl's had a crush on you for way too long. I didn't mind when she was younger because I knew you had too much respect for her—and me—to cross that line, even though you wanted to. However, my baby isn't a baby anymore and those feelings she has for you still run deep."

I open my mouth to say something, fuck if I know, but close it when his eyes narrow.

"Don't insult my intelligence by denying that, Nate. You might act like a little shit, but you have a good head on your shoulders. You fucked up, so what are you going to do about it?"

"Can I talk now?" I ask him after a moment of silence, my head spinning.

He doesn't speak. I watch as his jaw ticks and his eyes grow harder.

"I'm pretty sure she doesn't, um … have those kind of feelings for me," I hedge.

"I told you not to insult me."

"Right." I sigh, dropping my head and looking down at my booted feet. "Are you saying you don't have an issue with your twenty, almost twenty-one-year-old daughter crushing on a man who is almost thirty?"

"Didn't say that, did I?" he growls at me. He uncrosses his arms and steps up until he's in my face, and I brace, thinking he's changed his mind about that ass kicking. "What I said was my little girl's happiness means more to me than kicking your ass. Seeing her smile is the reason I fucking live, so when I see the reason for her smile runs hand in hand with her feelings toward you, I'm willing to put my own feelings aside, for now, to get that back on her face where it belongs."

"I respect you there, Maddox, I do, but what I'm asking you isn't about her smile."

"You want my little girl."

His response is enough to shock me stupid. The venom in his voice says enough. He knows my 'want' is a fucking lot more complicated than that. I fucking crave her.

"I'm going to ask you again because I would really like to not have any surprises here. You do understand what you're saying … right?"

Again, he doesn't talk. His eyes don't even blink as he continues to level me with those black orbs of intimidation.

"I've been in love with her since before it was legal to feel that way," I tell him honestly, voicing my feelings for her for the first time out loud.

One eye twitches, and on the opposite side of his face, I see his jaw tick.

"She hates me."

That gets him, and he steps up until we're chest to chest. "She doesn't hate you, you clueless fuck. She's hurt because you fucked up major. That's my baby girl, so I really don't like talking about this shit, but she's a woman and I'm not stupid. Remember. Think really fucking hard, Nate, and remember your sister's reception. Fix this shit and bring back that smile, but I warn you … the next time you call my daughter *babe,* you're going to know how she felt that night before she ran off and her smile died."

What. The. Fuck.

No. That's not possible.

My breath stills in my throat when his implication hits the

mark. Vivid images of that night—that dream night—hit my brain, only this time I know the same thing that's kept me up night after night has also been keeping her up, but for different reasons.

And as if that wasn't enough, I know now that her very overprotective father knows I fucked his baby girl without realizing whom I had in my arms.

"Oh fuck," I grumble.

"Yeah, oh fuck is right. You fix this and me and you … we aren't done with this shit," he tells me with another intimidating look before turning and walking back into my parents' house.

Chapter 6

Ember

PLACING THE LAST BRUSH BACK in its designated drawer, I look over at the sunrise landscape that I had been working on for the last two days. I study it with a critical eye and a deep exhale.

It's beautiful, stunning even, but looking at it just causes me to feel nothing but sadness when it should inflict the exact opposite.

I started with the tall maple trees lining each side of the canvas and the center focusing on the rising sun. The sun is and should be the spotlight, but for me, the grassy field that takes up the whole bottom half is. The sun's rays hitting the empty field cast an entrancing effect, as each blade appears to be glowing.

I've always had a talent at making my work look as if it was a picture rather than a painting, and this one is no different. My fingers itch to reach out and see if I could feel the light sheen of dew covering the valley between the trees.

The bright green blades look just like Nate Reid's eyes.

I know exactly why I escaped to my art after the family dinner two nights ago. Painting has always been the only thing, other than being near him, that made me feel like I was complete. An outlet that I can channel to express the feelings I never know how to separate in my jumbled thoughts. I've never been the type of girl who wants to go out every night and party.

To me, art is something I can understand when people never have been. I don't need to pretend to be someone else to get some sort of approval when I get lost in an introvert's heaven. But because of that, a loneliness I just can't shake always lingers.

I hate the knowledge that the only other time I've felt safe enough to be me outside of my painting was when things were normal between Nate and me. I never had the feeling of judgment from him. He never looked at me as if he had no clue how to deal with the shy, quiet, awkward girl.

Some people might think I'm insecure, but I'm not, even though it has taken me a while to realize that. Getting past the fear of being accepted as the weird artsy girl will probably always be with me, but I'm ready. I'm just lonesome. A little lost maybe, but I know something needs to change. I need to learn not to care what people think and live my life for me, no one else.

It doesn't take me long to tidy up my workspace now that my brushes are clean and stored in the large wooden storage chest that my dad had made for me. I'm meticulous in the order of that chest. Each paint pot, tube, and brush is stored in its labeled spot before I leave the room. When I push the last drawer closed, I run my hand across the bright teal of my name inscribed on the top of the white painted box. It's the only purposely-placed color in this whole room, aside from my canvases that is.

Of course, that chest is the only thing that's neat and tidy in this room. I deliberately decorated this room in all whites from the ceiling to the floor including every piece of furniture in here; that way, if paint spilled or transferred from me as I moved around, the room would take on a life of its own. My own little piece of living art. Little smudges on the couch, chair, and table. Splatters dance across the floor in random successions. Even a huge smear of bright red graces the center of my ceiling courtesy of a very overeager new tube of paint exploding when I tried to open a jammed top.

I can't wait until the day that this whole room is a collage of my career.

With a smile on my face, I move over to the sink and wash my hands before picking up my phone and turning it on. A few notifications start popping on the screen as the signal wakes up. I give them a quick glance, reminding myself to open the Uno with Friends app I've been obsessed with lately so I don't lose my daily accumulative rewards.

A few messages from Levi come, letting me know what time he's picking up Nikki and Seth before coming for me, but before I can open his message to reply, another one pops up.

Nate: Call me, Ember. I've been trying to get in touch with you, but I need you to work with me. Call me, text me, just do something other than continue to ignore me. Please.

Yeah, no.

After the family dinner and a pity party I'm not proud of, I decided no more stupid thoughts of something that will never be. I should have moved on and I had done a good job of that after my graduation night ... until his sister's wedding and one too many drinks.

Inhibitions and fears went out the window as old feelings and dreams started trying to mend my broken heart that night. I had been coming around the side of the house, laughing to myself about getting lost on the way back from the bathroom, when I found myself colliding with a hard body. I'm still not really sure how things progressed from there; all I knew was that my panties were on the ground and I was burning from the inside out.

Then, of course, there was the figurative bath of cold water when I realized Nate had no idea who he was pushing his hard dick inside. The next thing I knew, I was no longer in his arms as I rushed from the darkened corner blindly.

Not even wanting to think about everything that followed, I ignore his message and go to Levi's text.

Ember: Sounds good. ;) I'll be ready in an hour. See you soon!

I don't get a reply, but I didn't think I would since Levi is the worst at responding. I shoot Nikki a similar message while walking to the back door and letting an overexcited Bam in from his run in the backyard. I leave my back room to head to my bedroom and get ready for a double date night.

I look across the table at Levi and try to focus on the conversation around me. He and Seth have been going on and on about some new training program they've been on to 'bulk up.' Whatever the hell that means. Something about their muscles getting bigger ... or was it sharper? More defined? I don't know.

Nikki nudges my foot under the table, taking a sip of her beer, and rolls her eyes.

"I hit the gym twice yesterday, man. My veins looked like they were going to pop through my skin by the time I finished."

"So, Levi," Nikki interrupts him and turns her attention to the man next to me. "How are things at the fire department?"

"Good," he says, giving her a small glance before looking back across the table to Seth. "So I told Allen I would be there at six in the morning tomorrow to work my legs some more. Since I'm working a double this weekend, no gym time until Monday."

Nikki gives me a shrug, not really caring that she was dismissed, and we both continue to eat.

The look of displeasure that I got from Levi when I ordered pasta almost made me regret my decision, but I've never been one to shy away from a hearty Italian dish. Just because he's a health nut doesn't mean I have to be. I should be annoyed that he tries to control what I eat, but I don't really care. I'm not going to become someone else just to make him happy, even if my knee-jerk reaction is to do just that. I'm not a skinny girl, but I'm also not big. I'm just me, soft in all the right places.

"Are you sure you can't get someone to take your shift?" I ask him before taking another big bite and smiling at him when he frowns at me. He gives me one of his devastatingly handsome grins when the noodle slurps loudly, just shaking his head at me. After two months, I might still get the looks and a few comments, but he knows I'll be the last one who starts to worry about what goes in my mouth.

"Sorry, babe," he responds, and I succeed in hiding my grimace at the pet name. "I tried to get Trenton to switch, but his little sister is getting married so it was a no go."

"I can't believe you're letting her go party on her twenty-first," Seth chimes in.

"Letting her go?" Nikki questions with a harsh tone.

"Yeah, letting, Nic. I remember how wild things got at mine. Fuck, dude, there were strippers that—"

"I probably wouldn't finish that sentence." Levi laughs.

"No, please … tell me all about the strippers, Seth," Nikki sarcastically drawls, leaning back in her seat after placing her fork down and crossing her arms over her chest.

"Seriously? What's the big deal?" Seth looks clueless as to why his girlfriend is pissed, which is sad.

"The big deal is that you probably shouldn't be talking about the strippers you had that night when your very pissed girlfriend, the same girlfriend you had three years ago during said birthday full of skank happened, is sitting next to you."

Levi and I burst out laughing at Nikki's smartass response.

They continue to fight and I soak up Levi's attention as he gives me a soft, chaste kiss before returning to his meal.

Nikki pushed me toward Levi almost two months ago. I'm not sure what made me say yes, but I knew it was largely in part to the loneliness I was sick of feeling. Our first date was great. We had dinner at a local Mexican place before following that up with a movie. He left me a few hours later with my first front porch kiss experience. He was easy to be with and the relationship progressed from there.

I say relationship loosely because lately, he's been acting so weird. I think the only thing that Levi really cares about having a relationship with is his gym membership. A few other little things lately have also been making me question if being with him is the best thing for me.

Nikki and Seth continue to bicker, and I look over at Levi as my thoughts darken. He doesn't notice my attention, which is also something I've noticed a lot of lately.

He looks like such the boy next door. All-American type with the looks that could probably put him as the front cover model for J. Crew or something, but underneath is a simmering anger I've only recently been privy to. He wasn't always like this. When we first met, he was amazing, and I really had high hopes that he would be someone worth exploring a relationship with. But I'm not sure what to do with this new easily angered and controlling side of him.

"Are you excited to hit up Nate's place?" Nikki asks me, clearly done fighting with her boyfriend since she's now taking a big forkful of her own pasta with a look of pure pleasure. She doesn't notice that her question has now caused a dark cloud to settle over my side of the table.

"Who is Nate?" Levi asks her in a hard tone. His question might be directed at Nikki, but the anger is all for me.

"A friend," I tell him, ignoring him much like he's been ignoring me for most of the evening.

"What kind of friend?" His words come out sharp and forcefully.

I shrug and keep chewing. I look up when I see Nikki stop her fork's upward path to her mouth; the utensil paused halfway to her mouth as she looks at him with wide eyes, not used to seeing this side of him.

I take a fortifying breath for patience and turn so that I'm looking at him. He's so handsome, even when he's pissed. His blond hair is cut short, but long on the top. His blue eyes are narrowed, but that just makes the sharp edges of his facial features stand out more. Add the tan that I'm pretty sure he gets with the help of a tanning bed, and he really should be making my heart beat with desire.

But it doesn't.

Because it only does that for the man I can't have.

Yet another reason I can't keep dragging this on with him. It's very clear that I'm just not feeling like a girl should when she's in a relationship with one man, but still in love with another.

A cold flash of rage flickers in his eyes when I continue my silence and I shake off the chill that skirts down my spine.

What the hell was that?

"I grew up with him," I finally say, feeling the goose bumps pebble across my skin. "He's a childhood friend and nothing more," I assure him.

"Let's hope so," he says through thin lips. "How come I haven't met this friend before?" he adds.

I look back at Nikki, her fork still in the middle of its journey to her mouth; only now, half of her fettuccini is hanging off. Her eyes say it all, but then she mouths *creepy,* and I can't even deny it.

"We aren't that close anymore, Lev. I see him once a month during the family dinner."

"If he's close enough to attend the infamous family dinner, I would say he's someone I should have met by now," he growls through clenched teeth.

I give him what I hope is a reassuring smile, not interested in having to deal with his one of his 'dark moods' when we're in public.

"Don't be like that. I told you, I grew up with him and his parents are good friends with mine. He's just a friend." *A friend I'm in love with*, I silently add.

"Maybe it's finally time you took me to a family dinner then, babe. You've kept me from your *family* long enough, and it's time they meet the new man in your life."

I can tell he's seconds away from the rage in his voice becoming a scene, so I do the only thing I can to stop the train wreck from happening. I lie through my teeth.

"Of course, it is. Next time, I promise," I placate him.

Yeah, I'm thinking it's definitely past time I call a stop to things between Levi and myself.

Things didn't get any better from there. He returned to his meal after a good two minutes of just looking at me and breathing hard. He only talked to Seth and even that was with short and impatient responses. If Seth noticed, he didn't care. By the time I had finished my food, my head was throbbing with what promised to be one hell of a migraine, but it wasn't until the bill came that the pain exploded in a burst so painful I thought I might throw up.

"I forgot my wallet, babe, you got this," Levi tells me instead of asking, not even a small amount of shame present. He doesn't wait to hear my response before tossing his napkin on the table and standing. He looks down at Seth before jerking his chin toward the front of the restaurant.

"Here," Seth says to Nikki, handing her his wallet and standing, following behind Levi as they make their way out the door.

"Stupid son of a nutcracker," she mumbles under her breath, opening Seth's wallet and pulling out enough cash to cover both of our tabs. "Serves him right for being friends with that tool."

"Need I remind you, that tool is the same guy that you told me was my soul mate just a few months ago?"

She leans back in her seat, and I feel bad when I see her face get soft. "I know, I know. That was crazy intense, Em." She places Seth's wallet in her purse before looking back at me. "I knew he could be a jerk sometimes, what guy isn't, but I've never seen something like what just happened. That was creepy as hell. More creepy than the weirdness he's been oozing lately."

"I know." I sigh, rubbing my pounding temples. "He's been doing stuff like that more and more. Getting excessively controlling and possessive the last few weeks, but ever since we slept together, he's become … well, that," I say and point toward the door.

"Has he ever—"

I stop her with a shake of my head, knowing where she's going with this. "No, Nikki. I wouldn't still be here if he had put his hands on me. I'm smarter than that," I tell her. Even though I'm reasonably sure that's the case, I know now the loneliness I had felt for so long was the only reason I had allowed things to get this far between us. Instead of me breaking things off when I first noticed how over-the-top he would get when it came to me.

"He got really mad when I brought up Nate. I figured he'd met him already. I didn't know you hadn't brought him around anyone. I mean he wasn't just mad … he was *mad*. He bent his fork," she says and points at where his discarded fork is lying on the table. Sure enough, the metal is bent slightly in the middle. "Are you okay?"

"I'm okay. I don't know why you assumed he had been around Nate when I've been avoiding him for the better part of the last year. After Maddi had taken an instant dislike to him, I figured I would hold off on my parents. Look, I'm going to talk to him after this weekend. Since he's covering for someone else, he's working a double and we won't see each other until Monday."

She doesn't look happy, but she gives me a weak nod before we move from the table and walk together outside. Not surprising, Levi and Seth are already in the SUV. I can see them talking as we walk around and get in the back of his Tahoe, Levi's eyes never leaving mine until he was forced to in order to keep facing forward.

We continue our silence as we drive through town, and I'm thankful my house is on the way to Nikki's apartment, so I can avoid being alone with Levi. How I have allowed myself to get this deep in our relationship is beyond me.

No. That's a lie. It isn't just on me. He did a damn good job of hiding his true colors from me for weeks. It's just my fault that I let it go on as long as I have. The signs have been there for a while now, and I would rather be single with an occasional case of the lonelies than have to deal with this.

"You missed my street," I whisper from my seat, the blinding pain slamming around my skull and making me feel weak.

"I didn't," he responds.

I lean my head against the window and try to argue, but Nikki takes my hand with a gentle squeeze.

"I think Ember needs to get home, Levi. She isn't feeling well."

"And she'll get there when she gets there, Nikki."

"Which should be sooner than later. Seriously, Levi, turn around."

I squeak when the brakes compress harshly. I had been resting my head against the window, but the second the seat belt cuts into my stomach, I lose the battle with my nausea and hurry to open the door before losing my dinner on the street.

"Like I said, she isn't feeling well," Nikki snaps, unbuckling her seat belt and shifting to the middle seat to help me hold my hair back.

I had just finished heaving, feeling another wave of vomit fighting its way up my throat, when he slams on the gas. The door, not able to stay open with the power of his acceleration, bangs into my already pounding head. I have to choke down the vomit as the pain becomes something of the likes I've never experienced.

"It's okay," Nikki tries to reassure me, scooting back over on the seat and pulling me until my head is in her lap. I focus on the feeling of her fingers running through my hair, and it isn't long until the hypnotizing movements have me asleep in her lap. Just as the pain dulls enough for slumber to take hold, I hear her mumble under her breath. "You're a fucking motherfucker, Levi Kyle."

I have no idea if he responds; my last thought is that she couldn't be more right.

Chapter 7

Ember

I WAKE UP IN A FOG.

It takes me a second to realize that I'm no longer in Levi's backseat but instead laying in the middle of my bedroom floor. The revolting taste in my mouth is enough to make me want to vomit all over again. My head is still pounding, but not like it was when a monster migraine rushed through my skull.

I've always had trouble with migraines. They don't hit me as often as they did when I was in high school, but high-stress situations always have been a big trigger for me.

Pulling myself from the floor, I notice how weak I really feel as I move to the bathroom.

The second I'm upright, blackness tugs at the corners of my vision.

Well, that's new. I can't remember a migraine ever doing that.

I stumble with my first step, and I fight with the exhaustion that washes from the top of my head all the way to my toes.

"Jesus, what is wrong with me," I mumble to the empty room. I look for Bam, but I don't see him anywhere. "Bam-A-Ram," I weakly call out but still nothing. He's probably pissed at me for not giving him the rest of my lunch yesterday.

Ignoring the fact that I'm becoming overwhelmingly more exhausted with each moment I'm up and moving around, I turn the shower on. It takes me forever to get my jeans off, pulling my underwear with them and kicking them to the side. My arms get caught in my shirt as I pull it over my head, and for a second, I wonder if my arms had turned to Jell-O at some point while I slept.

The second I step into the steaming hot shower, I take a deep breath and try to remember how the hell I got home. The last thing I can recall is getting sick, then Nikki's soothing touch helping to ease the pain enough for me to fall asleep.

Then nothing.

I don't spend much time washing, just putting in the good old college try of hitting the hot spots with the bar of soap. It falls from my hand in a loud clatter the second I finish. I had the fleeting thought to ignore my hair, but the memory of puking in it last night is all the motivation I need to push through my exhaustion and reach for the shampoo.

I cry out in pain when my fingers push against a huge goose egg on the side of my head. The shampoo from my hands running down my face and into my eyes as I rinse it off just makes me cry out again.

"Shit, shit!"

I raise up, opening the shower door and jump out to grab a towel. When I'm standing in front of the mirror, I turn my head and move my thick hair out of the way. When I part my hair, I see the painful bump I had felt in the shower as well as a small cut in my scalp. That explains the headache, I guess.

I rush out of the bathroom and start searching for my phone. It takes me a few failed attempts, but I finally find it tossed behind the couch, just inside the front door. I fumble with the stupid thing before pressing the right prompts and holding it to the uninjured side of my face.

"Someone had better be dead," Nikki grumbles in greeting.

"How did I get home last night?" I breathlessly ask.

"Ember?"

"Nikki!" I yell, closing my eyes when a pain shoots through my head. "How. Did. I. Get. Home."

"Uh, you're freaking me out, Em."

"I'm freaking *myself* out!" I scream. This time, my head doesn't just give a burst of pain. Now, I feel a joining wave of nausea.

"Levi dropped you off. Well, we dropped you off. After you got sick and passed out, I kind of went a little nuts and threatened to cut off his balls if he didn't take you right home. I figured he was over it when we got to your house. Seth was pissed about how Levi was acting, but he got your door unlocked and Levi carried you in."

"I don't remember any of this," I tell her. "Did you come in too? Or just Levi and Seth?"

"Seth made me stay in the car. I think he was worried about

Levi going off the handle because I got a little lippy and wanted to keep me away from him. He just unlocked the door and came back to wait for Levi. You scared the shit out of me, though. I know you need your migraine meds and your bed when they get that bad. I just had to make him listen."

"Did you take Bam with you?" I ask, still trying to figure out how I'm missing a huge chunk of last night.

"No, why would I take that beast with me?"

"I can't find him. I can't find him, and I don't remember anything. On top of all that, I've done something to my head and I CAN'T FIND BAM!"

I hear her move around, the groaning of Seth complaining before she speaks. "I'm on the way."

I hang up, drop to the couch, and look around my living room.

"What the hell is going on?" I ask the empty room.

I must have zoned out, or passed out is more like it, because the next thing I know, I have a frantic Nikki banging on the front door and screaming my name. By the time I was able to pull myself from the couch, she must have remembered she had a spare key and she was bursting into the door.

"Joe Jonas on a stick!" she screams, bringing a smile to my face. She loves using Jonas's name in vain. "You scared the ever-loving shit out of me, Emberlyn Locke!"

I look up at her, hair wild and frizzy just sticking out in a million different directions, as she stares down at me. My head is still spinning, but I managed to sit and lean forward on the couch. My elbows propped on my knees and my head hanging between my legs.

"I found Bam," she tells me, bending down so that she's at eye level with me. "He's limping a little but seems fine. He was tied to the back fence. Why would you tie him to the fence?"

"This makes no sense, Nik. You know I would never do that. I just woke up, and it's like a whole chunk of my night is gone."

She looks at me, worry flashing in her eyes. "What's the last thing you remember?"

"The ride home. I remember the ride home, throwing up, the car door hitting me ..." I trail off and reach behind my head and feel another, smaller knot on the back of my head from where the door slammed me. "I have a bump from when he took off after I was sick, but where did I get this one?" I question her, feeling my eyes go wild as I push my head up, grabbing her hand and pushing it gently into my hair so she can feel the larger bump.

"Holy Madonna." She gasps, reaching forward and poking around the injured skin. My head jerks away from her touch instantly. "Em, that didn't happen when you were with me."

I just look at her, and I can tell by the scared look in her eyes that we're both thinking the same thing.

Levi.

Levi had something to do with this.

Bam nudges my knee, and I look down at my beautiful beast. He whines when I rub his furry head, and I know without a doubt that if Levi is responsible for my new aches and pains, he most definitely had a part in Bam's.

"Let's go get you checked out, Em. I would feel a lot better if you went to the hospital."

I shake my head and look up from Bam's brown eyes. Nikki,

clearly thinking her suggestion is a done deal, is gathering some more clothing out of the neat laundry stacks I had made earlier yesterday before running out of time to put them away. I look down and realize that I'm still wearing just my huge bath towel knotted at my chest. Luckily, it's large enough that even sitting as I am, I'm covering everything important.

Bam whines again when Nikki almost steps on him, moving away with a limp that makes my heart hurt.

"Here," she starts. "Let's get you changed."

"I'm not going to the doctor, Nik. I can tell you right now that I most likely have one hell of a concussion. Whether that's from the door or whatever happened to me when I got home, I'll never know. But if I show up at the emergency room, this will get back to my dad, and I just can't deal with his overprotectiveness right now."

She frowns. "I don't think that's a good idea."

"Maybe not, but it's not going to change anything."

Sighing, she drops the clothes on the couch next to me. I look over at the yoga pants and tank top and move to stand before dropping the towel. Nikki ignores me as I cover up my nakedness. We've been friends for so long that we lost our shyness a long time ago.

"I'm not leaving," she tells me with determination so I don't try to persuade her otherwise.

"Good. You can drive me to the vet when they open later this morning so I can have Bam checked out."

She makes a sound of annoyance and throws up her hands. "So you'll check on your dog but not yourself?"

I nod, pulling my top down and looking back at where Bam is licking his back leg with slow swipes of his tongue. He looks up, his eyes trusting, and I give him a smile.

"Yup."

Chapter 8

Ember

AS MUCH AS I LOVE Nikki, I'm going to kill her in about three seconds. She's refused to leave my side, being a constant shadow since my early morning phone call a day and a half ago.

Annoying, smothering, and overwhelming with her mothering.

"Nik, you need to go home. I need to get started on my final piece for the exhibit before everyone comes over for the big secret plans tonight."

She looks at me with determination and maybe even a little uncertainty concerning leaving me alone. Even though I've been fine, save the little headache that is just finally receding.

"I'm fine, Nik!"

Bam barks at my outburst, and I smile at him. He's still limping slightly when he moves around, but the vet assured me that he just had a nasty bruise.

"You aren't fine, Emberlyn. You hardly have any energy."

I huff out a growl type noise and place both my hands on my hips before giving her a look that clearly shows my losing battle with patience. "I would have plenty of damn energy if you weren't still here waking me up every hour to make me recite my name, alphabet, and the presidents' names in order of office term!"

She has the decency to look sheepish, but before she can voice some sort of comeback, I continue.

"And I should add I wouldn't ever be able to tell you the presidents' names in order of office term without freaking Google! So your argument that I must surely have brain damage because I couldn't complete your asinine tasks is just ludicrous. I'm fine, but I need a nap to make up for my lack of sleep, Nik. Especially since you guys are still set on me going out to party tonight."

"They weren't asinine! You know damn well that I know what I'm talking about. You don't just forget first-aid training."

I narrow my eyes. "First-aid training that you got when you were twelve in 4-H!" I scream.

"Well, it still makes me more qualified than you are to make that decision, now doesn't it."

"I'm going to kick your ass if you don't go home."

She smirks before picking up the nail file she had been using and continued to shape her nails. "No, you won't."

My hands fly in the air, and I toss my head back to let out another groan.

"I'm going to go back and work. You need to go home so that I can finish in peace, get a nap for a few hours without you waking me up, and come back tonight with everyone else."

I turn from where she is sitting at the kitchen table and walk to my studio. The second my feet touch down on the white floor, I let out a calming breath, instantly feeling at home.

Looking at the clock hanging over the doorway, I make a note of how much time I have before I need to stop. Since the sun has just now touched the top of the trees, I know I have a good five hours before I need to stop. My sister told me earlier, through text, that they would now be over to my house around six tonight with dinner before starting our prep to go out.

I turn on my music before setting my timer for just after lunch. I go about getting all my paint and brushes set out in front of the huge canvas that is bigger than I am tall. The curator of the gallery where my exhibit is being housed didn't even bat an eye when I asked her if I could change the featured piece at the last minute. The idea came to me last night during one of the rare moments Nikki let me sleep, and I hadn't been able to stop thinking about it since.

The first thing I did, before calling her, was go through the blank canvases that are stored in my guest room to find *the one*. I remember when I bought the six-foot-by-four-foot canvas; I never thought I would find something to put on it, until last night.

Placing the canvas so that it's horizontal on my easel, having to adjust the custom-made brackets in order to hold the monster, I instantly pick up my brush and drop it into the gray paint.

It isn't long before the music, my mind, and my arm against the canvas are synced together in a beautiful dance. Each stroke is made without thought; each dip into the paint is made without looking away from the swirling arches and twists of black, gray, and white paint.

Never have I created something that wasn't full of color, full of life. All of my paintings are known for being vibrant and as lifelike as a picture. But not this one. This one is as abstract as it gets.

My timer goes off, and I step back to look at the work that has held me captive for the last five hours. I take a deep breath and move from one side of the canvas to the other, taking in the unfinished work. I'm surprised that I managed to get as much as I had done today, but really, I shouldn't be. It's been a long time since I was that captive in my zone.

I make quick work of cleaning up my supplies and moving the unused paint mixtures to the pods that will keep them fresh until I can return to my work tomorrow. I ignore the grumble in my stomach as I drop down on the couch with a heavy sigh and give in to the exhaustion that I've been pushing off.

My dreams are full of the black, gray, and white world I just knew would be my best piece of art to date.

"What?" I ask around a mouthful of pizza.

My sister just continues to look at me with narrowed eyes.

"Seriously, what is your problem?" I snap, dropping the crust after tearing off the last delicious bite.

"Dad is going to shit his pants when he sees your head," she tells me, crossing her arms over her chest.

"Yeah? And how is he going to find out unless someone opens her big fat mouth to tell him?"

"You two annoy the shit out of me," Stella bluntly states, causing my sister to snap her eyes over to where she is finishing Dani's hair. "I'm so happy that my dad didn't have more kids. I could never handle that crap."

Dani laughs, earning a scowl from Stella when her head moves too much. "Just imagine having to deal with a miniature version of my dad as a brother!"

"Yeah, no. No way in hell I could handle that shit," Stella continues, curling another long piece of Dani's hair around her flat iron.

"You have it all wrong, Stel." Lyn laughs. "There is no way a sibling could have handled *you*!"

Everyone laughs, and Stella just shrugs, sprays another lock of Dani's hair with hairspray, and continues without disagreeing.

"He's going to find out," my sister continues as if she hadn't just been interrupted.

"Shut up." I groan and move to walk into my living room where the rest of the girls are hanging out in various forms of readiness.

Dani and Stella had been doing everyone's hair since the moment they all arrived two hours ago; now, the only two left are the both of them. My hair had been first and the beginning of my sister's annoying chatter about my dad potentially freaking out. The second Dani moved the shorter hair that always brushes over the side of my forehead and got a look at the now yellow and green bruising, she hadn't stopped.

I can hear her muttering under her breath as she moves around the kitchen to clean up the last of our group's dinner mess, but she wisely stops giving me a bunch of what my dad refers to as our 'sass.'

Megan and Lila are talking softly on my loveseat, and judging by the way she keeps turning her phone in Lila's direction, I'm assuming she is showing off pictures of her newborn son, Jack.

They're both wearing black dresses, but where Lila's is on the shorter end of slutty, Megan's is not. Megan's is a beautiful shirtsleeve dress that hits her right in the middle of her thighs. Loose in the skirt and hiding what she refers to as her stubborn baby weight.

Lila's is sleeveless, but with thick straps and a deep neckline that shows off her cleavage impressively. And where Megan's is loose, Lila's is skintight and hits her just under her bottom.

Nikki, Lyn, Dani, and Stella are in similar dresses as Lila's, each a little different from the other but all black.

"We look like we're going to a funeral," I mumble before attempting to sit on the couch next to Nikki. But before my bottom hits the cushion, she is pushing against my back and shoving me forward. "What the hell, Nik!"

"You need to go get dressed!" she snaps.

"She's right," my sister says, coming in the room. "You're the last one!"

She pulls me forward and down to my bedroom. When the light snaps on, illuminating what has been laid out on the bed waiting for me like a snake ready to strike, I feel my stomach start flipping nervously.

"Uh," I start.

"Nope. No. No way in hell," my sister starts to fuss. "You will put that on and freaking like it."

"That," I say, pointing to the blood-red fabric on my bed, my voice getting a little manic as I continue, "is not a dress. That looks like something a toddler would wear."

"It's stretchy," she tells me as if that's all that matters. She starts to unbutton the shirt that I had put on over my strapless bra earlier and I slap her hands away.

"I'm not wearing that," I screech.

"Yes, you are," I hear behind me and turn toward the doorway to see Stella. "My pops spent a ridiculous amount of time hunting for the perfect birthday outfit for you for as he says *hours and hours, darlin' girl*," she says, mocking her pop's voice perfectly. "You know what happens when you ignore the advice of that man." She stands up straight, tosses her long curled hair over her shoulder before continuing in Sway's voice. "There's certain times in a woman's life when she needs to make sure to work the goodness God gave her with no hesitation whatsoever, darling girl. Just flaunt all that beauty and make every man you pass die a little inside because he will just not live another second if he can't have you. For little Miss Emberlyn, that moment will be tonight, and Sway demands pictures and pictures before you hit the town." She relaxes her posture instantly and shrugs. "So let's do this."

Chapter 9

Nate

OPENING NIGHT IS IN FULL swing.

I'm sweaty and hotter than fucking hell, but the smile on my face hasn't left for a second since we opened the doors three hours ago. Even before the six o'clock opening time, the line had been so out of control to get in the door that we went ahead and opened up the holding room at almost four in the afternoon. The girls and guys had been working together in perfectly synchronized movements ever since.

I see Shane the second he starts to climb the stairs to my office, where I've been observing the insanity while I cooled off some.

"Fucking madhouse," he rumbles with a smile on his face.

"We did it," I tell him, not looking away from the packed floor below us. Even the areas that hold the tall tables and beyond are packed with bodies undulating with the pounding bass flowing through the speakers. The house DJ, Thorn, changes the song to another fast-paced tune and throws one arm up and down with the beat. The bodies surrounding his staged-off area begin to move together a little closer. You can tell without being down there that things are getting heated, which isn't a surprise since each bar has been passing drinks in rapid speed.

"We didn't do shit, brother. This is all you."

I move to deny his claim, but a flash of color by the entryway into the madness stills the words before they could even leave my lips. I squint my eyes and try to see through the dim lights and smoky air, but the vision was gone so quick I'm almost positive it was just a trick of the lights.

"Did you see the crowd during the bar dances?" Shane asks, moving to my side and watching the floor.

"Insanity." I laugh, and it had been. Complete insanity. The second the DJ had dropped the bass and cranked up the volume, our boys had sprung into action. The patrons didn't know what to think at first. All drink orders had been stalled, and instantly, they had their heavily booted feet up on the glossy wood. They pulled back their drinks and the surface was cleared for them. Even I could appreciate the show knowing that it was my brainchild that had held the masses captive and hypnotized as the guys moved like whatever was in front of them was a naked woman ready and willing to be fucked … hard.

"I think they're starting to anticipate them now. Every time we inch closer to the top of another hour, drinks start being pulled off the bar before Thorn even has a chance to drop the beat."

I nod. "You going to get out there tonight?" I ask him.

"No clue. Are you?"

I turn my back to the crowd beyond my window and lean back against the glass. "Depends, my friend. If the mood strikes, maybe. Not sure I see anyone worth getting up there and shaking my ass for anyway."

Shane laughs, dropping his hand heavy on my back. "Yeah, something tells me that motivation isn't going to be an issue for you," he oddly says and walks back to the doorway. "Let's go join the party, brother."

The second he opens the heavy steel door, the music thumps and pounds through the once silent space. A familiar rush of adrenaline fills my body as we both stalk down the stairs together and into the overheated floor. I see, but ignore, the females around us as they turn and attempt to gain our attention. I continue through the pulsing bodies that litter the massive open space and walk toward the bar.

"Yo, Nate," Dent yells over the music, and when I turn my head toward him, he slides a shot down the sleek wooden surface.

My hand shoots out and grabs the glass right when I hear Logan yell, "Bottoms up." Without thought, I bring the liquor to my lips. The burn travels down my throat, and when I settle the shot glass back on the bar, Travis is already there with the bottle of tequila in his hand, refilling it instantly.

I ignore the chick to my right and turn to look around the room. The small smile that had been playing on my lips drops when I see the woman dancing just a few feet in front of me.

"What the fuck," I mumble, dropping the once again empty glass down and stalking forward.

I look around when I lose her in the crowd, but continue to stomp through the crowd to the other side of the club where the other dance floor is moving like one giant wave to the music.

I see her again and instantly fume.

"You want to tell me what the fuck you're doing here," I rumble low in my throat when my head dips down until my mouth is right next to her ear and grab her by her forearm.

The thin arm is pulled from my grasp when she turns around. I stand back and cross my arms over my chest and wait for her to talk.

"What is your problem," she yells over the music.

"My problem?" I yell at her and bend down so that I don't have to scream over the noise. "My problem, dear sister, is that you're in my club dressed like … that," I tell her and point my finger at her dress. "Does your husband know you're here?"

She narrows her eyes and stops dancing to stand up on her toes and get in my fucking face.

"He sure does and I'll have you know that he will be here later."

I drop my head back and look up at the ceiling. I should have known they wouldn't stay away. It's not that I don't want them here, I do, but not if I have to look out for her while he's not here.

"Plus, we're celebrating," she yells before dropping down on her impossibly tall heels and dancing again.

"Celebrating what?"

Her smile goes all wonky and shit. She looks downright fucking evil.

"Ember's birthday, big brother," she tells me with a pat

against my chest before spinning around and vanishing through the thick crowd.

Ember's birthday.

And then it hits me.

Ember's *twenty-first* birthday.

Fucking shit.

And if I know my sister and her gang of misfits, she's up to something a lot bigger than just celebrating. Of all the places they could have ended up tonight, they picked my fucking club knowing damn well that things between Ember and me are one giant mess. Dani isn't stupid, and since she was the first person I ran into after my chat with Locke the other night, she knows exactly what's going on between us.

With a single-minded determination, I start to scan the room for Dani, Ember, or any of the other girls that I'm sure are tagging along for the showdown they're hoping for.

Each pass my eyes makes around the room just coils the tension in my gut tighter until I'm determined to find them and kick them out. If I were smart, I would find Shane and make him take care of it ... but clearly, I'm not of sound mind because the second my eyes lock on Ember, I know the last thing I'm going to do is let her walk away from me again.

I feel my cock jump when I see past the group dancing between where I'm standing and she is laughing with the girls around one of the tables just off the dance floor. Then I get my first good look when the definition of living sin meets my eyes.

"Holy fucking shit," I breathe out in a rush of words, feeling like I've just been punched in the stomach.

The possessiveness that fires through my body at the vision before me is nothing like I've ever felt before. The anger that anyone else in this room is free to look at her slams into my body with a force so strong I almost reach out to steady my footing ... almost.

My feet are moving just as rapidly as my racing heart as I move toward her. Dani, facing my direction, drops her jaw as her eyes widen. I see Stella roll her eyes in a bored way before giving Maddi a nudge and nod in my direction. I don't look at Ember's sister long, but I don't for a second miss the small smile that hits her face when she sees me fuming behind Ember. I pay no attention to the rest of the girls in their group but reach out to spin the little devil in front of me around gently.

She teeters on her feet, and I glance down with a frown. Each bare inch of her tan legs has me clenching my jaw, but when I see the tall-as-fuck heels on her dainty feet, whatever blood I had left in my brain blasts to my cock. I groan when my eyes travel back up to a dress that shouldn't be allowed past the bedroom as my balls grow painfully tight.

"What the fuck are you doing here?" I growl.

Fucking growl. Like a goddamn bear.

She doesn't respond, but she also does a shit job at hiding the hurt that flashes in her eyes.

Shit.

"Don't be a jerk," I hear my sister yell.

I lift my gaze and narrow them on her. "You had better watch it before your nose is in the corner for a much-needed time the fuck out, Danielle Cage."

She rolls her eyes, and I make a mental note to deal with her later, looking back down into Ember's pissed face.

"You shouldn't be here." The second the words are out of my mouth, I feel regret slamming into me. *Fuck yeah, she should be here*, my mind keeps screaming over and over. "You don't belong here," I continue to speak. I can't stop the words coming out of my mouth, and I know the second my heart starts to pound at an unnatural speed that I'm fucking up major here.

"You're a son of a Bieber's biscuit!" I hear a drunken screech from my side and look over to see Ember's best friend, Nikki, reach out to poke me. "Son of a Backstreet Boy," she oddly screams next and brings her offending finger to her chest to cradle it as her brow furrows in pain.

Weird girl, that one.

I take a deep breath to fill my chest with the smoky, raw air around me, before doing what I should have done in the first place. I bend, and before Ember can react, she is over my shoulder and I'm stalking back to the stairs that will lead to my office. My hand splays out against her backside so that the short-as-shit dress she's wearing doesn't give a view to the room that should be for my eyes only.

My eyes only? Where the hell did that thought come from?

I feel her small fists beating on my back, but I ignore her as I climb the stairs, trying my best not to think about the heat of her pussy against the palm of my hand. The second I slam my office door shut, closing us in the room, she launches herself off my shoulder. Luckily for her, I was near the couch, so when she stumbled on those heels, she landed on the soft leather with an oomph.

"What the hell is your problem, Nathaniel!" she screams, launching herself up to stand and pushing me with both hands against my chest. "You have no right!"

Taking her tiny wrists in my hands, I bring them down and trap them behind her back. She struggles and my eyes drop to her chest as each heaving breath makes the material drop a little lower.

"How the fuck is this even staying up," I fume. Switching my hold so I have both wrists in one hand, I bring up one finger to pick at the thin fabric strap going over her shoulder. My eyes roaming over the exposed skin of her neck as I trail my finger down the thin strap until I hit the deep V exposing the silky smooth skin between her tits. All it would take is one real deep breath and her nipple would be on display.

"N-nate," she stutters, and I lift my gaze from the valley of tan skin to look into her eyes. The anger is still there but it has dimmed, and in its place is pure fucking lust.

"No one should see this much of you. Not one fucking person but me."

"I'm not yours," she fumes, and I can see that the fury is winning over the lust.

"You're fucking wrong, babe," I respond without thought.

She snaps back and pulls one hand from my hold before I can even process her movement. In the next blink, that same freed hand cracks against my cheek and I feel a red-hot burn.

"I *am not* your fucking *babe!*" she shouts.

"I'll give you that one, but only that fucking one, Ember."

"I'm not yours, Nate. You had that chance, and you didn't

want it."

Bending down so my eyes are level with hers, I give in to the possessive need to claim her. "You were fucking born to be mine, little firecracker, and mine you will fucking be." My words coming out in a thick rumble, and I watch in satisfaction as her pupils dilate.

Check. Fucking. Mate.

Her shocked gasp works in my favor, and in the next breath, my lips are on hers as my tongue slides into her mouth and caresses the slick heat of her own. My hands hit her hips, and with a flex of my fingers, I pull her against me roughly.

The body that had been rigid in my hands goes weak the second our bodies press tightly together, and she kisses me back with a fervor that surpasses my own. Her arms, no longer hanging limp at her side, move up until her hand is pushing into my hair and the tie that had been holding it up behind my head is ripped out as she pulls me closer to her mouth by my now loose locks.

This kiss is all about domination, and at the moment, I'm not fucking sure I want to be the one to win this war. Our moans are mingling together and the wet sounds of our mouths feasting drown out the dull thump of the music. Letting her own silky lips take the lead, I hum deep in my throat. My erection rubs against her belly as my hands slide down to the point where the fabric meets burning smooth skin.

The second my fingertips curl around her dress and begin to lift the fabric, she jerks in my hold. The hands that had been tugging through my hair drop to my chest, and with a strangled sound, she pushes me away.

We stare at each other, chests heaving.

When I move to take her back in my arms and give us both what we clearly want, her arm comes up and stops my movement with one palm against the center of my chest. I look down at the offending hand with a tilt of my head, trying my fucking hardest to get my brain to turn back on. Or at least, will some of the blood that is currently lacking from my head to leave my hard-as-shit cock.

"No," she whispers hoarsely.

"Yes," I demand, my eyes snapping back to hers.

"This will not happen."

Again, I'm struck dumb and I just tilt my head again like a confused puppy that just wants his bone.

"Nate." She sighs with a small shake of her head. "This won't happen. I have a boyfriend."

I feel one of my brows go up as I continue to look at her.

"Not only that, but you had your chance ... twice ... and both of those times ended disastrously for me. I'm not willing to put myself through that again."

Shaking my head, finally getting some sense back in my system, I clear my throat before speaking. "You *had* a boyfriend, Ember. But that's going to change real quick. You've ignored me since dropping that bomb on me the other day, and trust me, firecracker, we will be talking about *that*. One thing you need to get through that pretty little head of yours, though, is that this will be fucking happening."

She's silent but not for long. She comes up on the balls of her feet the best she can in order to level her eyes with mine, but she just ends up with the top of her head getting there before dropping back down with a huff.

"I handed myself to you years ago, Nate, and the only thing that was missing was the silver fucking platter. You rejected me. Like a stupid little girl, I thought my crush on you was this big grand love, but you proved me wrong, and I was *crushed*. You get that? Then, when I had finally put that behind me, you treat me like a faceless slut *YOU DIDN'T SEE* as you almost took my virginity against a fucking wall. So, no ... this will *not* be happening."

"You're mine," I grunt deeply. "Fucking mine."

"I'm no one's but my own, and I'm definitely not yours. I'll never be *yours*."

She storms past me and wrenches my door open before disappearing down the stairs.

"We'll just see about that," I mumble to the empty room as the door slams in her wake.

Chapter 10

Ember

THE FUCKING NERVE.

My lips burn and I can feel the wetness between my legs with each step that pulls my underwear against my bare sex.

My core throbs with the climax I had in his arms from that kiss alone.

I should feel terrible that I just came apart in a man's arms who didn't belong to my boyfriend, but I don't. That could be because my mind had already put Levi in the ex category, the actual breakup just being a formality.

The crowd seems to part as I push through the room and back to where the girls are still drinking and laughing as if Nate hadn't just carted me off over his shoulder.

How embarrassing.

Not a word is spoken as I snatch my purse from the table and reach in to grab some cash before spinning on my heels and making quick work of getting to the bar.

I don't look around, too afraid of what I'll see on the faces I pass. My eyes go up to the black glass above me, and I know without being able to see him that those eyes are tracking my every move.

"What'll it be, babe," I hear, bringing my focus away from the wall of windows.

Babe.

I'm so sick of people calling me babe. I feel like that word alone is going to drive me to the edge of sanity.

"I don't care. Just make it strong," I yell, slapping the bill down on the bar.

The shirtless man just nods as he turns around to grab one of the bottles of liquor behind him and a shot glass. He slides it forward, but when I push the money toward him, he shakes his head and walks away.

With a shrug, I lift the cool glass to my lips and take it down with one swallow. My eyes sting as the liquid burns down my throat and into my belly. I blink a few times to clear my vision as I slam the glass down and wave the same man over.

This time, he takes my money, and I wave him off when he goes to get change. I shoot the drink back before pointing at the glass again, silently demanding another.

He leans against the bar and just tips the bottle over the glass again.

Three more shots and no more cash, I'm finally able to handle the burn without wanting to gag.

Of course, that would be when I open my eyes expecting to see my new best friend the bartender's brown eyes, but instead, I see the emerald fury of Nate Reid.

Maybe it's the shots or maybe it's just the hold he's always had on me, but I don't move. Not even when I see him moving his arms as my old friend, brown-eyed bartender, hands him a cup and a few bottles. He does something with them, but I couldn't tell you what because my eyes never leave his face.

When a body collides with mine from behind, pushing me against the bar painfully, the trance he had me stuck in is broken, and I look away to watch some drunken man stumble after a group of girls. Before I look back at Nate, I peek over at the table our group of girls is occupying. Gazes locked on us, they all wear expressions with slack jaws.

Well, everyone except Nikki. She looks like she just discovered Santa was real and won the lotto in the same sweep.

I feel something cold hit the hand I have resting on the bar, and I turn back around, glancing down to where Nate is pushing a drink into my hand. I look at the colorful drink instead of the man pushing it toward me. He's swirling the drink around with a stick, mixing the colors inside the glass for a second before he pulls his hand up. I watch as the stick becomes a lollipop, then follow its path up until Nate's smirking lips open to suck the candy in his mouth once before popping it out and dropping it back down into my glass.

My gaze doesn't look at the drink this time, nope ... no sir, this time, I study his mouth as his tongue dips out and wets those thick lips that had me coming undone just minutes ago. I feel my breath pull in a choppy inhale and look up to meet his eyes. I'm not sure what to make of the expression on his face, and if I'm honest, fear and self-preservation are what keeps me from trying to figure it out.

At that moment, all rational thoughts die a shocked death.

Nate reaches forward, tags the lollipop from my drink again, and before I realize what's happening, he begins to paint my lips with the wet, sticky candy of the lollipop, and the music changes from some Justin Timberlake song to something I haven't ever heard before. His features morph into a sadistic grin and an equally wicked gleam shines in his eyes before pulling the candy away and dropping it back into the glass.

Call it intuition, but the second I see both his palms press against the bar's surface, I reach out and tag the glass in my hand, pulling it toward my chest just as he literally jumps from where he had been standing on the ground to a crouched position with his feet on the bar.

I hear the whole club go electric and notice just out of the corner of my eye that my brown-eyed friend is also standing on the bar as the song's lyrics hit my brain. Something about lollipops.

Holy shit.

Nate stands, his body moving with the music, and I back up to see him a little better. A small step, but that's all that is needed. He reaches up, his eyes never leaving mine, and grabs some handle thing that is hanging above him.

You know that scene in *Magic Mike* when Mike is spinning and all that on the stage … well, that's the only way I can describe what Nate does next. One large fist around the handle holds his huge body up while spinning him in quick circles. I gasp when he lets go and slams his feet back down on the bar. He doesn't even look the slightest bit dizzy when he drops down to his hands and knees against the wooden surface.

He flips his loose hair from his face and turns his head to look directly into my eyes, pulling his thick bottom lip into his mouth as he starts to fuck the wood under his body. I have to squeeze my legs together with the vision before me because I know, I just *know*, if I were under him with my legs spread, his dick would be drilling into my body, deep and hard.

When he pushes up and spins on his knees to face me, his crotch eye level with my face, he slowly starts to move his shirt up. As he reveals each deliciously hard ab, I can hear the screams around us getting louder.

I hear the music increase in tempo as he leans forward, dropping his shirt and covering his beautiful body. I stand there in shock as he pulls the lollipop back up from my drink and presses the cold, wet candy against my lips. They part without conscious thought to take the lollipop inside my mouth.

The song ends and he gives me a wink as he pulls the candy from my mouth and into his own before he jumps from the bar to the space in front of me. I feel lightheaded when he leans down and runs his nose against the shell of my ear, making me gasp.

"You.Are.*Mine*," he growls before taking my earlobe between his lips and biting my flesh roughly between his teeth. A moan rumbles from deep in his chest and his breath echoes in my ear.

And what do I do?

I stand there and come, again, from just the simplest of touch-es.

Well, fuck me.

Chapter 11

Ember

"STOP MOVING," I GROAN AND pull my covers over my head as I pray for my stomach to stop swirling.

"I'm not moving, the world is," Nikki rasps from behind me and rips the covers from my face to cocoon herself in some weird blanket burrito.

She wiggles some more and the movement makes my stomach instantly revolt. I jump from the bed, almost tripping over where Bam is laying on the floor. I'm sure if I could see the weird dance I make to keep from stumbling to the ground, I would laugh, but instead, my eyes start to water as I run through my dark bedroom and into to the bathroom. My knees slam on the ground so hard it feels like my teeth rattle in my mouth. Ignoring the pain, I lift the lid and vomit violently.

"Oh, God!" I hear Nikki scream and the sounds of her rushing from the bedroom. I can hear her own sounds of being sick echo through my house and hope she, at least, made it to the guest bathroom before losing the contents of her stomach.

Long, agonizing minutes later, I finally feel like I can move my head from the toilet. I drop to my butt and lean against the wall as I test my ability to move without getting sick again.

Slowly, I crawl on my hands and knees until I reach the bed. Bam gives me a sniff before ignoring me to go back to sleep. Lifting my arm, I glance at the clock next to my bed and see that it's just past four in the morning. With a groan, I reach up and pull my comforter down from the bed before curling up next to Bam's furry body as the world continues to spin.

I fall back to sleep just as I hear Nikki stumble back to the bed. She mumbles about having no covers, but then her snores fill the air, and I join her a beat later.

I hear my phone vibrating against my nightstand. Peeling open my eyes, I see that the sunlight is now shining through the slats in my blinds. Feeling marginally better, I reach up and grab my phone without moving much of my body.

"'Lo?" I utter into the phone.

"Be quiet," Nikki grumbles.

"Well, don't you two sound pleasant this morning," my sister practically sings in my ear.

"Do you have to be so loud?" I question.

She laughs and I pull the phone from my ear. "Get up and drink tons of water, brat. Take some Advil and trust me when I tell you that you'll feel better with something bland in your stomach."

"There is no way in hell I'm putting anything in my stomach," I force out when just the thought makes my stomach revolt.

"I'm on the way." She sighs and hangs up.

I drop the phone and curl back up with Bam.

This time, instead of getting a little peaceful sleep, my visions are full of Nate. That kiss. That *dance*. And his words.

By the time my sister is poking me with her foot, I was so worked up I was seconds away from shoving my hand down my sleep shorts and taking care of my arousal.

He's put some voodoo curse on me.

My body seems to be stuck in some sort of Nate-induced provocation of lust and need.

"Time to get up, Em!"

I jump at Maddi's outburst and glare up at her.

"Here," she says and thrusts a huge bottle of water in my face.

I take it with greed-fueled need, as the dryness in my mouth seems to intensify at the sight of water.

"Slow down," she says when I take huge pulls and gulps of water, the excess running from the sides of my mouth and onto the top of my shirt. "You're going to get sick if you drink that fast. Slow down and take these," she stresses, pulling the bottle away from me and pushing two pills into my mouth before pressing the water back to my lips.

She continues to stand over me until I've drunk almost half of the bottle before giving me a piece of toast. I give her a look of disbelief—doubting I'll be able to actually keep that down—but I take it and slowly nibble. By the time I had finished the second piece, I was feeling less zombie-like and closer to a lukewarm human.

"Better?" she asks knowingly.

"Don't be a bragger."

She just laughs at me and helps pull me up from the floor. I look over at Nikki with a smile when I see her finishing some toast of her own.

"Don't worry, she got to me too. She's like the hangover Nazi."

"Go clean yourself up, then meet me in the living room so we can chat," Maddi says before leaving the room.

"Well," Nikki says with a mouth full of toast. "You heard the tyrant. Get your ass in gear before she comes back in here with more demands."

"I heard that," my sister calls from further in the house.

"I meant for you to!" Nikki yells back.

Rolling my eyes, I drag myself into the bathroom and go about 'cleaning myself up.'

"So …"

I groan, pulling the brush through my hair, and ignore my sister.

"Yeah, I second that so," Nikki adds when I don't make a move to speak.

I finish brushing my hair before dropping the brush down on the coffee table. I curl my legs up and wrap my arms around them before looking at the two of them sitting on the loveseat together, waiting none too patiently for me to give them what they want.

"So he just danced a little. What more do you want?"

"Uh … no. I want you to start with when he pulled you over his shoulder like Tarzan and you disappeared up those stairs. *Then* you can end with what happened when he 'just danced a little,' which in turn caused you to put so much alcohol into your body that you had to be carried out to the car and put to bed without so much as moving a muscle."

I gasp at my sister in shock. "I had to be carried out? I don't remember that."

She laughs. "Well, I would think not since you were basically comatose when Cohen helped you in the back of his truck. You didn't even move once. Which, bravo on taking your twenty-first down like a beast."

"I'm never drinking again," I vow.

"Sure … that's what everyone says." She laughs.

"Would you two shut up and get to the good stuff."

I roll my eyes at Nikki, look down at my toes, and make a mental note to repaint them later.

"I'm not even sure I understand what happened," I tell them honestly.

"How about you start at the beginning, and we can help you figure that out," Maddi says compassionately.

With a sigh, I do just that and start from the beginning. Well, more like the middle since both of them know what started all of this—that being my humiliating graduation night.

I gloss over the night of Dani and Cohen's wedding. I'm not

sure why, but deep down, I know that moment should be left be-tween Nate and me. "We had a run-in almost two years ago. It wasn't pretty, and no, I'm not going to give you more than that. It's been … hard, you could say, for me to be around him since."

"I knew it," Maddi exclaims. "I knew there was a lot more to why you weren't coming around when the family was all togeth-er."

I narrow my eyes. "Are you going to let me finish?"

She holds up her hands. "Sorry, proceed."

"Anyway, I reminded him earlier this week why things had been strained and he's been trying to get a hold of me since. I ig-nored him because I really wasn't ready to face that stuff yet. Hell, I'm not sure I am now. Then … well, then last night happened."

"I'm not really sure where to go with that, Em. That's pretty vague."

I drop my head to my knees at my sister's words and try to organize my thoughts.

"He threw my love for him in my face years ago, Maddi. Then hurt me even worse a few years later. Then, without mem-ory of even doing that, he hurt me again a few days ago. Until last night, he's never even hinted at feeling anything more than a friendship type bond toward me. Now, my mind is running wild because last night he dragged me to his office, kissed me to the point of death, and then ended it with that dance. Then he left me standing there stunned stupid as he said to me, and I quote, 'you are mine.' So … where you might not be sure where to go with that, I can assure you that *I* most definitely feel even more lost than you do right now."

Looking up, I stop avoiding them and take in two very stunned faces.

"He did *what?*" Maddi gasps.

"Well, way to go Nate-Dog!" Nikki yells.

"What about Levi?" my sister continues with a bitter look on her face, ignoring Nikki's outburst completely.

"I know it doesn't make it better, I mean I did kiss another man last night. Well, he kissed me, but I didn't push him away immediately, so I'm at just as much fault, but for what it's worth, I was breaking up with him tomorrow. It's been a long time coming, but I've just been putting it off to avoid the confrontation."

Maddi tries, but she does a crap job at hiding the happiness in her expression.

"You didn't do anything wrong," Nikki says softly, her face a mask of understanding as she nods gently. Of course, she understands. She knows everything that's happened between Levi and me that has led up to that decision.

"When did you decide this?" Maddi asks hopefully.

"A few days ago, for sure. But I've been thinking about it for a few weeks. I would have already broken it off, but he's been working all weekend. He got off this morning and went right to bed. Hell, maybe the gym, but regardless, we don't have plans to see each other until later tonight or tomorrow."

She nods, looking over at a still nodding Nikki before her nod turns into a shake of her head at my weird friend's theatrics.

"Okay," she starts, and I hold my breath. I would hate it if she were disappointed in me for the way I'm handling the men in my life. Shit, men in my life? When did I become one of those girls?

"I'm going to have to agree with Nikki, Em. You aren't exactly an angel in this situation, but you didn't instigate things between you and Nate. And if I'm being honest, if I were in your shoes, I'm not sure I would have been able to resist the kind of sexual tension you two have going on."

"But?"

Her face goes soft before she stands and walks over to the couch, sitting down next to me and pulling me into her arms. "No buts, little sister. You're in one hell of a complicated situation, and the only advice I can give you is to follow your heart."

"My heart needs to stop and ask for directions," I mumble against her chest.

I feel her laugh before she speaks. "Then you know what I think?"

Lifting my head with a sniffle to keep my emotions in check, I wait for her to continue.

"It's time to call Mom."

Chapter 12

Nate

MY COCK IS GOING TO fall off.

I grab the shirt I had thrown off last night and wipe my come off my abs before tossing it in the general direction of my laundry hamper.

I look down at my still hard cock in disgust and wonder if this is one of those moments I should call my doctor because my erection has lasted longer than four hours.

Hell, it's lasted longer than twelve.

I frown when I watch it grow even harder at the memory of why I've been in this predicament for so long.

Ember.

My little firecracker.

She lit up like the Fourth of July just from my kiss.

She might think I didn't notice, but when her body got tight in my arms just seconds before those sweet fucking tremors took hold of her, I knew.

I reach out and grab my lube, again, and get ready to fuck my fist when I would give just about anything to have Ember here in my bed. Just when I'm wrapping my fist around my cock, my phone goes off and I sigh, looking sadly at my crotch.

"Dude, you're going to have to just stay hard," I moan before placing my cell to my ear.

"Son?"

"What's up?"

"Do I even want to know what you were just saying?"

"Probably not, but hey … how long do I wait for my dick to go soft before I need to worry?"

Silence meets my question, and I pull the phone from my ear, checking to see if the call was dropped.

"Uh," my dad starts, and I drop back on the bed, feeling my cock bounce against my stomach.

"Not something I'm exactly excited to have to ask, but I would rather ask you than call the doctor."

I hear my mom say something in the background. My dad's voice sounds muffled when he says something in return, then I hear him moving around the house before responding. "Nate, did you take something?"

I laugh without humor. "Fuck, no. I wish that were the problem."

"If you didn't take something, do you want to tell me why you're having this little issue?"

"It's not a little issue," I mumble looking down at my cock again to see just how far from little my issue really is.

"Smartass."

"Let's just say, I had a run-in with a woman who started this problem, and I haven't been able to get soft since."

"And you didn't take anything?"

"Jesus fucking Christ, I don't do drugs!"

He chuckles softly, and I try not to be annoyed that he thinks this is a time to be cracking jokes.

"I remember when I first met your mother," he starts, and I quickly shut that shit down.

"I'm going to need your advice to be void of anything that starts with a sentence like that," I boom into the phone.

His laughter rumbles louder.

"Not even that took care of your problem, huh?"

I look down, my cock still angry fucking red, the tip wet with pre-come when I shouldn't have anything left in me, and groan.

"Hate to break it to you, son, but you're going to be walking around like that until you can run back into the woman who started the problem."

"That's what I was worried you were going to say," I groan.

He's silent, but I know it's more about him weighing his words than not having anything to say.

"Care to fill me in a little? I might be your dad, but I could also be able to help even if it's uncomfortable as shit for both of us to be talking about your dick."

"I'm not really sure this conversation would get any easier if I filled you in a little more, old man."

Ignoring the pain in my crotch, I pull myself from the bed and grab a pair of sweats, carefully tucking my hard buddy in and walking to the kitchen to make a protein shake.

"Try me," he says.

"It's Ember."

This time, I know the silence is a lot more than weighing his words. "Ember as in Emberlyn Locke, Maddox Locke's baby girl?" he grumbles deeply through the line.

"One and the same," I respond, before taking a long swallow of my shake.

"Shit," he murmurs under his breath.

"Yeah … that about sums it up. Oh, I think the kicker would be that Maddox is very aware of what is going on between Ember and me."

His humorless laugh comes first. "Of course, he does, Nate. There isn't much that has ever gotten past that man."

"He's going to kick my fucking ass," I tell him.

"Without a fucking doubt," he confirms. "How's that help your problem?" he adds with a laugh.

"Not even slightly better."

He laughs even harder, and I just roll my eyes, grabbing a banana and taking half down with one bite.

"Ignore your dick, Nate," he says after a minute of solid belly laughs. "Ignore that shit no matter what until you know what you want to do when it comes to Ember. If you don't intend to start something solid with her, well … then your dick should be the last thing that you give attention to."

"I don't think it matters what I want with Ember," I complain.

"And that would be why?"

"Because I fucked up when I thought I was doing the right

thing. I fucked up even more a while ago without even realizing it, and I'm not sure which one was worse, but I'm pretty sure them both together means my wants pertaining to Ember mean jack shit."

"Tell me," he says with seriousness. "When you fucked up the first time, did you do it to protect her or because you would rather be a little punk?"

"Nice," I grunt, finishing my second banana. "I pushed her away because not only was she way too fucking young, but also because I wasn't ready to see what was right in front of my face."

"And now?"

"And now, I'm not just ready to see it, I want it more than I want my next fucking breath."

"Well, son, if you ask me, I think you have everything you need to know right there. We're men, we're going to fuck up, but the beauty of finding that one woman meant for you is that no matter how much you fuck up, she will always be there to help make it right. So it's up to you to do what you can in order to right the wrong turns you made and then spend the rest of your days doing everything in your power to only make right turns."

"What the hell does that mean?"

He laughs some more. *Fucking asshole.* "Let me make it simple for you. Find out what you want from Ember. Look in your future, picture her completely out of it, and ask yourself if you can live with that. If not, work your ass off to prove to her that no matter how badly you fucked up, you'll do anything to make it up to her."

"Easier said than done."

"It's pretty fucking easy when all a good woman ever really wants is the unconditional love of her man."

I stare blindly out my front window, looking into the woods that surround my property while rolling his words around in my head. "Her dad is going to kill me."

"Nah, he knows that would hurt his girl too much. He'll make sure he doesn't leave any marks that can't be covered up."

"Not helping," I grind out through clenched teeth.

"Learned my lessons a long time ago, Nate. Lessons that hurt with so much vicious pain that sometimes I still feel the tug of them. But one thing I will never take for granted is that love, true love, is always worth fighting for even if you're fighting the one person who holds the key to taking all that pain away because, in the end, love conquers all, Nate."

"No one said anything about love, old man," I respond without conviction because it would just be a lie. I've loved that girl since I lied to her face and broke her heart.

"You didn't have to," he softly says. "I'm here if you need me, son. It won't be easy, but don't give up until you've won."

"Never," I say, this time having no trouble with the conviction in my tone.

I hear the call disconnect and I drop my phone down before collapsing on the couch with a deep sigh. With one more sad look toward my crotch and tented sweats, I start to plan.

Chapter 13

Ember

MADDI HASN'T STOPPED SMILING AT me since she called my mom and asked her to come to my house and bring lunch for us. Nikki, sensing this moment should be between a mom and her daughters, left shortly after that call.

While waiting for her to show up, I busy myself in the bathroom to brush my teeth again and go about freshening up in the attempt to feel just a little more human before I bared my soul for not just my sister, but my mother as well.

Hell, it could be worse … it could be my father too.

"Sweetie?" my mom calls into my bedroom with a soft knock on the door.

"Come on in, Mom," I respond with a smile that only grows when she pops her blond head through the crack in my door.

You would never guess that she's in her mid-fifties. My mom

still doesn't even look a day over forty, if that. Her blond hair doesn't hold a single gray, and her freckled skin is wrinkle free. She's the most beautiful woman I know.

"You okay?" she asks, walking into the room and shutting the door. I'm silently thankful for the privacy, something she clearly sees judging by her next words. "I sent your sister home, honey. Now, give me all your worries and let me make them better."

A sob bubbles up before I can stop it, and I step into my mom's arms. She holds me while I get it out, maneuvering us until she is leaning against my headboard and she has her loving arms wrapped around me.

Sometimes, no matter how old you are, the only thing that makes you feel like you can manage all the things spinning around you helplessly is to have your mother's arms wrapped around you.

"Is this about Levi?" she hedges.

"No ... yes. God, I have no idea how to even answer that."

"Well," she says and pulls back to look into my eyes. Her light brown eyes full of love and understanding. "Give me everything and we can pick it apart and figure out what needs to happen next."

"Directions ... I need directions," I mumble through my sniffles.

Her blond brows pull in slightly and a small frown hits her lips. "Directions to what, baby?"

"How to follow my heart." I hiccup.

Her frown disappears instantly replaced with a wide smile. "Then directions we'll find."

I drop back into her arms and give her everything, not leaving a single detail of it out, and when I finish, I don't feel any less confused.

"Oh, my sweet girl. You always, even when you were a tiny baby, overthink any and every challenge placed in front of you. That is something I'm afraid you came by honestly. Your father was the same way. Overthought everything and let his fears and insecurities overrule what his heart was screaming."

I lift up and move to cross my legs, facing my mom as she mirrors my position.

"What changed?" I ask, searching her eyes, having a hard time picturing the strong and confident man I know like that.

"Your father did." She laughs. "Well, I think it might have been a little of my stubborn will mixed with his and his steadfast determination mixed with both our fears and endless love, but in the end, it was the same result."

"I'm not sure I follow," I return.

She laughs again, the sound like little bells ringing, and my heart lightens some.

"You know that your dad and I didn't have an easy start. I was insecure and feared many things because of the way I was raised. Your father, well, he had many similar feelings, but also had some stupid, misguided beliefs that I was too good for him and he would ruin me. Silly man."

I gasp, thinking about just how similar that sounds to Nate's and my situation. "And … what changed?" I ask again.

"He woke up. I didn't give up. He didn't give up. A lot of the same, but it was just our love being too big to ever ignore."

I look down at my nails, picking at my polish, but I don't

speak.

"And a lot of sass," she continues.

I throw back my head and laugh, feeling lighter.

"So this isn't about Levi, exactly, but more about you and Nate?"

I nod, still not looking up.

"Sweetheart, look at your mama."

Instantly, I give her my eyes. She's still smiling. "Nate's a good boy. He has a huge heart and isn't afraid to laugh. He's one of those live big and live loud people. I've watched him grow up from a baby into the man he is today, so I can say with certainty that he is a man worthy of your love. But I can also see how Nate, being the man he is, took the youthful, innocent love of a just turned eighteen-year-old young lady and panicked. His age difference doesn't seem like a big deal right now when you're both in your twenties, but then, that difference was a bigger deal to a lot of people."

"He said he would ruin me."

"Baby." She sighs. "Nate's seen a lot of bad things happen to people who loved each other completely. He might have been young, but he was still around while each and every one of your father's friends fell and fought for their love. He's seen his sister go through terrible things for love. Watched Lee and Megan fight for what they have. If I had to guess, that boy is afraid of what could happen if he was to give in to what his heart is saying."

I frown and think about what she's saying. It makes sense. No one in our 'family' has had an easy go at falling in love, but they all took on that beautiful war and won.

"So what do I do now? How am I supposed to listen to my heart when it's been broken to bits by the one and only man who holds the power to fix it."

"That depends. He hurt you, and I understand it, baby, I do, but in order for you to follow your heart, you have to forgive him. You just said it yourself; he's the only man who holds the power to fix the hurt."

"And what if this is just a game to him? What if I am just some conquest?"

She reaches out and takes one of my fidgeting hands in her own, rubbing my knuckle with her soft thumb.

"Make him prove to you that isn't the case. Open your heart, cracks and all, and give him a chance to validate what you feel. Don't give up on him, even when it hurts, because you could be throwing away something truly beautiful."

"God, that's terrifying."

"That's because love is never easy, sweetheart. But it's worth every single bump, scratch, and crack in the end. Now, sit back here and tell your mama all about this lollipop dance."

I toss my head back and laugh.

By the end of our chat, my heart feels a little less heavy, and I know that I need to give Nate a chance. If anything, we need to sit down and talk.

But first things first—I need to break things off officially with Levi. There is no way, even if I hadn't been thinking and working toward this moment for weeks, that I would feel good about waiting another day when it is clear we have no future.

After the heavy conversation in my bed, I pulled my mom to

the kitchen and settled in to catch up with her over the lunch she had brought.

Chicken salad sandwiches, my favorite.

The rest of our early afternoon time is spent with her curled up on the couch in my studio, watching me get lost in the heartbreaking canvas I had started the day before. I was so tuned in to what I was doing that I had completely forgotten she was still there until her soft voice broke through my tunnel vision.

"Okay, sweetie, give me a hug. It makes me feel good to see that dark cloud hanging over your head starting to clear away. Promise me that the next time you need me, you'll pick up the phone?"

I don't hesitate to wrap my arms around her and agree.

"I love you, Mama."

"I love you, my sweet Ember."

Chapter 14

Ember

M Y PHONE HAS BEEN GOING off for the last few hours, annoying, but easily something I can tune out when I've hit that sweet spot in my painting. I hit that magic spot while my mom was still here, and I haven't stopped since, even with the lingering hangover that still haunts my body.

More often than not, when I've hit that spot, not a single thing can tear my focus away. Everything is falling together like magic and the once blank canvas is now beginning to look exactly how I envisioned.

I was right yesterday when I thought this might be my best piece yet.

So much haunting beauty in this large glory.

Heartbreakingly sad, but alight with a hopefulness for something 'more' swirling between the brushstrokes.

Today, I had concentrated on the two outstretched arms meeting in the center of the canvas as the focus. Each finger on the opposing hand extended, trying desperately to reach the other, but never getting close enough. Being as close as I am to the piece now, I can see the outline of the man and woman starting to take shape beyond those two hands.

When I'm finished, the abstract piece will be more blur and fade around the edges, the two bodies becoming clearer the closer you get to those two perfectly painted and in focus hands.

This is me.

This is Nate.

It's us.

So much beauty and pain in one huge piece that I can't help but think it is eventually my soul stripped bare and splattered against the canvas.

"A Beautiful War," I declare to myself with a smile, knowing instantly that the title for my piece has been born.

Bam bumps my leg, and I look down, smile still in place. "What's wrong, handsome man?"

He whines before moving to the door of my house. With a laugh, I clean off my brush and close the tops of my paint before moving around my easel.

"Come on, beast." I snicker when he starts to wag his tail in excitement.

When I push open the door that leads into my kitchen from my studio, he rushes through the house and I hear him barking at the front.

"I'm coming, I'm coming," I complain, almost tripping over

the chew toys that he had strewn all over the kitchen floor. "You're worse than a child, Bam," I chide with a chuckle, picking up the few toys on my way to the living room.

I can hear him whining as I turn the corner into the living room from the small hallway and come to an abrupt halt when I see the imposing figure sitting in the middle of my couch. His arms are over the back in a relaxed manner, but his face betrays him. I can tell by the tick in his jaw that the calm he is portraying is a mask, but why he's looking at me with eyes cold and calculating is beyond me.

"Ember," he drawls, his deep voice thick, the way it always is when he's angry.

"Levi, hey … I thought you were going to call me later tonight?"

He doesn't speak, but I watch his jaw clench now as his lips thin. The unease that I had felt when walking in the room grows to a burning ball of anxiety in my gut.

"How was work?" I hedge nervously.

"Fine."

"Would you like something to drink?" I continue, moving to settle in on the loveseat opposite from him.

He leans forward, dropping his arms from the back of the couch and placing his elbows on his knees, never dropping his eyes from mine. "No."

"Okay." I gulp, not understanding his mood today. Hell, I haven't seen him since the other night, and even though we didn't leave on good terms, the brief texts that we've had since haven't given me a clue to why this is happening now.

Unless he knows you're about to break it off.

I ignore the inner voice and will my hands not to start fidgeting as I shift in my seat.

"How was your *party*?" he questions, deadly calm as he continues to leer at me.

"Good," I respond. "Well, good until I figured out that the hangovers are never worth the buzz," I clarify in an attempt to lighten the mood.

"That's nice. I didn't hear from you after you told me you would be going to that new club in town," he accuses.

Losing the battle with my nervous fidgeting, I twist my fingers together in my lap. His eyes cast a quick glance at them before they flit back to my face. "Yeah, sorry about that. After the girls got here, things just kind of went crazy. They had me busy from the second they opened the pizza boxes until I got home last night."

"Hmm," he remarks.

"Anyway, how was your night?"

"Interesting," he discloses ominously.

"Did you have a lot of call outs?" I ask, trying to ease the alarm I feel over his calm anger.

"Not really. Just one."

"Are you okay?"

He studies me for the longest breath before leaning back with one side of his mouth tipped up. Instead of looking like a smile, it only makes his face look like an evil sneer.

"Levi?" I coax when he doesn't speak.

"Tell me, Ember," he starts. "Would you think for one second that I would be okay with my fucking woman dressed like a slut while some man had his hands on her?"

"What?" I gasp in shock. I don't take my eyes off him, but I have a bad feeling things are about to get ugly.

"Did you fuck him?"

"Levi! No, of course not. You know I'm not that type of girl." Except, I'm not really sure what would have happened if rational thought hadn't returned after the touch of Nate's lips to mine last night. If I'm honest with myself, we were, in fact, seconds away from becoming a tangle of naked flesh.

"I'm not sure I believe you, Ember. Imagine my shock when we get a call to come check on that new fucking club because of the crowd size, and I walk in to see my girlfriend in the middle of some weird bar lap dance. I have two goddamn eyes, and I would be a fool not to believe what was right in front of my face."

Shit.

Damn.

Well, this wasn't exactly how I had pictured this going, but I might as well get it over with. Rip off the Band-Aid and finally make the long overdue move to end things between us.

"Nothing like that happened, Levi. I'm sure that Nate was just putting on a show because he knows the girls would think it was hilarious to embarrass me."

His eyes flare at the mention of Nate's name, and I feel my heart pick up speed and my skin flush cold with chills.

"Nate?" he bursts out, the sound like a deep rumble of thunder, making Bam bark. Levi's head swivels toward where Bam is sitting, and I hear my poor baby whine, which is so unlike my sweet-natured pup. He loves everyone.

My mind goes back to the other morning when I found out he had been tied to the fence, and I know, somehow, deep in my gut, that Levi was responsible.

"Look, Lev. I had hoped that we would be able to go out to dinner tonight to have this talk, but clearly, this just needs to happen now. I've felt this way for a while now, but we're just not working. I think it would be best if we broke things off."

There. I said it and the world is still spinning away.

His head twists from Bam, and he studies me with his stoic and quite frankly terrifyingly calm mask still in place. I wait with bated breath as he continues his silence. The clock on the wall behind me ticks away. Bam's panting echoes against the walls. My heart is in my stomach as trepidation climbs up my throat.

I watch as something dark dances across his face, briefly, before he gives me a nod and stands. I lean back in my seat at his sudden movement.

"If that's what you want. I'm not going to stick around if you would rather whore yourself out around town and look like a fool."

He stomps toward the door before stopping when his body is in front of the small entryway table I have next to it. His hand comes up from where he had been clenching his fist at his sides, and I watch as he picks up one of the many frames that decorate the surface. I try to visualize the order of my framed memories but can't seem to recall what could have possibly drawn his attention.

The muscles in his back ripple with tension, pulsing through the tight fabric of his dark tee shirt, before he turns to lock his evil gaze on me. I don't have time to comprehend his movement before the picture is sailing through the air and crashing into the wall, just barely missing my head.

"Family friend, my fucking ass. Have a nice life, bitch," he seethes before opening the door so hard that the doorknob sticks in the drywall.

My breaths come in rushed gasps as I stare in fear at the open doorway. Bam rushes to my side and lays his head in my lap with a gentle whine meant to soothe me. I hear the sound of Levi's truck start up, but it isn't until the sound of his engine had long since faded away that I rushed from my spot and muscled the door out of the wall before slamming it and throwing back the locks.

I scramble around my vacated seat and bend to grab the broken and shattered photo from the ground, gasping when I see which one it was.

I don't even remember who took the picture, but I had never been able to take it down and put it away. It's been one of my favorite images and cherished memories for so long that I should have realized it was the one Levi had seen.

It was a few months after Nate had started tutoring me. Everyone had been enjoying a long day at the Reid's. My skin was pink from being out in the sun for hours, but I didn't mind a second of that sunburn later that night.

I had been standing at the edge of the lake; you could see the out-of-focus people peppered in and out of the water, but at that moment, the camera caught me laughing at something Nate had said to me. My head was thrown back, hair down my back; my bikini had been a new purchase that I got in so much trouble with from my dad. I looked beyond happy and carefree.

And Nate … he was standing next to me, his board shorts low on his hips in the most delicious way. But I loved his face the most about this picture. He wasn't laughing with me. Instead, he was looking at me as if I was the most precious thing he had ever seen.

That look helped to convince me months later to take a chance and tell him how I felt. I was desperate to see that look again with my own eyes, but it wasn't until last night that he ever gave me a chance to see it once more.

There is no doubt in my mind that Levi saw the same thing I had built all my hopes on when he saw Nate's face, and as twisted as it is to feel this way, the only thing his outburst has done is given me the verification needed to see the direction my heart wants me to follow.

Chapter 15

Nate

NIGHT AFTER NIGHT FOR THE last week, Dirty has been insane.

A good insane. The kind that solidifies the fact I knew in my bones for a long time coming that this place would be a success.

But it's also been somewhat of a double-edged sword.

The madness kept me there for the past seven days while I've had to fight with myself every second of that time not to say fuck it and rush off to find Ember. I hadn't even had time to jump over to CS until now to finish the cases I still had to close.

I spent the first day after my chat with my dad still struggling to get my cock under control. The day after that, I kept going over and over what he had said. Picturing my future without Ember in it. Visualizing her meeting someone, getting married, having his kids … and in the end, I felt like I would be sick. Hell, I almost was.

There was no doubt about it; the thought of her with someone other than me was unfathomable. At that moment, I knew that my old man was right. I had to work my ass off to make up for the shit I had done that not only hurt her and pushed her away, but also get to the bottom of that night at my sister's wedding.

My memories still start and end with the dream that had haunted me for months, but until I hear it from Ember, I'm not sure how to make up for that.

The only thing I know for sure is that I'm going to fucking do it.

I hear the door open but don't look away from the monitor in front of me. I had neglected my responsibilities here at CS for a week now, and regardless of my responsibility to be at Dirty, I can't let my dad down.

"What's wrong with your face?"

I look up from my computer at the sound of Maddox entering the room.

"Shit," I mumble under my breath.

"I can hear you," he says, walking around to drop down on the chair at his desk. I look up in time to see him scowl at the picture of his girls, the same picture that I had turned slightly so I could see Ember better earlier, and wince when he grumbles low in his throat before shifting it back—only this time so I can't see shit.

"You want a picture on your desk of my girl, you need to earn the right to have it there."

"Yes, sir," I smart.

"Nate," he calls, and I pause my typing to focus on him. There's no way in hell I'm going to do anything that could piss him off when he knows I'm after making his baby girl mine, so I wisely give him one hundred percent of my attention. "Did you fix things with her?"

A lesser man would have looked away when Maddox Locke turned his penetrating black eyes on them. He's a hard man; rarely smiling unless it's at one of the three women in his life, but that silent dominating hold his very presence commands hits hard. He has a dark side; a side you don't ever want focused on you.

"Working on it," I respond, my voice strong and true.

"Work harder. I don't like seeing her upset, Nate."

My brow furrows. "I wasn't aware that she was upset," I add.

This time, his expression darkens, and I know I fucked up, even if I didn't mean it in the way it sounded.

He opens his mouth to speak, but I stop him with a sigh and one hand in the air. "Don't. I understand that you mean well right now, and I respect the hell out of that, but from now on, what happens between Ember and me will stay that way—between us. Before you assume that I didn't know she was upset because I had been avoiding her, let me set that straight. I've been working at Dirty from noon until almost four in the morning for seven days straight, and I finally pulled myself away from that to give up some much-needed sleep in order to close these cases out. I already told Shane, my manager, that I wouldn't be in tonight because I needed to take care of something. Now, it isn't any of your business, but I had planned to go see her tonight. I'll also share that I've talked to her briefly during the week, and she understands that I couldn't get away until tonight. So if she is upset still, respect *me* enough to know I'm working on it."

"You done?" he probes when I stop talking, an odd look crossing his features.

"I think so."

He nods, looking down at the frame before reaching out with one tan finger and pushing the corner of it until it is—once again—facing in a way that I can see Ember's beautiful face.

I take a deep breath, slowly, so he doesn't see I might have been seconds away from shitting my pants.

We continue to work on our respective cases in silence, the hours passing quickly. I look down at my work, making sure to finish my notes up in as much detail as possible before hitting the enter key with so much force that it echoes around us.

I lean back with a satisfying smile when I think about the hell storm that is about to rain down on the CFO I had been investigating. Now, with that strike against the keyboard, not only will our client know the depths of his employee's deceit, but the FBI will as well.

Now that my work is done, the rest is up to them.

And that officially ended my work at CS for the foreseeable future.

I look back at the turned frame and let myself relax knowing that even if she puts up a fight, now that I'm finished here, I can go there and then, I'm one step closer to getting my girl.

"Nathaniel."

I look up at Maddox and pray he isn't about to kick my ass now. I would rather not have to explain to Ember that her father tried to kill me before I even had a chance to win her.

"Sir?"

"I'm proud of you," he declares, causing me to pause cleaning up my files. "I'm not an easy person to stand up to and the fact that you had no problem putting me in my place shows me just what kind of man you've become. You might play the part of the carefree clown, but you have a strength about you that shows me if my baby girl decides to give you her heart, you're worth holding on to it."

I almost lose control of my body and drop dead in shock at his words. Fuck me, but I never thought I would get his *blessing*. I figured winning Ember would be the easy part—winning her father's approval being the fight.

"Thank you, Maddox," I reply, pretty damn proud that I'm able to keep myself from pumping my fist up in victory.

"That being said," he continues, his voice taking on a threatening tone. "If you hurt her in any way, remember that I know how to kill you and make it look like an accident. Don't make me have to kill one of my best friends' boys, Nate."

"Uh," I hesitate, my eyes widening.

"Nothing to say. I know where you stand and you know where I stand. You have my blessing to make her happy, but with that comes the promise of what I'll do if you fuck that up."

I nod, swallowing the pool of saliva that had gathered in my mouth.

I place the last folder of my closed cases in the tray on the side of my desk and grab my phone off the charging dock before turning to leave, only to stop in my tracks when Maddox calls my name.

"Coming from me as a man and not a father, know I speak from firsthand knowledge that women don't take kindly to being pressed against a wall unless you actually remember doing it to her too."

Fuck me. He did not just say that.

"And," he continues, looking down at his monitor. "My daughter deserves better than being pushed up against a dirty wall. Don't do that shit."

Without knowing what in the fucking hell I'm supposed to say to that shit, I give him a gruff sound of acknowledgment before turning and walking with just a little more speed than normal out of the dungeon.

Chapterr 16

Ember

Nate: I'm on the way.

I LOOK DOWN AT MY PHONE but decide to finish my task before responding.

I pull the latex glove down onto my hand and grimace when I reach out to pick up one of the two dead birds right outside my back door. I had already cleaned up the broken bird feeder that had been hanging on the overhang leading into my house. My heart broke thinking that I had been responsible for two little birds dying because I hadn't secured their feeder well enough.

This week has been full of me cleaning crap up, it seems.

Five days ago, a branch had fallen off one of the oak trees outside my bedroom window, shattering the window above my bed before landing in the middle of my mattress with enough force to puncture the damn thing. That, fortunately, had happened when I had been up late finishing my last piece for my show, trying to make up for the two days I missed after my birthday and subsequent hangover. Still, I made a point to have the men delivering my new mattress help me move my bed to the other side of the room—the one without a window near it.

Three days ago, in what would appear to be one hell of a night for some bored kids, my house and two surrounding it had met the sun with a yard full of toilet paper. Enough toilet paper it almost looked as if we had a snow day.

Not wanting to even deal with that for a second, I hired someone to come clean up the mess. I had enough going on with getting my painting done in half the time I would normally spend on a piece.

Yesterday, my mailman had apparently decided to try his hand at crash test dummies. I got home from the grocery store to find my mailbox trampled in a vibrant display of shattered wood and crushed metal.

And now, the damn bird feeder is murdering my feathered friends.

I swear nothing is going my way this week. I can only hope that with Nate coming over now, I'm not about to have another wave of bad luck.

After grabbing the second bird and carrying it to the trashcan with my arm completely outstretched, I snap off my glove and throw that in as well. Bam trails behind me the whole time, his thick head looking all over the yard as his tongue hangs lazily out of the side of his mouth. The big beast has been attached to my side since Levi almost took my head off last week. I've almost broken my neck more times than I can count because he decided to move his bed in the corner of my studio and drag it directly behind where I stand. I've even woken up to him in my bed four times this week, which is something the big pup had never done before. You would think that when a two-hundred-pound dog clambers up to your bed at night, you would wake up, but not me.

"Ember?" I hear called from the front yard, and I look down when Bam takes off with a bark around the side of the house.

So much for being my big shadow, I guess.

I follow his path, going around the house instead of inside. When I find Nate crouched down, Bam is happily soaking up the attention as he scratches him from head to tail.

"Bam, here," I call sharply, but just roll my eyes when he flops his huge mass down on the grass and sticks all four legs up waiting for Nate to give his belly the same attention.

Nate laughs but gives Bam what he wants for a minute before standing and brushing his hands against his jeans. Jeans that I should note are molded to his thighs and highlight the bulge in his crotch. I watch, my eyes almost crossing, when the bulge in question visibly twitches beneath the denim.

"Em, please don't. I can't handle another reminder that my cock doesn't know how to behave."

I snap my eyes to his, wide with shock at his words. "Uh … I'm sorry?" Really, what else could I say right now?

"Long story, but please don't be offended if I end up walking funny soon."

I can feel my cheeks heat the second I visualize him having

to walk funny because of an erection.

"Did you want to go get a bite to eat?" he asks, making me stop thinking about his dick and try to form big girl sentences.

"I cocked. I mean I'm cocking. *Fuck.*" I bet my face is bright red now. How embarrassing.

"Right, so you're making dinner?" he questions, moving his hand to adjust himself. I watch his long fingers work the raised denim with a groan deep in his throat. "Let's go inside, Em, and please let me go first. I'm not sure I can handle seeing those shorts going up the stairs."

I follow mutely, not really sure what just happened.

Nate walks in and follows Bam as he excitedly rushes through the house and into the kitchen, his nails tinkering across the wooden floors as he leaps and jumps in front of Nate.

I watch his ass.

He freely admitted he would have done it to me, so it's only fair.

And what an ass it is.

He moves around my space as if he's spent every day here. He grabs Bam's food bowl, filling it up, and then repeating the process with his water. He moves to the stove and lifts the lids, stirring the pasta sauce before grabbing the spaghetti noodles I had been waiting to put in until the water boiled. I just stand there mutely as he makes himself at home.

He turns after the putting the noodles in and leans against the counter with a sigh. My eyes move from the stove, to Bam, and back to the huge man making my kitchen seem like it had shrunk in size.

"I'm guessing spaghetti is good with you?" I question.

"I love spaghetti."

And he does. He especially loves my mom's sauce, something I had spent the whole day cooking at a low simmer.

"That's good."

My fingers twist together as my nerves get the best of me, and I look down at the floor. I've always wanted to see him moving in my space with me, but I never in a million years thought it would actually happen. It's one thing for us to be together for family dinners or even when the gang got together to go out as a big group but never have we been alone in our own homes.

"Why are you nervous?" he inquires, pushing off the counter with a shove and walking forward until his booted feet meet my vision.

"You're here," I weakly exhale.

"I am."

"I'm just trying to figure out why. Why now." And it's the truth. Even with the knowledge that I would open my heart to whatever was happening between us, I would be an idiot not to have a little bubble of nerves about it.

I close my eyes when I feel his fingers brush my hair behind my ear. His warm palm slides down from my cheek until he's cupping my neck with his thumb resting just under my chin. My head is pushed up gently and his fingers tense and flex where they rest at the back of my neck.

"I'm a smart man, but not always a bright one. I have a lot to prove to you, but I'm here because it's where you are."

I shake my head while he speaks, but he smiles, and without saying another word, he bends down to kiss my lips soft and quick.

"Dinner first, then we get to the heavy stuff, okay?"

I nod, not really trusting my voice, and move around him to stir the noodles. We work together as if we've been doing it forever, and in no time, everything is done and we're sitting at the table with huge plates full of spaghetti.

"God, I forgot how much I loved this sauce," he moans, with his mouth full of his first big bite.

"It's just store sauce," I lie, twisting my fork in the sauced coated noodles. Inside, I love that he realized, with his first bite, that it wasn't just any sauce.

"Store bought, my ass. I would recognize this sauce anywhere. I used to beg your mom to come over and make it for my mom, but she would just smile and give me another huge helping. I think she thought I was joking, but let me tell you, my mom could never get it right."

I feel my nerves recede some and smile at him. "It's a tricky one. You have to cook it for hours, but I loved smelling it all day when I was living there, so it's nice when I cook it myself and have a little of my childhood memories filling my own home."

He drops his fork, his mouth red from the sauce, and just gapes at me. "You made this?"

I tilt my head, chuckling to myself as I swallow my bite. "Of course, I did. How else would it have gotten here?"

He mumbles something about a ring before shoving another huge forkful between his lips. I watch him chew, his eyes closed in bliss and his moans deep. I mutely hand him a napkin before the sauce that had been trailing down his chin could fall.

"I figured you had just heated up some frozen shit you had from your mom."

I gasp. "Uh, no. The first thing my mom did when I was old enough to walk was pull a chair to the counter while she cooked to teach me everything she knew. I can make her chicken fried steak and mashed potatoes better than she can."

His fork falls on his plate and he looks at me with awe.

"What?"

"Good God, woman, don't tease me."

"Promise, even my dad says so. I'll make it for you tomorrow, er ... I mean some other time. If you want, that is."

He reaches out his hand, his face going soft and his smile growing big. "Tomorrow sounds good, baby, but you'll have to bring it by Dirty. I need to get some paperwork done, and Shane won't be there to cover for the night."

Baby?

Oh.My.God.

"I can do that," I squeak.

"Good, it's a date."

"A d-date," I stutter.

He just continues to smile, and even when he picks up his fork and continues to eat, that smile never leaves his lips.

Of course, the one on my own never left either.

Chapter 17

Nate

AFTER THE LAST POT WAS dried, I grab Ember's hand and pull her into the living room. She stumbles at first, and I hate that she is looking at everything I do and trying to figure out what game I'm playing. I saw it in her eyes earlier when I told her we would make a date out of dinner at Dirty tomorrow. It was written all over her face when I started the pasta, and then again, when she admitted she didn't understand why I was there.

She was justified in her thoughts, I muse as I drop down on the couch and pull her down to sit on my lap. I fucked up and I'm just now beginning to see just how much.

"Ask me," I stress, shifting her so that she is sitting sideways with her back leaning against the armrest and put one arm over her shoulder to twist one of her long locks of hair around my fingers, while my other hand comes up and rests over her fiddling hands, halting her movements.

"Ask you what?" Her eyes widen, and I watch as her chest starts to rise and fall faster with each breath.

"Ask me what I was thinking when you told me that you loved me the first time."

She jerks in my arms, and I fight back the groan when her weight rubs against my swollen cock. I tighten my hold on her with a squeeze of the hand that is holding her two captive and pull her closer to my chest.

"I can just tell you, but I need to know that you actually want to hear it."

She sighs, and I know she would rather be saying anything else right now, but she does it. "What were you thinking?" There's a slight tremor in her soft melodic voice, and I say a silent prayer that she doesn't start crying. I'm not sure I could handle her tears.

"I was terrified out of my mind. I had been fighting my feelings for you well before you turned legal. It didn't matter in my mind that you were finally eighteen; there was still a gap between us that wouldn't have been easy for us to overcome right then. You were still finding yourself, and we both know that I needed to stop being a punk and grow up. I had been drifting, content in life, even though I had dreams that no one knew about. Dreams that I've only now made a reality."

She continues to search my face as I speak. I pause to collect my thoughts, pulling her hands apart and clasping one of her tiny hands in my larger one. She sighs and I take a deep breath before continuing.

"That wasn't the only reason, Em. I had some stupid fear

in my head that pain always comes with love. I watched some fucked-up shit happen to Dani only months before, and seeing how lust, love, and all the feelings in between can turn sour real fast, I let that fear rule me. But I also knew, even if you didn't see it, that there was no way us being together wouldn't cause issues within our families."

"It wouldn't have," she rushes out quietly.

"Yeah, it would have. I wasn't the same man I am today three years ago. I needed to wake the hell up and make something of myself. I can tell you, the man I was then wasn't worthy of you."

"You're so wrong." She sighs sadly.

"Yeah, well … I see things differently now, but I still think it would have been a damn hard road for us then, and I'm not sure I would have been strong enough to make sure it was one we traveled with no trouble."

"You hurt me, Nate."

I take a deep breath and give her the rest of it. "Yeah … I hurt me too."

She jerks in my arms, visibly shocked at my admission.

"Denying what I felt. Hurting you to push you away. Knowing deep down that I would regret that moment for a long time coming. *Being without you* for the last three years, yeah … that hurt me too."

She pulls her hand from my hold and shifts in my lap until she is facing me with her knees on either side of my thighs. "You never acted like it," she accuses, her hands coming up to rest on my chest as she searches my eyes, running her gaze down my face and over my features.

"Because it was easier to act like I didn't have a care in the world than to admit that I was wrong and risk you rejecting me like I did you."

And that's the truth of it, something that I didn't even realize until recently when I forced myself to really think back to why I pushed her away. The reasons behind denying us what we both wanted.

"I never—" she starts, but I stop her with a shake of my head.

"It's in the past, Em. A wise man once told me that looking back wouldn't do anything but make the hurt grow a little bigger."

"I'm not sure I agree with that," she tells me.

I smile. "Yeah, maybe not, but my dad's got some years on him and he's been through enough shit that I'm going to take his word for it. If we're going to make anything of our future, Em, we're going to have to stop looking in the past. All that's going to do is stop us from creating our forever."

Her face is comical when I finish. Her beautiful brown eyes round and huge in disbelief. Her lips parted slightly and I don't even need to look down to know that her tits were heaving beneath her tank top. A thought that I should have tried to ignore because, not even a second later, I watched her face flush when my cock jumped against her core.

She shifts, and it jumps again. I quickly take hold of her thin hips with one hand grasped tightly on each side of her waist. "Don't you move," I demand through clenched teeth.

Her eyes leave mine, and she drops her head. A submissive move that I don't miss in the least. My cock pulses violently at the thought of taking control of her while I fuck her in this position.

Not letting her top from the bottom while I show her who holds the reins.

"Look at me," I command in a hard tone, fucking thrilled when she instantly gives me those eyes again. "You need to let that go. For us to move on and forward, we can't do that successfully if you're holding that against me. I can't change it, but I can promise you that I will never willingly hurt you again. Understand?"

She nods, swallowing audibly, and I know the controlling and dominating side of me that I normally only let out when I'm in the bedroom is turning her the fuck on. I always thought that Ember might be a sexual submissive but to have that confirmed feels damn good.

"Time to move on?" I probe while looking into her eyes and caressing the soft skin at her hips where her shirt had ridden up. "This next part isn't going to be better, but we need to clear the whole table, and in order to do that, I need you to fill in a whole bunch of blanks I have right now."

She goes wooden in my arms, and I fucking know she understands where I'm going with this.

"Nate," she whimpers.

"I know, Ember, but I need to explain myself and I need you to be honest with not only me but yourself after I do. Got it?"

She relaxes her body but only marginally.

"For months and fucking months, I've woken up from the same dream. I'm with a soft and willing woman hot for me against a wall. My eyes never open in the dream, but even then, your face and scent filled my senses. I had never pictured anyone but you. I would wake up with the scent of lemon and wildflowers so strong in my nose that I was convinced it was real, but it always ended the same. Me opening my mouth and asking that woman's name."

With every word that leaves my lips, I watch as she struggles, and loses, the fight to control her emotions. When the first tear slips over her lids, I want to kick my own ass. Hell, by the time the second one spills over, I was ready to call her dad myself and tell him I was ready to take what he had to give me.

"When you," she starts but has to pause when a giant hiccupping breath steals her words. "You didn't even see me, Nate."

"Baby, I was so drunk, I didn't even see *me*. Even in that damn dream, I'm aware of how drunk I am."

"When you pulled my arm as I was coming back from the restroom, I was startled at first because I didn't know who it was. It was so dark on that side of the house, but the shadows you pulled me into made it almost impossible to see. But then you grumbled something about not being able to wait any longer. I thought you knew, Nate. You said you couldn't wait to have me, and I thought you knew!" she screams and drops her head down on my shoulder. She turns, resting her forehead against my neck before she continues to speak. "The second you said those words and pushed me up against the wall, I didn't even care that I was about to have sex for the first time with my family and closest friends around me in the middle of the shadows. None of that mattered because it was *you,* and I knew that I would be safe. Then …" She sucks in a stuttered breath. "Then in the same second I thought I would die of happiness, you pushing your thickness inside me just a bit—a place no man had ever been—you asked me *who I was*. There I was experiencing the best moment of my life with the man I had loved *forever*, and he didn't even know who he was about to fuck. That. Killed. Me."

"God, baby." I exhale through the pain her words inflict on me.

"Then after I pushed you away, you just fell to the ground like nothing had happened. I can't tell you what you did after that because I was too busy running away as fast as I could. Which, awkwardly for me, just happened to put me on a collision course with my own father. It was the worst moment of my life, Nate."

Her breathing continues to come in choppy gasps as I hold her tightly to me with my arms wrapped around her back. I never would have believed that damn dream was just a drunken memory. Had I known, fuck, I would never have let this much time go—the hurt fester—without making it right. Now, I'm not even sure how to fix this.

"I understand now," she says with a hitch to her breath. "It doesn't take away all of the pain it caused, but it goes a long way in dulling it."

"I'm so sorry," I lament. "It sounds like a weak thing to say, I know that, but fuck, I am … so sorry."

She pushes off my chest and lifts herself until her face is level with mine. You would never know she had even shed one tear. Most chicks I know turn a hundred different shades of swollen red when they're crying but not Ember. Her face is just slightly flushed, but other than her wet eyelashes, you would never know.

"I'm terrified, Nate, honestly terrified. If what you say is true and looking back on painful memories only makes that hurt grow, then I need to get over it. But I don't know how. In my head, I'm convinced that you're just going to drop me if I blink too long. My heart, though, is telling me to wrap myself around you and never let go. I feel like I'm being torn in two different directions."

She is silently begging me with an expression mixed with fear and hope to provide her with all the answers, but I know nothing I can say will give her what she needs.

This is something I need to show her.

Prove to her.

Fight for her.

I frame her face in my hands, feeling her pulse beat wildly at the base of her neck as I lean forward and press my lips against hers. I don't deepen the kiss, but when I take a deep breath through my nose and my senses are full of everything that is her, this kiss feels more intimate than anything I had ever felt before.

"Keep following your heart, Ember. Follow it—*me*—and let me worry about guiding the way. Allow me to prove to you that I'm worthy of you giving me your love back. How does that sound?"

Chapter 18

Ember

I'M A BUNDLE OF NERVES.

I called Nate about an hour ago and told him I would be there around eight and he told me just to pull up out back and he would meet me there.

When I drove up, passing the entrance, I was shocked to see so many people lined up outside. There were so many people; it looked like they were pouring out of the club. I never thought that Tuesday would be a popular club night, but apparently, it is.

When I was here for my birthday and first witnessed what they called the holding room, I thought it was a brilliant idea to have a whole building designated for the people waiting to get into the actual club. But seeing all the people lined up outside, I feel an instant sense of pride that Nate's club is so popular that they can't even make room for everyone, and that's just in its second week of operation.

Pulling my car beside Nate's huge truck, I turn the key and take a huge gulp of air in an attempt to calm the butterflies swirling around my stomach like a tornado. Stepping out, I walk to the trunk and pull out my picnic basket. Before I can shut the trunk, though, the basket is being taken from my hands and Nate's scent hits my nose.

Whatever cologne he uses is so distinctively *him* that I've caught myself over the years following the trail when I would catch a whiff of it in random places. If I knew the name, I'm pretty sure I would buy a bottle just to spray on my sheets.

With that thought, coupled with those damn butterflies, my mouth opens and I speak without turning. "What cologne do you wear?"

His low chuckle rumbles against my back as he kisses me on my temple before leaning in and breathing right next to my ear. His scent becomes stronger instantly.

"Acqua Di Gio," he hums against my ear, the reverberations washing over me, and I shiver instantly.

"Who makes that?" I ask breathlessly.

"Giorgio Armani."

I'm definitely buying a bottle and spraying every inch of my house.

"Give me some time, baby, and I'll transfer it on every inch myself. Just need you to help."

"Shit," I hiss when I realize I spoke that out loud.

His free hand comes up and turns me gently before pulling me to his side. "Hey." He laughs.

Embarrassment forgotten, I look up into his handsome face

and echo his greeting in a whisper. He shakes his head, his hair moving around his angular face, making my palms itch to run my fingers through the silky strands. I'm so used to seeing him with it up in one of those sexy man buns that the rare sight of it falling free makes my mouth water and my core clench.

Damn, he is so sexy.

His lips twitch, and I know I did it again.

"Come on. I've been starving for you, and it hasn't even been twenty-four hours since I left your house."

He grabs my hand, the other holding the basket full of our dinner, and pulls me toward the door that I just now notice the bartender who served me shots on my birthday is holding open.

"Dent, meet my girl, Ember. Ember, my friend, Denton."

I go to reach out my hand to take the one Denton is offering in greeting, but jerk it back when I feel Nate growl low and deep. Denton's head goes back, and he booms out a thundering laugh.

"Did you just growl like a dog?" I ask Nate in shock and turn to look up at his face.

He keeps his narrowed eyes on a still laughing Denton, not answering me.

"That's a little much, don't you think?" I continue.

Nate looks down at me like I'm the crazy one for even asking him that, and I ignore him by returning what I hope is a hard look of my own. He shrugs and pulls me through the door and into a dark hallway.

"It's nice to formally meet you, Denton!" I call over my shoulder while still being pulled behind Nate. I hear another animalistic sound from him and just roll my eyes.

He's crazy.

When we reach the end of the hallway, I can see that the club is just as packed as it was the last time I was here. I continue looking around while keeping up with Nate's huge steps as he leads me to the stairs that I know will lead me to his office, only letting go of my hand long enough to wave me ahead of him.

I look down at my outfit, a short summer dress that I picked after an hour of throwing almost everything out of my closet, and wonder if I miscalculated when settling on this one. I hadn't thought about the long climb up. He probably wants me ahead of him so I don't flash anyone.

When I look back up at him and see the mischievous twinkle in his eyes, I know that I was wrong. He wants me ahead of him so that *he* can catch a flash of what is under my skirt.

Well, he's in for a shock. I wink and laugh when I see him frown in confusion before moving around him and starting my climb. The hissed breath that I hear over the music at my back gives me a rush of power and confidence. I put a little extra swirl in my hips with each step, and by the time I'm halfway up, my lips are curled in a smile so wonky and big that it hurts my cheeks.

Just when his warm palm hits the inside of legs, I reach out and push the handle on his office, about to come out of my skin when the tip of his thumb touches my bare sex.

"Oh my God," I gasp and stop just inside the door of his office.

He hits my back, and I hear the contents of my picnic basket shift. "What the hell?" he explodes behind me when he finally sees what stopped me in the first place.

Oh, how I wish it were just because of his hand.

The skirt of my dress had ridden up from the jerk of his arm when I stopped abruptly, and I hastily pull it down. Lord knows, one half-naked woman in his office is enough.

"Oops," the sickly high voice says from his couch and she stands slowly. Her naked breasts sway as she bends to pick up the black corset top.

I look back at Nate and see him just barely keeping a leash on his anger. I know whatever we just walked in on isn't something welcomed by him, even if I wasn't here. He moves into the room and tenderly—despite his very raw anger—moves me out of the way so he can shut the door and silence the music that is pounding up from the club below.

"You want to tell me what the fuck you're doing in my office, Julie? Without your top on, no less."

He walks over to his desk, unfortunately placing him closer to her, and puts the basket down with utmost care. His hand runs across the top in an almost reverent caress, and I can't even describe what seeing him do that does to me.

Even though she's tainted our moment … whatever this is, he is still almost disbelieving that I'm here, with him. Well, he's not the only one, and I'm not letting this woman ruin a moment I've only dreamed possible.

She steps closer to him, her top still not on, and reaches out to touch him.

I don't even think. I move to stand in front of him, my wedges almost tripping me up in my haste to get between them, and I cross my arms over my chest with a growl low in my throat.

I feel Nate bend, his mouth going to my ear as one strong hand curls around my hips and pulls me flush to his body. "Did you just growl like a dog?" he mockingly breathes so low I only hear him before nipping the sensitive flesh behind my ear.

"Back up now," I fume when she has the nerve to look at me as if I'm the one intruding.

"Who the hell are you?" the woman—Julie—snaps at me.

"His."

"Mine."

We both speak at the same time, and her eyes dart back and forth between the two of us before narrowing and she addresses Nate. "That's not what you told me last night." One very thin blond brow attempts to go up, but judging by the way it just kind of twitches, she's got a little too much Botox going on. Her red lips tip up and what could have been a smothery look just makes her look like a devil.

A she-devil.

"Nice try, but you're going to have to work a little harder if you're going to try that kind of garbage with me because he never left my side last night."

I see my words hit her when some of that malevolent spitefulness dims. She doesn't know I'm lying, but I know she is.

"That was a nice try, *babe*," I tell her before reaching over and picking one of her blond hairs off her breast, my finger grazing her hard nipple and I curl my lip up in disgust. "Honey," I call over my shoulder, not giving her the satisfaction of looking away first.

"Hmm?"

"Do you think bleach would ruin your couch?" I ask, my brow arching high.

His laughter bellows from his chest, the richness fills the room instantly. The hand still holding my hip flexes and he pulls me closer, the other arm going around my chest to hold me to his body. Whether he's doing that to keep me closer or to keep me from *her*, I don't really care. The second every hard inch of him presses against me from top to toe, the woman before us might as well have been invisible.

He is finally able to calm down his hilarity to just a few bursts of air that I feel tickle the top of my head a few moments later. The woman is still topless and still fuming in front of us.

"You're fired. If I see you back inside or near Dirty, I'll make sure you're in the back of a cop car in seconds, got me?" His deadly calm tone causes a shiver of arousal to stream down my spine. He's doing it to intimidate her, show her he's serious and in control, I'm sure … but hearing him take a tone full of domination flips a switch inside me that makes me shift uncomfortably when I feel the wetness between my legs.

"What?!" she screeches and throws her hands in the air. "A few weeks ago, you were on the bar dancing for me, and now, you're throwing me out when we both know this is what you want."

Instead of allowing her words to cut me, I reach back and push my hand between our bodies until my palm rests against the bulge in his pants. He's not hard, thankfully, but he's obviously a sizable man if the heavy weight of his cock beneath my palm is anything to go by. He hisses out a breath when I squeeze my hand. I want him to know that her words aren't affecting me in the least and the only way I can think of is to remind him that I meant what I said yesterday. I still want him even with this clusterfuck in front of us. The old Ember, the one that let her past rule her, would have run the second I stepped into his office, but not the new me. I intend to live up to the nickname he gave me a long time ago.

His length hardens with my touch, but he just flexes the hold his hands have on me and lets me continue to play.

"You know damn well that I was giving a demonstration that day. Not for one goddamn second was I dancing for *you*. I don't know what sick fantasy you've built up in your head, but I promise you that it will never come to fruition. Get the fuck out of my club."

She hesitates.

"Now!" he roars, and she hastily covers herself with her top before running toward the door and down the stairs.

I feel him breathing rapidly against my back, my hand still holding his now very hard cock. I give him a squeeze, and it's almost as if someone stuck him with a cattle prod. He jerks back, his hands going to my shoulders, and he spins me around roughly. I would have fallen, but the second I was facing him, he bent, grabbed me at the back of both thighs, and had me up in his arms before I could blink. His mouth crashes against mine roughly before turning us. I feel my back press against the cold, hard surface of his windows before all rational thought flies out the window.

"I won't take you here," he rumbles against my mouth before turning his head and deepening the kiss. I try to roll my hips, desperate to ease the ache between my legs, but he pushes me harder against the glass. "No." The unwavering authority in his voice stops me instantly.

He steps back, gradually helping me to my feet until he is sure that I have steady footing. Stepping back and running his hand through his hair, I lick my lips when his brown hair falls back in a shiny curtain against his face. At the moan I must have let slip, he jerks and turns to face me.

"No, Ember. We're going to set the table," he commands, pointing at the table I hadn't noticed on the other side of the room. One single rose sits in the center of the black surface. "You're going to go over there and get everything set up before sitting down like a good girl. You aren't ready for the kind of time-out I have planned for you, but know that if you disobey me, I'm going to start adding that shit up. I'm going to the bathroom to take care of this problem you've created, and you're going to set the table, sit down, and wait for me so I can give you a proper first date you will remember for the rest of our lives."

The shock of his words is still slamming into my overheated body when I hear his door slam. *The kind of time-out he has planned for me?* Something tells me it will be a whole hell of a lot more fun than the kind of time-out that always ends with his sister having her nose shoved in a corner.

He wants a first date to remember for the rest of our lives? Something tells me that isn't going to be a problem at all.

Chapter 19

Nate

I HAVE THE ONLY WOMAN MY cock has been craving just outside this door, and here I am in my office bathroom fucking my fists roughly so that—hopefully—the bite of pain I'm giving with each thrust of my hips and twist of my wrists will be enough to calm me down.

I had my cock in my hand before the bathroom door had even slammed behind me, and here I am, not even minutes later, with my balls tightening and the tight coils of pleasure starting to unravel.

I move over to the sink, continuing to work myself with both fists, as I line myself up to empty my come into the basin. I feel my balls pull up and the blinding pleasure that shoots up my spine and wraps around my brain makes my vision go black as I roar out with each thick rope of come that shoots from the tip of my cock.

"Fucking goddamn," I moan deeply, feeling my knees lock.

I look down, blinking against the gray still clouding my vision to see that I'm still pulsing heavily. Relaxing the hold my hands have on my cock, I take one hand and slowly stroke my oversensitive skin, watching as the last few spurts hit the basin.

I swipe my thumb over the tip before letting my—thankfully—soft cock drop heavily against my undone jeans. Washing my hands first and ignoring the ridiculous amount of come painting the inside of the basin, I carefully tuck my cock and shirt in then zip my jeans and push my belt through the loops.

If what just happened is anything to go by, it might just kill me when I finally sink into Ember.

Looking in the mirror, I see the wild look in my eyes and I say a silent prayer that I'm able to keep the promise to myself that I won't take her until I know I've proven myself to her.

When I open the door and see her sitting demurely at the set table, I groan and almost stumble when the tip of my cock—still sensitive as hell from my release—brushes against the denim of my jeans.

Ignoring my needs, I walk around the table and stop directly behind her. I smile when I hear her suck in a breath only to let it out in a moan. My girl enjoys my smell. I reach up, pulling my hair back and holding it in my fists, and I bend. The side of my stubbled cheek rubs against the smoothness of hers on my descent. She shivers, and when I reach her tan, bare shoulder, I turn my head slightly before opening my mouth and sinking my teeth into the tender flesh where her neck meets her shoulder, sucking lightly. She whimpers and shifts her body the best she can since my teeth are still pressing against her skin.

"Good girl," I rumble low against her skin, kissing the teeth marks and pink bruise my mouth left behind. "It pleases me that you listen when I tell you to do something."

She doesn't respond; she just tips the right side of her lip up and looks at me with lust-filled eyes.

Taking my seat, I look down at the plate before me and wonder if I could come again just from the mouthwatering aromas swirling up from the hot food.

"To a first date to remember." She breaks the comfortable silence around us, picking up the Coke she must have brought with her and waiting for me to do the same with the one in front of me.

"And many more to follow," I add, touching the top of her can with mine before placing it back down and picking up my fork and knife.

"Better than Mom's," she smarts with a wink.

"We'll see."

She waits while I cut into the meat, dip it in the mashed potatoes, and bring it to my mouth. I couldn't hold back my moan if I tried because the second the flavor hits my taste buds, my mouth waters, and I close my eyes. I see her starting to cut into her own food, still smiling, but I'm incapable of talking at the moment. Not while I'm eating the best damn thing I've ever tasted.

"You're right," I mumble around the mouthful of food. "Better than your mom's, baby."

That damn smile just gets bigger, and she silently continues to eat.

It doesn't take long before I'm about to lick my plate clean, but she just reaches out and places the rest of her dinner in front of me with a knowing look.

"Next time, I'll make sure to bring more than one helping for you, honey."

My chest warms when she calls me that, something that I just vaguely recall her using when Julie was in the room, but now that I know she wasn't saying that for her benefit, I let the pleasure of it fill me.

"You know I didn't want her here, right?"

She nods, taking a sip of her drink and leaning back in her seat. "I'm not upset about it. I'm just glad I was here to let her know you aren't on the market anymore."

I give her a sly smile before asking, "Yeah? I got myself a woman?"

One of her shoulders comes up in a shrug and she laughs softly. "We'll see."

Oh, we sure will, Emberlyn Locke. We sure as fuck will. Knowing I'm not sure I can last much longer without hearing her agree that I do, in fact, have a woman, I mentally give myself two weeks tops to make it happen.

"Come with me?" I request.

We had finished our dinner about an hour ago and instead of pulling her to the couch as I would have liked, I sat in my desk chair, pulled her on my lap, and swiveled the seat so we could look down at the club below.

She turns her head and looks over her shoulder at me before giving me her smile and a small nod.

I help her to her feet before climbing to my own and pulling her toward the door, down the stairs, and into the madness. The crowd parts without trouble, and I make sure she settles safely at an empty spot I found for her at the main bar before jumping over the surface and behind the counter.

I hear the sound of her laughter over the music when my feet land. I look over my shoulder with a wink before grabbing a shot and pint glass. I place them both down in front of her before reaching around and grabbing the amaretto and filling the shot glass about three-fourths full before getting the 151 proof rum and filling it the rest of the way. Then I place the now full shot inside the pint glass. I feel Dent move to my side and hand me a beer, smirking a knowing smile when he watches me fill the pint glass up until it's level with the already full shot glass.

Her eyes follow my hand as I reach out and hold my palm up, knowing that Dent will be ready for the next step, and he doesn't disappoint.

Both of her dark brows shoot up the second I flick the lighter and hold it to the shot glass in the center of the pint, the flame sparking instantly as the liquor burns brightly in front of her.

While it burns between us, I catch her gaze, and with one finger, I point at the brightly lit sign above me.

I had one installed at each of the bars around the club last night. Luckily, I know enough people around town that when I want something done, it's done right away. Some sort of glowing backlight design illuminates the simple wording centered on both sides of the solid black sign.

Dirty Dog's Pleasure Elixir :: Ember Firecracker

I watch her jaw drop, knowing without words what I mean by that display. I'm claiming her as mine for everyone to see the second they step up to any of the bars inside Dirty. Well, I'm sure the majority of people who order Ember's drink will have no fucking clue except for those who know us personally. And honestly, it's more about making a statement to her anyway.

One that screams I, Dirty Dog himself, only find my pleasure from *my* Ember.

My firecracker.

Chapter 20

Ember

"COME ON, BAM!" I YELL across the expanse of my backyard as I wait for him to bring back the nasty, slobber-filled tennis ball that he loves more than life. I watch him frolic around; tossing his huge body up in the air before running in circles to chase whatever imaginary thing he's found.

Giving up on getting him to come inside so I can get some cleaning done before finding something to eat for dinner, I flop down on one of my outdoor chairs and give in to the thoughts that have held my mind captive for the last week.

After the night at Dirty when I brought him dinner, I've been burning for him, and it had nothing to do with the drink that he had created for me. A drink that I know in my bones was his way of letting me see just how serious he is about this newly created us.

I stuck around for another hour after his grand reveal of Ember's Firecracker, but I had a feeling that, by me being there, Nate was having a hard time focusing on what he needed to do, which was run his club. I made my excuses, even if I wanted to stick around, and after another explosive make-out session next to my car, I headed home.

That night, even with the shocking start we had with his office surprise, had been one of the best of my life. Unfortunately for us, the timing just hasn't been on our side for the last week. Not since he has to deal with everything that comes with having the most popular club around two weeks after opening their doors.

Over the week since, we've been able to steal a few phone calls here and there and texts when calls weren't a possibility, but I've had enough. I know he's busy, and it had almost been a blessing since I've spent almost eighteen hours a day working nonstop on *A Beautiful War.* I never dreamed a painting that scale would only take a little over two weeks, but if I keep up my pace, I'll be finished middle of next week. Just over a week before my show.

This afternoon, though, I hit my breaking point. All those calls and texts were officially not enough. I'm desperate to see him face-to-face. To feel his arms around me again and his lips against mine. Which is probably why I currently feel nothing but pent-up sexual frustration and eagerness for him to return my text … or plea, rather.

I bend forward to reach behind me to pull my phone from my back pocket and check it—again—to see if Nate had texted back, but not before seeing the message that I sent him an hour ago. My desperation for him had hit a peak so high I thought I needed to take a break with my vibrator.

**Ember: Come over when you're done at Dirty. I need you.
No matter the time. Key is under the mat.**

Would he think I was crazy? Probably not. Would he come?
Probably. Would he wonder what I'm really asking for? Absolute-
ly.

"Come on, Bam. Time to get your tail inside." I laugh when
he leaps again, this time chasing after a bug.

He turns, his tongue wagging, as he runs toward me.

When I open the back door, he charges into the house, and I
hear him rushing into the kitchen seconds before he greedily starts
lapping up his water.

Just when I shut and lock the back door, my phone vibrates
in my hand, causing my heart to pick up speed. When I look and
see Nikki's name on the screen, I can't help but feel a little disappointed.

"Hey," I answer.

"Hey, you. White or red?" she oddly asks.

"Uh, white or red, what?"

"Wine, Ember. Really? We skip a few wine nights, and it's
like you forgot what we do once a week."

"It's Tuesday." At least, I'm pretty sure it's Tuesday. The
downside to not having a conventional job is that time has no
meaning most days.

"Oh," she murmurs. "Really?"

"I'm pretty sure. At least, that's what my planner said this
morning when I was checking my deadline for the last piece I
need to get over to Annabelle at the gallery."

"Well, son of a Bieber," she complains. "Well, we might as well just have wine night anyway. I'm in desperate need of it since I've been two seconds away from killing Seth since last week."

I laugh, not surprised that they've been fighting … they're always fighting. And honestly, she isn't the only one who is in the mood for a much-needed wine night with her best friend.

"How about get one of each and we will just play it by ear. I could use a good night of relaxing with a glass."

"Or ten," she mumbles.

"I wouldn't go that far." I snicker. "I'll start dinner in an hour, so come over whenever."

"'Kay. Love ya, bye!"

"So did he ever text you back?" Nikki all but wheezes, her eyes wide as her mouth hangs open with shocked anticipation.

I had just finished catching her up on everything that's going on between Nate and me. Needless to say, she's been about to fall off the couch with every word I've spoken.

"Nothing, which is weird for him. Even when he's been busy, he doesn't usually take this long to respond to me."

She nods her head but doesn't speak.

"Should I try again?" I ask, taking another sip of the nasty red she picked out.

"Nope. No way. Don't look desperate."

"I *am* desperate!"

"No, you aren't. You're horny."

"And that's different?"

"Sure, it is," she muses. "You want some of his dick, which I bet is *huge* if I'm being honest right now. But I digress; you're horny for what he can give you, not desperate in the sense that you're going to die if it doesn't happen right this second. Plus, judging by what you've told me, I think you still have some doubts about his motives, which is stupid as hell."

I turn my head from where I had been looking out the front window, staring mindlessly into the dark night, and narrow my eyes at her.

"And you think I shouldn't?"

"I didn't say that. You've been hung up on that for a while now, so it makes sense you have reservations, but now that I've heard his side of things, I think it's time to at least take his advice and try to put the past in the past to stay. He makes a good point; the longer you hang on to that pain—remembering how much it hurt—you feed it the fuel it needs to grow bigger. Also, you were just out of high school, Em. Then and now are like night and day. I'm not saying you should just jump in head first without thought, but I don't think he would even be pursuing anything if he wasn't serious about you."

I mull over her words before responding. "You're right," I agree with a sigh of acceptance. "But we've had one, technically two, dates. If you call them that. How can I know he's serious in that short period of time? What if he finds something about me that he doesn't like? Hell, we haven't even done anything past kissing. He might not like what he gets if we take it past that. He's *a lot* more experienced than I am, and every time I've been with a guy, there wasn't even a spark, let alone fireworks. He could figure out on the next date that I'm not worth the trouble or risks."

She snorts, almost spilling her drink. "Yeah, no. First of all, you have known him your whole life. I doubt he's going to find something he doesn't like about you. Knowing someone that long means you know all their faults and just choose to look past them. Second of all," she continues, jabbing the air with her finger. "How does every other happily committed couple know anything after two dates? They don't, I'll tell you! They just take a chance and enjoy the hell out of it. You can't rush *that*. THIRD!" she screams, again stabbing the air between us. "You got Fourth of July-worthy fireworks from a kiss, Ember. You don't have those kinds of sparks only to find out that sex gives you something like a sparkler."

I open my mouth to respond, but Nikki is on a roll because before I can open my mouth, she jumps from her seat and throws her hands up in the air.

"AND! Let me tell you something, missy! He told you what 'risks' were holding him back before. Risks that I might add he is finding no trouble accepting *are* worth it to take now. He knows how close you are with your sister. He also knows Maddi can't hold a secret to save her life. The second he made that play, he was accepting those risks with the confidence that he *wanted* to make that trouble worth it when y'all's relationship went further."

She lifts her wine glass and downs the contents of the half-full glass before wiping her mouth with the back of her hand.

Only then does she flop down on the couch and lean her head back with a sigh.

"Ohhhkay," I droll, my heart pounding as her words take root and the understanding and acceptance blooms.

Her head rolls on the back of the couch, and she narrows one eye at me, looking ridiculous instead of intimidating. "You know I'm right. But I also know that you overthink everything. It's time to stop that shit. If you need a little more time, then take it, but don't question him or his motives until he gives you a reason to. A current reason to, I should add. Forget the rest of it and just give him a chance."

"You're right," I begin, but I'm forced to stop talking when her finger hits my lips to silence me.

"Of course, I am. And now that you've listened to reason, I think you should sleep with him and get that silly thought it won't be explosive out of your head. Since you've already established you're horny for his dick AND you know damn well that you're holding on to your crazy excuses about his motives as a shield of protection, drop it and be the one willing to take risks this time."

"You don't think it's too soon?" I wonder out loud; it's something that's been on the back of my mind since I did just get out of a relationship, even if that relationship had been very short-lived.

"Too soon?" She snorts and starts to cackle loudly, slapping my thigh as she cracks herself up. "You've been in love with the guy for *forever*. You've known him *forever* and you've been dreaming of having him—in every way possible—*FOREVER*. Too soon? More like it's about time!"

I roll my eyes.

"Don't be a brat. You know I'm right … again. If he doesn't text you back today, call him tomorrow or go see him at Dirty. Make the move. No one says you have to wait on him to do it."

"Okay. You're right," I say with a slight shake to my voice. I take another sip. "If he doesn't text me by tomorrow night, I'm going to him."

"That's my girl!" she screams, and we both start giggling.

God, I love my best friend.

Chapter 21

Nate

I DRAG MY FEET AFTER SOFTLY closing my truck door and try to keep my eyes open. I've been on my last ounce of energy for the last two days, not that I'm complaining, but things have been so busy at Dirty that I hardly had time to even eat. Not to mention, I've been spending every second either at Dirty or passed out after I finally manage to drag myself home. Now that things are starting to move along, I'm confident that Shane is ready to handle the nightly operations himself, especially since we've already promoted Denton to give Shane the coverage he needs to have time off himself. I can't fucking wait to be able to go in during daylight hours to handle office shit and only have to stay a few hours at night.

If it hadn't been for a text earlier from a certain woman that has plagued my every thought for a week, I might have passed out behind the bar hours ago.

I need you, she had said. Well, she had said a bunch of other shit too, but nothing stood out more to me than seeing her say she needed me.

Those three words had lit a fire under my ass, and I had been busting tail in order to get out of there before closing. Thankfully, Shane was there to close because if I had to wait a second longer, I was going to come out of my skin.

I lift the mat in front of the door, and sure enough, a shiny silver key catches the moonlight. I snatch it up with the mental note to spank her ass for leaving a key there. She might as well put a big neon sign telling every lowlife motherfucker to come on in.

I enter the house silently, only briefly looking at the woman sprawled half on and half off the couch, the TV muted as some late-night infomercial plays on the screen. Nikki looks about as uncomfortable as can be, but judging by the drool pooling under her cheek, the girl is out cold.

Bam meets me at the mouth of the hallway, but after a sniff, he walks over to where Nikki is now snoring and climbs on top of her. Well, on top of the one leg that is still on the couch, but she doesn't even flinch when his head drops onto her ass.

Weird girl.

My booted feet are silent as I make my way down the hallway toward the doorway that is open at the end. When I step into Ember's room, I'm confused for a second since her bed isn't where I know it used to be. The same place it was when all the guys in our little family—at the demand of her dad—helped move her stuff in here two years ago. Looking away from that spot, I see it now on the opposing wall. The moonlight doesn't touch the bundle in the middle of the mattress, but I can see clear enough and what I see makes my mouth water and dick twitch.

Her covers must have slid down at some point, tangling with her bare legs. My eyes trail up those legs and I almost choke on my tongue when I see what is on display for me. The shirt that she's wearing twists around her stomach, and with the way she's lying on her side, you can clearly see one very naked ass cheek.

That's all it takes for me to silently start pulling layers of clothes from my body. I bend, making quick work of my boots before placing them against the wall near her bedroom door. I unhook my belt, pull the button at my waist, and slowly drag my zipper down. Wisely, I leave my boxer briefs on because if I allowed my painful cock the freedom he wants, I would be inside her in record speed. My shirt comes next and after pulling my hair free of the band, like I know she loves, I close her bedroom door. The only sound breaking the silence comes from the soft snick of her lock.

Nikki might have looked passed the hell out, but I'm not taking a chance that she comes to when I'm about to finally have my girl in my arms.

The first step I take toward Ember's sleeping form has me taking my swollen cock in my hand and squeezing through the cotton of my briefs as I look down at her. If she were to turn just a little, I would be able to see her pussy clearly and that thought alone makes a little spurt of pre-come leak from the tip of my cock.

Fuck me.

The second I lie down next to her, I'm going to be hanging by a very frayed thread. I know without a doubt that if she gives me what I need, by the time the sun is coming up in just a few hours, I'm going to be coming inside her body.

With one last squeeze to my very confused cock, I place my knee on the mattress and move to climb into her bed. When my weight makes her roll slightly, she turns. The one leg that's covering her up shifts and she moans. I still, waiting to see if she's awake, but when her soft breathing continues, I move and lie down next to her. This close, her legs open slightly, I can smell her—all of her, but I ignore the cravings that scent brings and turn to the side before reaching over her and pulling her closer.

The second her ass settles against my crotch, I jump. The soft flesh of her lush ass rubs once as she tries to get comfortable without waking. I should feel guilty about my next move—I should—but I don't because she isn't the only one who needed someone tonight.

With our bodies pressed tightly, my front to her back, I spread my hand open against the smooth skin of her stomach, the tip of my pinky hitting the soft, short hairs on her mound. I shift until my nose is in the crook of her neck and I take a deep inhale, my cock pulsing again when her scent fills my senses. My hand travels up, moving under the bunched up shirt, and I rest my palm just under her full tit as her heart beats steady beneath.

It took fifteen soft kisses to the silky skin on her exposed shoulder and neck before she started to moan. I counted. When I ran the tip of my tongue from the edge of her shoulder all the way up to the back of her ear, I felt her shiver in my arms. When I pressed my cotton-covered erection against her hot naked ass, she arched her back and rubbed herself against me with a deep groan of desire.

But the second that I lightly bit her neck, she vaulted out of my arms and with lightning speed, had me on my back with her straddling my lap.

"You came," she pants.

"Not yet, but if you keep rocking against my cock, I will."

"You never responded. I didn't think you would come." She continues to speak, ignoring my smartass response, but she also doesn't stop grinding her core against me, the heat of her making me clench my jaw.

"Ember, you need to stop."

"Nate, you need to *start*," she stresses with a moan.

It's taking every bit of control I have not to flip her off me and show her who is in charge in here.

"Em," I moan, my head pressing against the pillow when she gives a hard jerk of her hips.

"I need you," she pleads.

"You don't know what you're saying."

"Make me yours," she whines.

My heart thumps erratically. "Yours?"

"God, yes," she moans, rocking even faster.

Reaching out blindly, I find the lamp next to her bed and click it on. Her flushed face and unfocused eyes don't hide from me when the harsh brightness fills the room.

I curl my abs and lean up, forcing her with our new position to stop her movements. She pants, her chest heaving, and I know she was just seconds away from coming.

"Make you mine?"

She nods.

"You ready for that?"

She nods again.

"I take you, baby, and I'm never fucking letting go. You ready for *that?*"

She nods, but I don't miss the small hesitation. She wants this, us, but she still has some lingering fears.

"That's okay, my little firecracker, I'll have fun making you believe that."

Her hands move from where they had been resting against her spread thighs and she places each of them on my chest, pushing me back down to explore my body. She twists each of my nipple rings and her pupils dilate.

"I'm ready to be yours, if … if you're ready to be mine."

I feel my chest rumble, having a hard time hearing over the roaring in my ears, but I'm sure whatever sound I'm making right now sounds more animal than man.

"Yeah, Emberlyn Locke, I'm beyond fucking ready to be yours."

Chapter 22

Ember

THE SLEEPY DRUNK FEELING WAS just starting to recede when Nate spoke the words I've longed to hear for such a long time. Words that I had given up on ever hearing. Words that, if I lived to be a hundred, I would never forget how I felt when I heard them, finally, for the first time.

"Yeah, Emberlyn Locke, I'm beyond fucking ready to be yours."

His eyes drop to my mouth as I feel my lips spread into a wide, toothy smile. I watch in fascination as his green eyes seem to darken and the color on his cheeks gets just a little flushed when his attention comes back from my mouth. His expression, so open and easy to read, is void of the playful mask he usually wears.

The realization that he's been hiding his feelings, acting and trying to make everyone believe he is so unaffected by *anything*, hits me hard. How have I missed that? Probably because I've had my head up my ass licking my own wounded pride for the last couple of years.

I push back the thought that I could have changed things a long time ago and focus on here and now. His stare still holds me captive, just as the hands gripping my hips roughly are, but I have a feeling deep down that what I see in his eyes is love, not lust.

My thighs, still spread with his body between them, try to close when the enormity of the moment mixed with the adoration in his eyes hits me. All rational thought flies out the window and I know, I just know, if I don't have him right now, I might just die from the need overtaking my body.

"I want you so bad," I mumble through the arousal rushing and flowing over every inch of my body, tingling up every nerve and swimming around inside me in overdrive. "I've dreamed of this for so long," I continue, my words coming out in a pant as I rock my hips.

"Ember," he warns when I jerk my hips out of his unforgiving hold, giving us both the friction we're in need of when my wet and swollen lips slide against his erection. "Stop," he barks in a deep rumble, his neck straining as he takes my hips again between his hands.

"Never." I let my head roll back and start to pick up my movements, each thrust up getting the attention to my clit. The burn in my core starts to fire up my spine, wrapping around me as it climbs through my body, gearing up to explode.

"Fuck!" he roars.

Before I realize what's happening, he's flipping us. My head lands in my pillows, just a breath away from the headboard in the center of my bed. It takes me a second, still clinging to the climax that had been just seconds away from taking over, and I push my hair off my face with both hands. When I look down my body, I almost retreat when I see the feral expression on the man kneeling between my spread legs.

He takes huge body rocking gulps of air, his chest heaving with their power. His hair is a loose mess hanging free to dance at his shoulders, a few pieces falling into his face that he either doesn't notice or just doesn't care about.

And his eyes are focused downward.

If I didn't believe he was fighting the same all-consuming feelings as I was, I would have thought that his downcast gaze was for another reason, but seeing those brilliant emerald eyes locked on my very exposed and wet sex, I know that *I'm* the reason he's being slammed with a hungered need.

The power I feel seeing his reaction to my excitement is a high I never want to live without. Something that I will wake up thinking about and fantasize every second we're apart, trying to think of new ways to make him come alive like this. That uncontrollable, feverishly strong emotion he's wearing can only be an aftereffect of our chemistry. Until it burns so bright that it's exploding around us like a brilliantly beautiful display of fireworks.

And with that thought, he makes a sound low in his throat, pushing forward in the next breath to cover my body with his as his mouth takes mine in a deep, bruising kiss. His underwear still keeping him from me completely, but that doesn't stop him from thrusting against my body as if he were already inside me. Each time he slams against me, the headboard slaps against the wall and my eyes roll back in my head.

It was foolish of me to think I would ever be able to control this man once I saw the fierceness burning in his scrutiny break free of his careful control. When I try to push my hands into his hair, he breaks our kiss with a hiss and narrows his eyes at me.

"You're not to touch me, Ember. Not at all. I'm so worked up right now because of you. I'm about to fucking come all over myself and the only place that's going to feel my fucking come will be the inside of *your* pussy. Do not test me by putting those wicked little hands on my body until I can take my time to show you what it's really like to *take* while *giving*."

"Please," I rasp past my dry throat, needing that so desperately.

"No, not *please*. From this point on, the only word I want to hear from your lips is my name. Moan, groan, scream out your pleasure, but you say no other word than my name. I want to hear you scream *that*, Ember," he stresses with a hard thrust. "You don't come until I tell you to," he rumbles deep in his throat. I lose his eyes as he bends to trace my ear with the tip of his tongue before whispering against it. "And when you do, you had better do it loud enough to feel pain in your throat from the pleasure I'll give your pussy."

"Take me," I beg, trying to rock against him, but his weight on me restricts my movements.

"Nate," he grunts in my ear. "No more fucking words but my name. Know who is claiming you. Let the whole fucking world hear who is taking you and making you his."

He runs his hands up each of my arms, stretching them out until I can almost feel the edge of my mattress and his hands are curling around my fingers.

"Hold on," he commands with a wink.

My shirt is instantly pushed up until he's forced to stop because of the position he has put my arms in. I can tell he's trying to figure out if making me move from my position is worth removing the shirt completely. Then he looks up into my eyes before jumping off the bed and walking over to the desk in the corner.

He searches the top, looking through each pen-filled coffee mug, before pulling the drawers open. My eyes widen when I see him turn holding a pair of scissors. I open my mouth to protest, but at the hard look he shoots my way, I snap my jaw shut.

He stalks back to the bed, but when I thought he would climb back on top of me, he just places the scissors on the bed and hooks a thumb under his underwear before pushing the tight black material down his powerful thighs. His cock springs free, his red, angry tip wet with his pre-come, and I lick my lips.

One of his hands grabs the scissors and the other starts to stroke the hard flesh between his legs.

"I want to see you wearing my marks, Ember. Your hips already have my handprint and just seeing that on you makes the animal you've awoken inside me fucking pleased. But it's not enough. I *need* you to wear my marks." He starts to mumble some more under his breath, but I can't make out his words with my loud and harsh breathing echoing throughout the room. When he brings the scissors up and starts to cut my shirt up the center of my breasts, I cry out. Not in pain but in anticipated pleasure. He walks to the foot of the bed when he's done and looks up my body before placing his hands down and slowly making his way back to me. "I'm going to eat you now. With my hands holding your legs captive at the back of your spread thighs, digging my fingers in each time you try to deny me what I'm going to take. My tongue will make you so crazy you might come, but you had better not. Not until I've marked enough of this perfect tan skin."

Then, true to his warning, his hands are pushing between my legs and the mattress as he lifts and pushes until he's holding me to his mouth by the bruising grip he has on the back of my thighs. I can feel the wetness of our combined fluids running down the crack of my ass. My legs being pushed until I can feel the top of my thighs touching my belly as my toes touch the top of the headboard.

If I could find a way to open my eyes, I might find it funny that I can look at my toes at this moment, but when he opens his mouth and closes his wide lips over my core with a hard suck, I'm pretty sure I died.

I scream, pant, and almost black out as he moves his mouth against the slick wetness he's causing. My fingers cramp up as I hold on to the mattress for dear life. The only thing keeping me from coming right now is the look in his eyes that I see when I finally open my own. He's looking up my body with burning eyes. Eyes that are daring me to disobey his demand. For a brief second, I consider giving in to the need my body has to come, just to see what he will do, but when I open my mouth, his eyes narrow and his growls vibrate against my pussy. I almost lose my control, almost come against his mouth, and he knows it since his tongue is feeling the fluttering of my inner walls as I fight to hold on.

And just when I think I can't take anymore, he releases me with a pop. His tongue coming out to give one thick flat swipe before his hold on my thighs eases and my legs are tenderly placed on the bed once again.

"You ready for me to make you mine?" he asks, his voice thick and deeper than normal.

I nod, not willing to take the chance that he denies me if I speak.

"Ember, I want you to answer me with words this time and only this time. Are you on birth control?"

I have to clear my throat to get a sound out, the scream of my release just waiting in a giant lump. "Y-yeah. The pill."

"Thank fuck," he rumbles, dropping down to one hand placed next to my head as he leans to press the tip of his nose against mine. I can feel him running the hot tip of his dick up and down between the lips of my sex, and I open my mouth with a silent gasp each time he presses it against my swollen clit. "You've been a good girl, keeping yourself from coming even though I know you were close a few times. You quivered against my tongue, and I thought I was going to have to stop to put my mark on your ass for not being able to hold yourself back."

I hum low in my throat, and his pupils widen as he mirrors my noise.

"You like that?" he asks, and I nod. "Next time. You'll get my hands on your ass before I let you put your lips on my cock."

Another sound comes from me, and I almost lift my hips off the mattress when his thick, blunt head pushes into my pussy just a breath before he swipes it back up to my clit.

"Next time, I want your hands in my hair when I cover my chin with your wetness," he muses and rubs the tip of his nose against mine while I feel him enter me again, this time almost an inch of him. My eyes widen and I gasp, earning a brief kiss from him when I'm able to keep my silence. "Hold on, Ember. I'm going to claim this pussy, and when you scream my name like a good girl, know that you're giving me all of you when you take my come deep inside your body."

He lifts up and looks down our bodies. After lining himself up and pushing the tip of him inside me, he brings the hand that had been holding his cock up, resting it on my collarbone. His eyes watch his hand as he trails it down until he is cupping the underside of my breast, his palm on top of my heart.

Then he looks up.

His fingertips press and flex before he lifts his hand and puts one finger right above my heart. "All of you," he vows and thrusts himself inside me in one rough push. His thickness makes me see stars as the pain of his size mixes and swirls into the most intense pleasure I've ever felt. He doesn't move, allowing me the needed time to get used to him, all the while holding me captive with eyes that are almost glowing with intensity.

When he pulls out, almost falling completely from my body, I mewl and whine, needing him back inside. The feeling is short-lived because, in the next breath, he is slamming back inside so hard that my bed slamming against the wall is louder than the scream that bursts from my throat. One side of his mouth tips up at my cry and then his lips are on mine as he continues to pound his cock inside my body. The bed protests with each and every thrust. He lifts up when another raw scream comes out of my mouth and cocks his head at me. I whine, not even ashamed of it, because the need to come has so much intensity driving its power that I know it won't be long. My searching eyes plead with him.

"My fucking name, Ember. Come on my cock and *scream!*" he bellows before lifting up and taking hold of my hips. While kneeling between my legs, he starts to fuck me even harder. So hard that I'm not even sure I *can* scream; the force of my climax raging through my body is too powerful. My eyes water, not from pain, but because of the feelings he is bringing forth.

I want to declare that I'm his.

I want to demand that he is mine.

I want to scream for him to never stop.

I want to sob that *I love him*.

Instead, when I feel myself detonate into a million pieces, I open my mouth and do what I was told to do.

"NATE!" My voice breaks at the end, and I sob as I come, and come, and come. "Nate, Nate, Naaate," I continue, unable to even think about saying anything *but* his name.

Just when the intensity almost becomes too much, I feel his rhythm falter before he gives one final thrust forward. His fingers dig into the tender flesh at my sides, but all that is forgotten when I feel him pulse inside me as the heat of his come enters my body.

My vision clears to a hazy fog when he falls and covers me with his weight. The feeling welcome and wanted. I look up and search his face, unsure what to say after that, but words aren't needed, not when our bodies said everything for us. He adjusts his weight until he's leaning on one elbow and turns my head to look at him with a gentle touch of his hand cupping my face.

"Ember," he whispers, ghosting a kiss over my lips. "My Ember. I'm never letting go, baby. Not now. Not ever. And pretty soon, your head is going to catch up with your heart and you're going to understand that. I meant it; I want *all of you*. I'm going to make it my mission to show you, prove to you, that I'm worthy of getting that gift from you again." I open my mouth, not even sure what I'm going to say, but he just bends and gives me a slow, wet, and beautiful kiss.

A long while later, after he had switched us so that his back was to the bed and I was in his arms, I rested my head against his chest as he breathed slow and deep. Even in his sleep, he held me tightly, and at that moment, I knew he didn't have anything to prove to me because my head had already caught up with my heart.

He's had it since I was seventeen years old. Even when I thought it would never heal when he turned me away a year later, he still held it. He will *always* have all of me.

Always.

Chapter 23

Ember

MONDAY

"I WISH YOU DIDN'T HAVE TO go," I whisper against his chest, my body still coming down from the fourth climax he's given me. We haven't been able to get enough of each other since the first time he took me a week ago.

His arms tighten around me, and I feel him press his lips against the top of my head. He had just shown up a few hours earlier, right as I had been making my way out to the studio, and he took me roughly against the front door the first time until I was screaming out one hell of a hello.

The second time was when my back was on the couch; he held my legs apart as he kneeled on the floor between them.

The third was against my own hand as I swallowed every

drop of him as he pulsed in my mouth.

And the last, we had finally made it to where we are now, a tangle of sweaty limbs in my bed.

"I wish I didn't have to go," he agrees. "I thought it would be easier to spend less time at Dirty now that we have Dent on as a manager, but things have just been crazy. I shouldn't complain, but fuck, I would rather be here with you than doing a bunch of paperwork."

"We've had plenty of time together, Nate." We haven't, but I don't want to make him feel bad when I know he's stressed about finding a balance between being the owner of a very popular club and my boyfriend.

Boyfriend? Is that what he is? I mean he's said that he was mine and I was his, but he's never spoken the words.

"Slipping into your bed in the middle of the night does not equal plenty of time. I haven't even taken you on a date, Em."

I push up on the hand that had been resting against his chest and look down at him. "Did I complain?"

I feel the rumbles of his silent laughter against the palm. "It's been a week since I promised I would prove to you that I deserved the gift of you. Two weeks since we decided to be together, and so far, the only thing I've been able to do is have dinner at the club between the little time I had to take a break. You are worth more than a rushed dinner, Ember. It's frustrating the hell out of me."

"Nate, you don't have to prove anything to me." My belly flops, and I shift to lean up a little more, giving him a brush of my hand against his hair. "Don't be so hard on yourself. I understand and don't hold it against you that you're needed at the club."

"That might be the case, Ember, but you deserve better."

"I deserve you," I whisper.

His eyes fire, the reaction to my words so strong that I can feel his heart pick up speed under my hand.

"Yeah? And it's my job to make sure you never forget that, baby."

I shake my head, knowing that I'm not going to get him to realize that I don't care if all we've had time for the last six days is a few hours here and there that he's made to come to my house. Before I can speak, though, his head comes up and he flips us while taking my mouth in a deep, slow, kiss.

Then he makes me come for the fifth time.

TUESDAY

I hear my doorbell just as I had finished signing my name to the bottom right corner of *A Beautiful War*. Bam starts barking at the chime, and I drop my brush to go answer it.

After Nate left last night, I haven't left my studio. The sun set and rose while I worked feverishly to finish. I feel like I'm about to drop, the exhaustion so strong, but every bit of my sluggishness is worth it after the signature I just penned on the canvas.

"Flowers for an Emberlyn Locke," the gruff voice greets when I open the door. "Here," he continues and thrusts a clipboard at me, just giving me enough time to take it before turning and walking toward his truck.

"Oh, okay," I mumble and sign my name next to the huge X

he had scribbled.

"Here. There's more," he huffs and thrusts a huge vase of roses into my hands.

"More?"

"Yeah, lady. More. As in eight more."

I look at the roses in my hand, judging there to be about two dozen bright red buds before snapping my head back up. "Are you sure?"

"Been doing this for twenty years. I don't get my orders wrong. Nine vases, twenty-four roses in each, to an Emberlyn Locke at this address. The only way I'm wrong is if you're not really Emberlyn Locke."

"I am, but this is a lot."

He gives me a weird look, holding out the second vase impatiently. "I'm just doing my job."

I struggle to hold both, so while he stomps back to his van, I turn to place them down on the table next to my door. I wisely stop questioning him and hope there's, at least, a note on one of these.

His surly demeanor doesn't slip until the last vase is in my hands. Then I get a smile from him before he turns to leave. "See you tomorrow," he oddly says over his shoulder before slamming his door.

Tomorrow?

WEDNESDAY

Sal, my new florist best friend, showed up just as I was returning from dropping my last painting off at the gallery. When his van had pulled in, I had been juggling my keys and the bag of fast food I had grabbed on my way home after I realized it was past noon and I hadn't eaten yet. Since he had to wait for me to put that down before I could sign and take the next enormous floral display, I had asked and gotten a very impatient '*Sal, as in Sal's Flower's*' before he pointed with a weathered finger toward his van.

I just shrugged and took the flowers.

Since his order yesterday, I was quickly running out of space. I figured it was wiser to just place them on the floor until Sal left, then find somewhere for them.

When he handed me the last one, number nine, I got the same grumpy wave as he trudged to his van. "See you tomorrow."

Uh? He can't be serious.

I look down at my feet, seeing just the top of each rose. A sea of red that only two hundred and sixteen roses can make. The scent of roses has already overtaken my house, but all I can do is smile.

I don't look for the card right away, knowing it's here, but walk around my house trying to find a home for each vase. With the last one in hand—and no other option—I place the last four in the middle of my kitchen table before plucking the card I see off one of them.

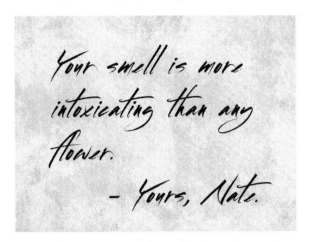

Your smell is more intoxicating than any flower.

— Yours, Nate.

His handwriting is rough and slanted, just as it was on yesterday's card. Of course, the one yesterday had just said, 'Yours, Nate.' Today's corny line makes me smile when the first made me melt. I drop the card on the table before pulling my phone from the back pocket of my shorts.

"Hey," he hums in my ear as the sound of shuffling papers comes over the line.

"You know, pretty soon I'm going to be sleeping on roses."

He laughs.

"Thank you, honey."

"You sound happy," he muses softly.

"And you sound tired. Do you need anything?"

He's quiet for a second, more paperwork shifting around. "Just you, Em. I'll be over later, but don't wait up."

"It's wine night with Nikki, so there's a good chance I'll still be up when you leave Dirty."

"I hope so. I miss my girl."

I laugh. "It's been two days, Nate."

"Two long-as-fuck days."

I don't respond because he's right. Instead, I change the subject.

"My mom asked if I would be at family dinner tonight. I told her no, but … uh," I trail off, not sure how to word what I really want to ask. Something I've been wondering, but not willing to ask and add to his stress.

"I got the same call from my mom. Not a surprise, but her question was actually whether *we* would be at family dinner."

"Uh …"

He chuckles deeply. "Em, what did you think was going to happen? You're not just some new girlfriend she's gotten wind of."

"Girlfriend," I echo on a squeak.

His hilarity grows, but I sense it's more sarcastic at this point. "Yeah, Ember. Figured that was clear."

"You just hadn't said and I … well, I didn't want to assume any titles had been placed."

"Yeah, I have, and now, I'm working on showing. Titles were placed the second you came on my cock, Ember. See you later, baby."

His disconnect is instant, and I pull the phone away wondering if I just screwed up by being all nervous and unsure.

My next call was to Nikki.

"So let me get this straight ... he sent you almost five hundred roses this week?"

I take a sip of my third glass of wine and look over at Nikki. She's about to fall off the couch as she leans forward with wide, excited eyes.

"Actually, it was four hundred and thirty-two. Not that I counted or anything."

"Holy shit." She gasps.

"I know. What does that even mean?"

"That's so romantic!" she screams, ignoring me.

I thought Nikki would be able to help me figure out what my mind couldn't, her experience with men being a lot more than the few short-term boyfriends I've had since high school, but I didn't think she would turn into a squealing and screaming freak fest.

"Yeah, but *what does it mean?!*"

She stops bouncing and narrows her eyes. "What does it mean? Oh my God, Em! If that isn't the grandest of gestures to show someone you love them, I don't know what is!"

"Love?"

Her expression gets a little crazy at that. Her eyes turn into angry little slits, as her head tilts to the side, and I can picture the wheels churning in her head. "Are you blind! Hell, I shouldn't be shocked you're confused when just last week I had to remind you of what the chemistry between the two of you would be like. Something, I might add, I was right about if the sounds that woke me up that night are anything to go by. Stop questioning his actions and just see them for what they are. He's trying to make up for the past by showing you how he feels first. My guess is that *he's* now the one worried about saying he loves you."

"Nikki, we haven't even been together for a month."

"And you've loved him for years. He made it very clear that he has had feelings for you just as long. Stop overthinking it and just enjoy the ride. You guys are being forced to date a little unconventionally with him being the uber-busy owner of the brand new most popular club around and all. If this were a normal beginning to a relationship, you guys would have been on a bunch of dates and you would be able to see how right I am."

I let her words sink in, and I have to admit she's right. It's been almost three weeks and had he not been so busy, my reservations wouldn't be warranted.

"Maybe he's waiting for me to say it?"

"So say it."

"You make it sound so easy." I laugh.

"What are you really all worked up about because I know it isn't the fact that he's sent you a ridiculous amount of roses."

"God, Nik. When he mentioned his mom asking about both of us, I freaked. I mean I know it's going to happen with us what we are now, but he had made it such a big deal when he rejected me. He said they wouldn't understand. How is it any different now?"

"Yeah, well, when he said it, he was probably right. A lot has changed in three years. You're not just a teenager fresh out of high school. You've been to art school, finishing well ahead of time. You have one hell of a career as an established artist now. You're an adult and even if your parents or even his thought something of you two being together, they have no say in it."

"Oh, I'm sure they'll have a say in it." I can picture my dad having a lot to say about it, actually. "I guess I'm really worried that he's going to cut and run when it comes down to standing up together in front of them."

She gives me a soft look of compassion. "I think you're underestimating him. The only thing I can tell you is to ride it out and let him do what he said he was going to do. Prove that he's worth giving your heart to."

We continue to talk about a whole lot of nothing after that, and by the time I felt him climb into my bed and pull me into his arms, my head was a lot clearer. I'm still a little nervous about what's to come, but seeing things through her eyes makes me look at them from another perspective.

One where he really might be the one afraid of getting hurt this time.

SATURDAY

By the time I realized that my daily deliveries weren't going to stop anytime soon, I started looking up places where I could share the happiness Nate was literally raining upon me. Sal showed up, surly as ever, and instead of taking today's nine vases inside, I had him help me load them in my car. It was a tight fit with all twenty-seven vases total that I had received since Wednesday, but we made it work. I think he actually cracked a smile when I told him I had planned to drop them off at the local nursing homes, but it was short-lived and he left with another promise to see me tomorrow. I didn't mention anything about it being Sunday and I would most likely not see him.

At this point, I wasn't sure when they would stop, but Nate was determined to make a point and I was loving every second of it. Which is why I decided to pass them out at nursing homes. Seeing the look on some of the elderly patients was the best feeling in the world, but hearing that I was the only one who had visited the vast majority of them in years solidified my decision to share Nate's love. Of course, I planned to talk to him tonight when he came over for dinner now that I had given the majority of them away. I probably would have kept each one, but after almost breaking my neck on one of them earlier, I realized that I couldn't keep the overwhelming amount I had.

I hear his truck pull into my driveway right when I pulled dinner out of the oven, and I felt giddy with happiness that he was here. I continue getting dinner ready as I dish out the lasagna onto our plates and the sounds of him greeting Bam reach my ears.

Just when I had put them down on the table, I feel him.

His arms go around my middle and his mouth presses against my exposed neck, making me shiver. I straighten and wrap my arms over his as he continues to kiss up my neck until he has his lips at my ear. "You smell good enough to eat."

"I think that's dinner," I joke.

"No, definitely not dinner," he rumbles and presses his erection against my back. "I love food, but food doesn't make me hard."

"You're a man. Food is like number one on the makes you hard list."

"Not true," he groans when I push against him. "You're number one through fifty on that list."

"And what's fifty-one?"

"Probably porn, but I haven't tested that since I haven't watched a single one in weeks."

I throw my head back against his shoulder and laugh.

"Damn, it's good to have you in my arms."

Still laughing, I turn to look up into his eyes with a smile. "You've been in my bed every night. Me in your arms. You're good for my ego when you act like you haven't seen me in years."

His lips are smiling as he gives me a brief kiss—one that had dinner not been ready, I'm sure we would have gotten lost in—before resting his forehead against mine.

"Hi," he whispers.

"Hi." I sigh.

"Thanks for making me lasagna. I've been craving that for days."

I shrug as if it's no big deal. The last thing I'm going to admit is that I hate cooking the dish and only did it for him. Hell, no. Not when he's looking at me like I'm the answer to his prayers.

"Come on; let me let you feed your man before I forget about dinner and demand dessert first."

He has to turn and literally push me into my seat after that comment because the thought alone is enough to make me want to forget all about dinner myself.

"Are you ready for your show next weekend?" he asks a little while later, after he's devoured his third huge plate of lasagna.

"As ready as I'll ever be, I guess. I'm nervous, but Annabelle seems confident that I shouldn't be."

"It's normal to be nervous, Em. This is your first solo show? Right?"

I finish swallowing my bite before wiping my mouth. "Kind of. I had one when I had just finished school, but it wasn't this big. Things kind of got a little crazy when Annabelle discovered me. She's featured my paintings for the last two years, and they sell within an hour of going on display, so I know I shouldn't be worried, but it's a lot different when you're the only artist on display. More pressure somehow, I guess."

"She's the one?"

I tilt my head in confusion. "The one?"

"The one who went to one of your art school's showcases and freaked out about you right in the middle of it, right?"

"How did you know about that?"

"Uh, I probably shouldn't admit this at the risk of sounding pathetic, but I was there."

I can feel the shock on my face. He was there? I knew that the majority of our group had been there, but I didn't remember seeing him. Then again, I had been about as close to freaking out as it got when the Annabelle Kingston, the owner of the largest gallery in Atlanta, had started dancing and screaming in front of one of my pieces. She had taken me under her wing before I even finished school, each of my paintings turning in a higher and higher profit. Here I am, two years later, debt free, in my own home, and my own show proving that I am—in fact—a successful artist.

Finally able to find my words, I open my mouth. "How come I didn't see you?"

He wipes his mouth before dropping his napkin over his plate and leaning back. "I didn't want you to see me."

"I see." The hurt I feel from his answer is not something I'm proud of.

"Stop whatever you're thinking, Ember. I went because I wanted to support you, but I knew things were still weird between us and I didn't want you to look back on that show and remember me making it awkward for you. I went and celebrated for you in the shadows."

"I wish you would have been at my side." I think out loud.

"Yeah, I wish I would have been too, but the time wasn't right."

"You're coming next weekend, though?"

He stands and offers me his hand. Once I'm upright, he bends to look into my eyes. "I'll be by your side every second. I'm so damn proud of you, and I want everyone to know that I'm the man in your life." I shiver—something he doesn't miss. "Clean up in here first or dessert?"

"Dessert. You could burn the kitchen down for all I care, just as long as I get dessert now."

He bends and with a squeal, I'm in his arms as he walks to my bedroom.

Chapter 24

Nate

"**I** WANT YOUR COME IN MY mouth," I tell her, feeling her hum against my cock. All fantasies I had over spanking her ass before she had me in her mouth vanished when I first felt her mouth take all of me. Her head moves up and down quicker, but I don't miss her hand moving between her legs. "You touch *my* pussy, and I'm going to spank your ass, Ember."

My cock touches the back of her throat before I feel her relax her neck and take me so far down that I feel the breaths from her nose on my skin. My head slams against her headboard when she swallows my cock. The sensation of her wet mouth sucking hard on me, her hand playing with my balls, and the hum of her enjoying the fuck out of this was becoming way too much.

"Jesus fuck. That's right, baby, take all of me."

She continues bobbing her head and hollowing her cheeks

until I fist her hair in my hand and thrust into her mouth. She whimpers against the bite of pain I'm sure my hold brings her, but just sucks a little harder before she pauses in her sucking to lick against the sensitive flesh she's consuming.

Through the narrow slit in my eyes, I catch her free arm moving, and I know she's ignored my warning. With a noise of protest from her, I pull her up off my cock, ignoring my own jolt of displeasure when I lose the heat of her mouth, and lean forward so that she is looking directly at me from her kneeled position between my legs in the center of her bed.

"I told you not to touch yourself. You don't come unless I tell you, and you damn sure don't get to take your sweetness from me by coming against your own hand." She doesn't speak, but her eyes spark with the knowledge of something, although it's a mystery to me what that something is.

"You're going to wear my mark on your ass now," I promise her darkly.

She shifts and I watch as she rubs her thighs together. Then, to my utter disbelief and fucking pleasure, she turns so her head faces the end of her bed, and bends so she is on her elbows with her knees still kneeling on the mattress. That ass I just promised to mark is up in the air, presented to me like a goddamn gift. The wetness coating her pussy makes my mouth water, and for a brief second, I forget why she is getting her ass pinked.

"You're going to remember what I said about taking your sweetness from me tomorrow when you can't sit without the burn of my touch heating your flesh, aren't you," I vow, my voice low and controlled even though I feel seconds away from losing my shit. The sight of her offering herself to me, ass up with her wetness begging to be filled, is unmanning me.

Shifting until I'm up next to her, my knees next to her legs and my cock pointing at her hips, I rub my palm softly against each of her smooth cheeks. I go back and forth as my free hand trails up her spine. I can feel the heat of her with each pass I take down her left globe, but I ignore her whines when I get close enough, and continue to caress her skin.

Just when I know she had started to relax into my touch, I bring my hand back and quickly slap one and then the other cheek before rubbing the sting. Her scream, of pleasure and not pain, hits my ears, and I give her another two quick cracks of my palm. It isn't long before she has the red imprints of my hands on her skin. I keep rubbing her flesh with my hand as I lean to the side and see that her arousal is now starting to drip down her thighs. She could come from my hand alone and that thought pleases the fuck out of me, but it won't be tonight. After another solid slap, I keep my hand in place, loving the way that her ass shakes.

My eyes never leave her red ass as I straddle her calves and take her hips in my hands. I lift her up with my hold and dig my fingers in while lining up my cock. The second I push into her, she lifts up her head and screams. Her cunt sucks me in even deeper before it clamps down tightly. I grunt, deep in my throat, and rock forward even though she has every fucking inch of me. That's all it takes for her to scream my name and coat my fucking balls as her juices leak from her body.

"God, yes," she continues as I pound into her.

I let go of her ass when I push in again, using my own hips

to hold her up and bring my palm down on her ass, loving when she clamps down on my cock again. "You're going to come again, Ember," I order before returning my hand to her hip and picking up my speed.

By the time I feel her start to tighten against me, I know she's close and I tilt her again so I'm hitting that sweet fucking spot inside her. The words coming out of her mouth don't even make sense, but the second I feel my come shooting deep inside her, she jerks in my hold and gives me what I want.

I slowly drag my spent cock from her wetness, loving the way that her cream coats it, and help move her so that we're lying on the mattress. She doesn't say a word as her fingers trace my abs. I place my hand on hers when I feel my cock twitch and hold it against my stomach, kissing her head, and tightening the arm around her back. She pulls one leg over my thigh and tilts her head up. Pressing my chin down, I look into her sated eyes with a smile.

"Thank you," she slurs, drunk from the pleasure I've given her.

"Thank you for what, baby?"

"For giving me you. For taking me. For giving us … us. I think my head is ready to catch up to my heart now, Nate."

And with that, she tucks her head back down and drifts off to sleep.

If only she knew.

The sound of my phone hits my ears before I could register Ember shifting in my arms, our bodies still on top of the covers where we had fallen asleep after 'dessert.' Not willing to let go of the soft woman in my arms, I ignore it and pull her closer.

"That's the third time it's rung, Nate," she sleepily mutters.

Shit. "Okay, baby. Let me grab it."

She moves so that I can slide out of bed, and I almost ignore the phone when I see the look in her eye when she sees my hard cock.

"Hold that thought." I laugh, bend, and grab my jeans and search the pockets for my still ringing cell.

"Nate Reid," I answer, annoyance in my tone when I see Shane's name on the screen.

"I need you to come close. I got a call from Lacey and I need to go home."

Fuck. Me.

"Does she really need you to come home or is she just pulling some more of her shit because she doesn't like you working at Dirty?" I question, knowing damn well his girl would do that shit. I can't stand the bitch, but I'm not going to tell him how to live his life.

He sighs. "I don't know, man. She claims she fell and hurt herself, but she didn't sound like she was in pain. I need to go check it out, and if she's pulling another stunt, I'll be back. I don't know what the hell her problem is lately."

"Dent?" I ask, hoping that I don't have to leave Ember on the one night that was supposed to be just for us.

"Still in LA. Won't be back until next week. Fuck, man, I hate calling you for this shit, but I don't know what to do."

I sigh, turning to look at Ember, expecting to see anger. However, she gives me a nod and smile, understanding that I need to go without even hearing the reasons. Supporting me and my responsibilities to Dirty without thought. Something that Shane's woman clearly doesn't understand. "I need to say good-bye to my woman. Give me thirty and I'm there."

I hang up, and when she stands from the bed and walks into my arms, I pull her naked body close.

"I hate leaving."

"I know you do, but you can't help the reason why."

"I wouldn't go if I wasn't needed, but Shane is the only one there and he has to run home."

She leans back and looks up with a smile. "You don't have to explain things to me, Nate. I'm not upset."

"How can it not bother you? We haven't had time to do anything but eat, sleep, or fuck when we're together."

Her eyes narrow. "Way to make it sound so meaningless," she snaps.

I open my mouth to soothe my comment over, but she shakes her head.

"First of all, I support you and Dirty because I know how much it means to you. Does it take you from me? Sure. But it also just opened and you guys are all still just getting your footing. It won't be like this forever. Hell, it might not even be like this next week. You will all find your stride. If you feel like it's taking too much from you personally in a few months, I'll still be here, and you can find another person to help hold the reins. Second, we have spent plenty of time together, and if anything, it's been better than if you were to take me out to dinner or whatever. We've had time to ourselves alone, sharing who we are now and getting to know each other as a couple and not friends. Third, if you would kindly find another way to express what we do when we're in bed and not sleeping, I would appreciate it."

Her gaze travels to my mouth when I feel my lips curve.

"I'll work on that, baby."

"That would be splendid."

I toss my head back and laugh, but when I feel her small hand smack my naked ass, my head drops forward and all laughter stops when I see the wicked look in her eyes.

"You're going to pay for that later," I threaten.

"That's what I'm hoping for," she smarts and pulls from my arms, grabbing her robe and walking out her door.

"Fucking Shane," I mumble under my breath and start to dress. I would kick his ass for pulling me from my time with Ember, but regardless of how I feel about his girlfriend, I know I would be doing the same thing if I were in his place.

Chapter 25

Ember

THE HIGH SCREAM OF MY smoke detector is the first thing that I hear.

Confusion fills my sleep-fogged brain, but when I feel Bam jump on the bed and whine in my ear, I wake with a start.

He starts leaping from the bed to the floor while the alarm continues to blast and I almost fall on my ass in my hurry. Luckily, when Nate left, I had pulled on some yoga pants and an old tee shirt, so it didn't take me long to leave my bedroom. As I cautiously walked down the hallway, the first thing that hit me was the smell of smoke. Panic started pulsing through me when I get to the living room and see the flames dancing around my kitchen.

I can't tell how bad it is from where I'm standing, but I don't dare go look. My house is newly remodeled, but it's an older construction and I'm not going to take the chance that something snaps and I'm trapped.

I turn on my heels and rush back to my room, where my cell is, before I sprint back to the front of the house and to the front door. I press a few keys before putting my phone between my shoulder and ear. Just when I reach the entryway, I hear the emergency operator asking me a question. I rattle off my address, telling her that there is a fire as I grab my purse off the entryway table and pull the door open. Right when I'm about to run out, I turn and grab the only other thing besides Bam that I care about.

She continues to ask me questions and I answer when needed, but the second I walk to the side yard and see the back half of my home blazing, I want to scream in pain.

Flames completely engulf the kitchen and my studio.

I drop to my knees as I watch the inferno continue to destroy everything it touches.

I distractedly think about the painting that I had just delivered to the gallery earlier that day, but knowing that everything else is most likely going to be gone is still crippling.

Sirens echo through the night, and I hear the operator tell me that they're almost at my location, but I don't respond. I feel the tears and roughness in my throat only after I register that I'm crying. When the lights of the firetruck, ambulance, and police car surround me, I climb to my feet and back from the house.

"Ember!"

I turn, phone to my ear and tears running down my face, and see Liam, Megan's husband, jump from his patrol car and rush toward me. I keep pulling air deep in my throat, feeling my vision start to blur as more tears come. He pulls the phone from my ear and speaks to the operator before hanging up.

"Are you okay? Hurt anywhere?"

I shake my head, still clutching my belongings to my chest and just look up at him.

"Come on, sweetheart. Why don't you come and sit in my car while I go get some information? Do you want me to call your dad?"

I shake my head frantically, grabbing for the phone that's still in his hands, and pull up Nate's name before handing it back to him.

He looks at the screen, his expression slipping slightly in shock, but just nods before walking away. I keep my feet on the ground next to Bam, the door open, and I watch as people rush around to put out the fire. Liam is moving around as he talks, and when I feel someone rush to my side, I look away from him.

"Holy shit, Ember! Are you okay? I just heard about the fire and came right over."

I jump when Levi pulls one of my hands away from my body, Bam making a noise deep in his throat. The simple touch is enough to knock the shock out of me, and I jerk back, dropping the contents I had been clutching for dear life on the ground.

He bends, ignoring my outburst, and picks up my purse, followed by the frame. The same frame I had just replaced when he had shattered it a few weeks before. He looks at the image, the one of Nate and me, and I see his jaw tick.

"Can I help you?" I hear Liam question, his voice full of authority as he walks back over, handing me my phone.

Levi stands and turns to look at Liam. "You can't. I'm checking on Ember here."

"It's okay, Lee," I interject before things get weird. "Levi is just an old ... friend of mine. He works with the Hope Town Fire Department and was just checking on me."

"Is that so? That's mighty nice and all, *Larry*," Liam sweetly says. "You just happen to be driving by?"

At Liam's question, I look over at Levi and notice that he isn't wearing his uniform. Instead, he has on a nice polo shirt and jeans.

"It's Levi." His nostrils flare and he stands a little straighter. "I had stopped by the station, actually, on my way home and was there when the call came in. Not that it's any of your business." He adds the last part under his breath, but I know Lee hears him because he gets a cold look in his eyes.

"Actually, *Levi*, it is my business. Not only because I carry this," he stresses while pointing to his badge, "but also because Ember is a close friend."

I ignore them, not interested in their macho bullshit, and look over at my house. They almost have the flames under control, and it looks like it didn't move far from the back half of my house. I take a deep breath and try to calm my frazzled nerves, but that all goes to shit when I hear the sharp scream of tires protesting. I look up and see my father jumping from his truck and rushing over, my mom not far behind him, and jerk my eyes to Liam.

"That wasn't the call I asked you to make," I accuse.

He holds his hands up, ignoring the man still standing next to the open doorway. "Don't look at me like that. I'm not going to get my ass handed to me because I picked the wrong order when it comes to the men in your life. Your father is scary as fuck, and I know he can kick my ass."

"He isn't who I wanted here," I hiss.

"Yeah, well the one you wanted here I imagine isn't far behind."

I narrow my eyes, and he just rolls his. "I have a wife, Em. You can't intimidate me with that look. Not to mention, Molly puts you to shame."

At the mention of his daughter, I feel some of my anxiety ebb, just in time for my father to take my shoulders and spin me until my nose is pressed against his chest.

"Are you okay," he huffs.

"Oh my God, baby!" my mom screams in my ear when she joins the huddle.

"Shit, Emmy, not so loud," my father scolds before pulling me back and looking down at me. "You're okay?"

"I'm okay, Dad. Just … in shock, I think. Bam got me out of the house before the smoke had even hit my bedroom."

He continues to look at me, his dark eyes probing as he makes sure my words are true. I can feel my mom fidget nervously as she watches them work to put the remaining flames out. He looks down, assessing me for injury, I'm sure, before pulling me back into his hold.

"Who the fuck are you?" he snaps, the sound grumbled against the ear he has pressed close to his chest.

"Levi Kyle, Ember's boyfriend."

"No, he isn't! Ex! *EX*-boyfriend. We broke up almost a month ago!" I yell, my mouth muffled against my dad's chest.

I try to turn around, but my father just holds me tighter against him.

"You're mistaken."

I shiver, the malicious tone in my dad's voice something that I don't often hear, but it never fails to cause me to tremble in fear. I've never had that tone directed *at* me either, and it's still scary as hell.

"Excuse me, I misspoke," Levi tries again. "We recently had a separation that I had been hoping to rectify."

"Oh boy," I hear coming from my mom, and I see her head pop in my line of sight, giving me a wink. She's loving this. Which shouldn't be a shock since she's married to my father and has taken great pleasure my whole life in 'throwing her sass' to get a reaction from him.

I finally push from my dad and turn to look at Levi. "At the risk of embarrassing you by doing this in front of an audience, I'm going to go ahead and say what I need to in the hopes that you'll hear me. I think it's nice that you came when you heard the call, but as you can see, I have most of my support here already. That being said, I think it was shitty for you to even say that during this," I stress and point behind his shoulder to where my house had been burning just minutes before. "But even if you had waited to do it somewhere else, the answer would be the same. I have no plan to rectify anything when it comes to us. Not now and not ever."

He makes a move to step toward me, but stops with a glance behind our little huddle, his eyes getting hard. I'm sure my dad is about to come out of his skin right now.

"You've had a rough night," Levi says, still not looking at me right away. "How about we talk about this in a week or so? Take all the time you want, but just promise we can talk. I miss you." He looks back at me with a smile.

"Are you stupid, boy?" my father snaps.

"Stop, it Maddox," my mom worries.

"I don't want a week, Levi. I don't want a day. Hell, I don't want even a minute. I really was trying to be nice, but I don't want you!"

"Damn fucking right you don't," I hear harshly barked and feel the instant rush of safety and relief rush over me at those words.

I turn to see that my father is still standing behind me with his arms now crossed over his chest, and I almost stumble with emotion when I look next to him and see the man mirroring his pose. Right down to the thin lips and narrowed eyes.

"Nate," I whisper on a sob, afraid to move without losing my shit and crumpling onto the sidewalk.

His eyes leave Levi's direction immediately, and he looks right at me. The anger that had been radiating from him dissipates the second he locks his eyes on mine. He takes a step forward and bends to pull me into his embrace. His head going to my neck and his mouth against the tender flesh as he lifts me with his hands on my ass until my legs wrap around his hips.

He doesn't move for a second, giving me all of him while my body shakes. Now that he's here, I finally let the enormity of tonight sink in; the fire could have been so much worse had Bam not woken me from my deep sleep. I feel the frame that I had been holding digging into our abdomens, but I don't dare ease up on my hold.

Soft kisses against my neck are the only warning that I get before he lifts his head and starts talking. "I know who you are, but you don't know who I am. This girl in my arms is mine, and buddy, you're one stupid motherfucker for letting her go. But you did and I promise you I'm not going to be that damn dumb. She said it nicely, but you didn't listen, so now hear it from me." I tighten my arms around his neck and press my nose into his neck, smelling his familiar cologne mixed with the scent of cigarette smoke from Dirty. A combination that I've become addicted to and it instantly makes me feel like all is right in the world. "You have no place in her life, and as nice as you think it was to come rushing over to make sure she was fine, as you can see … she is. You can leave now knowing that she's right where she needs to be. And, one more time, since you seem to need it really dumbed down—Ember is mine now and for the rest of our days on this earth, so you can fuck right off knowing that in no way will there ever be a break in that for the likes of you."

And at that, Nate turns with me in his arms and starts walking away from them.

He stops and turns his body until he's sitting. I lift my head up and see the back of an open ambulance before looking at him in question.

"You're going to stay right here in my arms and let them look at you. When we're done here, we'll see what else needs your attention before I pack up your and Bam's shit and take you home. And baby, do not argue with me because I've been holding on by the thinnest of fucking threads since Lee called me."

I just nod because really what else can I do?

Chapter 26

Nate

I WATCHED EARLIER AS SHE WAS checked out while her dad was saying a few things to that sorry piece of shit before he stomped off, got into his SUV, and left in a rush.

I could have fucking killed him earlier. The fear that I had for Ember morphed into a rage like I had never felt when I walked up to them talking around Liam's patrol car. He saw me, that fucking fuck, but he didn't let me being there stop him from running his mouth.

Not even the happiness I felt from Ember's response to him was enough to dull the rage that I felt. When I moved to step in, Maddox had stopped me with a hand to my arm, warning me without words to stand fucking back and let Ember speak her mind. So I did the only thing that made sense; I copied his stance in hopes that I looked even half as scary as he did, and that slimy fuck got the hint.

She shifts, her head almost falling off my shoulder, but I adjust her before it can. Her movement jolts me into the present and my mind away from the dark thoughts swirling in my head. Not for the first time since we sat down on a chair Liam had moved over from her front porch did I feel something dig into my gut. I move my hand between us and pull out whatever I've felt for the last thirty minutes but hadn't dared move to get it until I knew she was good and asleep in my arms.

I'm not sure what I expected her to have been clutching as if her life depended on it, but seeing a framed picture of us wasn't it. I hadn't ever seen this one, but to be honest, I hadn't really paid much attention to the shit she had around her house when she was the only thing I cared about looking at.

I remember the day this was taken like it was yesterday. I had been tutoring her for a few weeks, hell, maybe a few months, I don't know. The struggle to keep myself from her was getting to me, and when she showed up in that bikini, I almost forgot all the reasons to stay away. My eyes kept finding her throughout the day, and I kept finding reasons to be near her. I didn't know this picture was even taken, though. How had her dad not killed me before now? Because I know damn well if he had seen this picture, he had seen something between us long before I did.

I study the picture some more, overwhelmed that this was one of the things she had left the house with. Keeping it in my hand, I wrap my arms back around her and look up. Maddox has his wife in his arms, standing next to where Lee is talking to him at his patrol car, but his focus is on me and the woman sleeping wrapped around me. He looks at her, and even in the darkness, I can see the struggle he's having with himself not to come and take her from me, but when he looks up, I get the briefest of nods before he looks away.

It's one thing for me to have had his verbal blessing to pursue his daughter, but when she had picked *me* over *him* earlier, I had been a little worried. There is no doubt in my mind that he's been struggling with that since, but I have a feeling that the nod I just got from him was his way of letting me know that I now had his acceptance and happiness when it came to our relationship.

"I just got the okay to go in," Lee says, crouching down next to my seat.

"How bad is it?"

"Not as bad as it could be. There's some smoke and water damage to her living room, but from what I heard, nothing touched her bedroom and the guest room. The kitchen and the sunroom are completely gone, though."

"Studio," I grunt, hating that I'm going to have to tell her that.

"Pardon?"

"Not a sunroom, Lee. That was her art studio. The one room in the house that she basically lived in and one that I know means a whole hell of a lot to her."

"Shit, sorry, brother."

"Nothing to be sorry about. My woman is safe and the rest can be replaced."

He gives me a funny look. "Your woman, huh?"

I knew it was coming, so I just raise a brow, twisting my head to make sure she's still sleeping before responding. "More than that, Lee, if you know what I mean. She's my everything."

He smiles and gives me a nod. He's a happily married man who knows what it's like to find your everything. "Happy to hear that, Nate. She's good for you."

"Yeah." I sigh. "You took ten years off my life earlier with that call."

"I imagine, but she's okay and that's the only thing that matters. I'm going to go with her mom to pack up some of her stuff. I'm going to just go on and guess that she's going home with you? Or should I send her home with Maddox?"

At the middle finger he gets in response, he climbs to his feet with a laugh.

Her dad takes care of talking to the official looking people while I wait for her mom and Lee to get some shit packed. For that, I'm thankful. I don't want to let her go, needing her against me to remind me that she's fine.

"I'll check in with them tomorrow," he says, walking to stand in front of me and looking down at his daughter. "I suspect, had this not been the first time I had seen her in a few weeks, that I would have seen she had gotten her happiness back?"

"That would be right."

"You going to fight me on where she goes tonight?"

"With everything I have."

He smiles, a ghost of one that is almost not even noticeable. "I wouldn't expect anything less. Remember what I said, Nate. Accidents happen."

I nod, lifting the frame I still have in my hands and hold it out to him. He takes it as I wait for him to see what I'm hoping he does. His throat works as his eyes roam over every inch of the picture. I wait and hope that he sees it.

"Even back then." Not a question because even a fool would know the answer to that.

"Even back then," I parrot.

"I see. Take my advice then. Don't wait to tell her that you love her."

He continues to hold the frame when I see Emmy and Lee walking from the front door with three suitcases and two huge duffle bags between the two of them. I'm not sure which one of them I need to thank for making sure she was heavily packed because if I have things my way, she won't be back here even when the repairs are done.

"He really didn't say anything to you?"

I laugh at Ember's question, something she's been asking since we got out of our shared shower and climbed into my bed.

"He didn't, baby. He's a smart man, and he knew it was time to let you go."

"Oh, wow."

"You expected something different?"

She lifts her head from my shoulder and studies my face for a while, not giving anything away with her expression.

"Well, yeah. I mean it was one of the reasons that you said

we could never be together. I just assumed that you could see something in him that I couldn't. I've been worried about how he would handle us now because of that."

Well, shit. I feel like she just kicked me in the balls.

"Damn, baby."

"Don't say you're sorry, Nate. I didn't bring it up to make you feel bad, just pointing out that is what I had worried about when it came to us coming out, so to speak, and what his reaction might be. I understand why you said it back then, and I even agree."

"You do?" I ask, shocked.

"Yeah, and it doesn't matter now. We came out on top in the end."

"Yeah, I reckon we did."

She settles back down and starts to rub her hand on my torso. "Do you think my flowers will make it?"

I smile into the darkness around us. "Not sure, Em. Doesn't matter, though. I need to call in the morning and get your last couple of deliveries moved here."

She jerks in my arms. "There's more?" She gasps.

"Two more."

"Two more," she breathily repeats.

"Yeah, baby. One thousand five hundred and twelve in total. That's roughly one rose for every day I've missed since the night you graduated."

Her silence stretches out so long I wonder if she fell asleep, but when her breath hitches violently in her throat, I adjust our bodies so I can see her tear-streaked face.

"Ember?"

"That's the most romantic thing I've ever heard," she sobs.

Without a clue as to how to calm her down, I frame her face and just kiss her deeply.

Chapter 27

Ember

I HANG UP MY PHONE FEELING like, if he were in the same room as I was, I would physically hurt my father. When I showed up at my house two days after the fire—one that had been ruled an accident by faulty wiring—to find him directing a cleaning crew and movers, I snapped. Well, actually, I just gave him a hard look and got into my car to head back to Nate's without a word. With my show only a few days away, I need to focus on making sure everything is in order with Annabelle and the gallery.

But now, hearing that he's already hired contractors and the likes, without talking to me, I'm about to blow a fuse.

"You okay?" Nate asks, coming behind me and wrapping his arms around my chest. The scent of his deliciousness distracts me from why I was in a mood to begin with.

"Fine," I breathe, trying to take more of his scent in.

"You know, I learned really fast with a sister that when a woman says that word, she means the opposite, but at the risk of making you more upset, I'm just going to leave it at that."

I sigh. "It's my dad. He's taken over the rebuild at my house and even went as far as to move everything I own into storage."

He hums but doesn't respond. Instead, I feel his hand start to push up my shirt.

"Nate," I groan, pushing his hand when I realize something. "Nate!" I try again when he doesn't stop.

"What?" he says against my neck, biting the flesh between his teeth.

"Stop trying to distract me," I attempt but only end up moaning shamelessly when he cups my sex through my leggings and starts to move his fingers around through the fabric.

"You like it."

"Stop," I pant, shoving out of his wicked hands and turning.

His eyes are burning and his chest is rapidly moving when I look up at him. My eyes move from his chest to the sweatpants that are riding low on his hips, the erection tenting the fabric jerks when my eyes hit it, and I feel a noise deep in my throat in response.

"You're trying to distract me with your talented fingers and huge penis, aren't you?"

His face doesn't lose its intensity, but his lips twitch at my words.

"Do you know why my father moved everything I own into storage?"

He sighs. "I don't know for sure, but I can only assume."

"And your assumption would be what?"

"That he's doing what he would have done in my shoes, taking a guess at what I want, and doing it correctly."

"You're talking in riddles," I whine, tossing my hands up with a huff.

"Actually, I'm not. But I'll expand on that. He hasn't asked me how I feel about that fire or how I felt knowing that you could have been taken from me had you not got out. He does, however, know how serious I am about you, and with that being said, he decided to act as if he knew what I wanted to happen and make sure it's done."

"Seriously, Nate! How is that any clearer?"

He laughs, low and not with much humor. More like a sound that one would make if they knew something that the other person didn't. Which, duh, he does.

"In his shoes, if it had been your mother, he would have packed up her shit, repaired the house, sold it, and never let her out of his sight again. Her shit would stay in storage until she decided what to keep or donate, but her ass would stay in his house … forever."

I gasp, his meaning starting to become clear.

"Are you saying my father is preparing me to move in with you?"

"Like I said, he's acting as if he knows what I want."

My heart in my throat, I ask, "And what do you want?"

"Exactly what he would in my shoes, baby. The exact thing."

"It's been a month!"

He steps closer. "One month or one day, I would still feel the same about us."

And then his mouth is on mine, and I lose all ability to even form a thought, let alone another word.

"Come on," he says against my lips, taking my hand and pulling me from his living room and up the stairs to his bedroom. "I have you for another two hours before you need to head over to the gallery. How about we make good use of that time?"

And good use he does.

Over and over again.

"I think I like this one in here," Annabelle says, looking away from the series of landscape paintings to the few still-life ones that I have.

"Are you sure? I thought you wanted to mix them up some?"

She hums but keeps looking at the pictures she had cataloged of my artwork, placing a few against each wall in preparation to hang the respective canvases.

The way that her gallery is set up, it is essentially one large room with different 'walls' erected to hold various pieces. Normally, she has a good mix of art, even some freestanding displays for other mediums, but for my show, she has cleared off the whole floor.

We've already placed half of my collection, starting with the vivid colors of my nature scenes and ending now where we have the landscapes and still-life paintings scattered to make way for the huge abstract piece that will be the big focus of the event. The black wall that holds the picture solely takes my breath away; just seeing it up there with the spotlights on it and the tiny plaque that she had attached to the right corner.

It's a showstopper, and she knows it. When she told me that she was putting a fifteen thousand dollar price tag on it, I almost choked on my tongue. It's normal for some of my larger pieces to go for a couple of grand but never *that* much. However, now that I see it up there in all its huge glory, I now can see what Annabelle sees in those brushstrokes that make it worth that kind of price tag.

Hell, if she sells my whole collection, I could make almost seventy-five thousand dollars. And if this show goes off as she is saying it will, it's going to push my art to a whole new level when it comes to pricing. I've been waiting for this show. No longer selling five to ten paintings a month but selling that in a week. It will mean that I no longer have as much free time as I have now, but I'll be doing what I love, and since I already paint for fun seven days a week, this will mean that my 'fun' will now be sold instead of sitting in closet.

It's an overwhelming thought, but one that I'm ready for.

"I think we've pretty much got it all settled, Ember. We just need Daniel and his crew to come and hang the rest of your pieces. I can take care of placing the plaques tomorrow. You just need to spend the day focusing on getting ready for our big night. I'm so excited for you, honey."

"Are you sure you don't want more help?"

She laughs and places her hand on my arm. "You've done more than I ever would have asked. It's time you go on and enjoy some relaxing before tomorrow night."

"If you're sure." I look around one more time, seeing everything start to come together, and smile. "If you change your mind, just call."

She nods and walks away, dismissing me as her mind starts to wander with tasks, something she has a bad habit of doing.

When I first met her, I wondered how such a beautiful woman had never settled down with a family of her own, but I realized really fast that Annabelle Kingston is married to her work, and at fifty-two, she is perfectly content with her clients being the children she never had.

I grab my bag, pulling out my phone as I walk to the door and checking my messages as I climb into my car and start the engine. When I left Nate's house earlier this afternoon, he had said he was going to stop by Dirty but would be home for dinner. Seeing that it's now five, he's either finishing up there or already back at the house. Either way, the state of his fridge is scary, so my first stop will have to be the grocery store.

After the night of my house fire last week, Nate had been spending less time at Dirty, something that seemed to just happen naturally, even though it had been a big stressor in his life. He still goes in every day, but it is rare that he's there past midnight.

"Hello?" I answer, not looking at the display when my phone starts ringing through the speakers.

"Hey," Nikki says, her voice low and a little wobbly.

"Hey, you. What's wrong?"

She sniffs and I frown. Nikki isn't a crier. I often joke with her that her tear ducts are broken, but she just says it's a side effect of her black soul.

"I broke up with Seth." She sniffs again before blowing her nose loudly into the receiver. "Found that jerk in bed with some chick from his gym."

"Oh, Nik. I'm on the way to Nate's. Meet me there in ten, okay?"

She sniffs again, it coming out more like a snorted wheeze, but agrees before hanging up.

Pulling up to a light, I grab my phone and press Nate's name before placing it back down on the seat next to me. While I wait for the light to change, the phone rings a few times.

"Is it time for phone sex already," he drawls in a sexy rumble over the line, and I hear some deep masculine laughter break out around him.

"One of these days you're going to answer the phone like that and I'm going to make sure I had been playing with myself for long enough to just come in your ear as a response," I smart with a smirk when he grumbles a complaint.

"Get the fuck out of my office," he barks, and I hear his heavy breathing as footsteps echo and the sound of his door closing. "You've been told not to take my sweetness, Ember. Do you need me to remind you who that pussy belongs to?"

"Yeah, yeah, promises and all that. Listen, big man, Nikki's upset so she's coming over. Is that okay?"

"I told you that you don't have to ask permission to do shit. I want you to feel at home."

I roll my eyes. The same argument we've had since I all but moved in. "I'm still asking. It's your house, Nate."

He mumbles something, but his words are too low for me to make them out.

"I just wanted to warn you that you might be coming home to some pretty high estrogen levels and all that."

"What's wrong with Nikki?"

"All I know is that Seth cheated and they broke up. I told her to meet me there. I figured I could feed her ice cream and wine, the normal post-breakup comfort foods, and then see what else I could get out of her."

"Sounds good, baby. I'll stop by the grocery store when I leave here in ten. I have your back."

I laugh. "I'm pretty sure you're going to regret encroaching on a scorned woman's emotional breakdown time."

"Pfft. Don't doubt me, woman!"

He hangs up as my laughter booms around the cab, and by the time I pull up to his house, I'm actually looking forward to helping my friend if only for the reason that I know Nate has no idea what he's getting into.

Chapter 28

Nate

"AND THEN SHE JUST KEPT bouncing around on his dick like it was the next best thing to sliced bread. Just bounced and bounced. I really was worried that one of her fake freaking boobs was going to pop!"

"What did Seth do?" Ember asks, her voice low and comforting. My eyes keep pinging back and forth between them, trying not to focus too long on Nikki for fear of my life when she gives me one scary ass look.

Nikki doesn't even notice Ember, though. She's too far gone remembering walking in on her man fucking some chick. I shift when she gives me another squinty-eyed look of contempt just because I have a dick.

"He didn't do jack crap because his hands were tied to the bed!" she screams, still looking at me as if she would carve my eyes out with the spoon she's eating her ice cream with.

You would think that she would be thankful; I mean I did stop by the grocery store and buy them ten different flavors of ice cream, but nope. The second I walked into the house, she looked like she wanted to murder me along with her ex.

"So," I start, attempting to make my excuses and escape into my bedroom with some SportsCenter, but I snap my mouth shut when she stabs the air with her spoon. I watch Bam follow the utensil helplessly hoping that something, *anything*, will fall to the ground for him before looking over at Ember and praying she has the answers as to how I can get out of here.

"Would *you* let some hoochie tie you to the bed?" Nikki questions me with an evil tone.

Again, I look at Ember. I'm not really sure the truth right now will help my chances of getting out of here alive. She just winks and I know I'm on my own.

"Uh …" I clear my throat. "No. I would not. I'm more of the one doing the tying in this situation."

Ember stifles a giggle before Nikki can notice, but I don't miss it. She's going to pay for that later.

"You would tie up some hoochie?! You son of a Cher!"

"Huh?" Son of a Cher? Good God, this girl is strange.

"Ember! Did you hear him? He's just like all the other ones. Just thinking about his dick and some hoochie."

"Actually," I interrupt, and she jerks her eyes from Ember to where I'm sitting. I briefly consider all my points of exit options that I have and figure no matter what, my legs are longer, and if it comes to it, I have no problem running like a little titty baby from this spoon wheedling woman. "I never said I would tie up some 'hoochie.' I just meant that when it came to being tied up or doing the tying, I would be doing not receiving. And the only woman I'm going to tie to my bed is here," I finish in a rush and point over at Ember.

She gives me a big smile, distracting me for a second, but a second is all that was needed. I feel the spoon hit my forehead before falling to the hardwood in a loud clatter.

"Oops." Ember giggles.

"What the hell was that for?" I ask, rubbing my head.

"That was for having a penis."

"Why am I being punished because I have a dick?"

"Because you're breathing and thinking about using it. That's where it all begins," she sobs, and I watch as she drops her head to her hands as her hair falls into the almost melted container of chocolate ice cream.

"I'm just going to go … uh, somewhere, anywhere."

Ember's chest moves as she silently giggles, but she just waves me off as she moves from the chair she had been sitting on to the couch where Nikki is wailing and pulls her hair out of the ice cream. I see her look at her wrists for a hair tie and not wanting to stick around longer than necessary, I rip the one holding my hair in a bun and toss it in her lap on my way out of the room.

What a fucking mess.

With nothing on TV, I decided to pick up one of the books Ember is always reading. I used to make fun of Dani for reading 'mom porn,' but this shit is shockingly good. I've already made some mental notes of shit I plan to do to Ember. If she enjoys reading it so much, she's had to have thought about reenacting some of the scenes.

I had been thoroughly enjoying some bum fun when the door opened and a very tired looking Ember walked into the bedroom. Her white tee shirt was streaked with what I'm hoping is chocolate ice cream. Her bare feet are silent as she turns to pull her shorts down her legs, giving me a great view of her ass.

"How is she?" I break the silence, and she jumps a good foot in the air.

"I thought you would be sleeping," she says tiredly.

"I decided to do some light reading instead." I hold up the book, and she just shakes her head with a small laugh. "I thought about getting a highlighter but didn't want to piss you off by marking your book up."

"Thank you for that," she sarcastically drones.

I put the book down, making sure to mark the page I'm on, and pat the bed. "Come on, you look tired."

"I'm exhausted. Things just got worse when you left and she's been crying between mouthfuls of ice cream for the last two hours. I finally had enough and crushed up a Benadryl in her wine. She passed out thirty minutes ago."

"Is that safe?"

"Yeah. I called the twenty-four-hour pharmacist and asked if it was okay to take a Benadryl after a few glasses of wine. She's just going to take a good, much-needed nap."

She climbs into bed, one of her arms going over my stomach and her head dropping to my shoulder. She shifts a few times, bringing one leg up and over mine until I can feel the heat of her knee near my balls.

"I don't know this ex of hers, but is this something that came as a shock?"

I feel her finger push against my nipple ring and I remind myself why I need to calm my dick and be the sensitive boyfriend who listens instead of just fucks his woman every time she breathes near him.

Easier said than done.

When she gives it another tweak, I almost forget all my good intentions.

"I'm honestly not shocked. I've always wondered why she stayed with him, but she didn't have the best life growing up and I think she stuck around out of fear of being alone."

"I could kick his ass for her."

Her laughter tickles my skin, and I have to clench my jaw not to shiver like a little girl.

"That's sweet, honey, but I think her honor is safe and all that."

"Is she going to be okay?"

Ember lifts off my chest and shifts so that her lips press against mine.

"She'll be fine. She's a strong one. Just needed to get it out. Don't be surprised if she never brings it up again and just moves on like she hadn't just been betrayed by a man she had spent the last few years loving."

"That's not healthy, baby."

"I know it's not. She works on things her own way and I just make sure I'm there if she needs me."

"And what do you need?"

Her smile is instant. "Just you."

"Always."

She curls back against my body, her hand going still a few minutes later as her exhaustion wins. It's been a crazy night, but hopefully, it helped distract the nerves that she's been fighting as her show gets closer.

It's been on the tip of my tongue the last few nights, especially after the fire, to tell her how I feel, but because of the bullshit I had done in the past to hurt her, I know that she needs to be shown. I fucked up and because of that, my biggest fear is that my words won't be enough. Actually, that's a lie. The thought that I might feel what she did all those years ago when she bared her soul and I let the pain come to it is a very real insecurity for me. I know deep down that won't happen, but until I can make her say it again and prove to her that I won't take that gift for granted, I'm going to keep proving my feelings for her.

Hell, any fool can say those three little words but not all can show it. It took me a while to figure out what I needed to do was demonstrate that having all of her is something I not only want but also crave. Turning her down will always be one of my biggest regrets—even if it was the best thing for her at the time—because now that I have her, I know the only way I would have ever felt true happiness is in her arms.

Everything I have ever wanted is coming true. I have Dirty, and already, I know with no doubts that place will continue to thrive. My family is healthy. I have my own home, a badass truck, and friends with a bond that most people would kill to have. Everything that money could buy, I have. But getting the gift of Ember's love will without a doubt solidify that I've made it.

Nothing in the world is worth having if it isn't with her.

I know that now, and it's my job to make sure that any lingering doubts she might have are erased.

With a smile on my face and a plan forming in my mind, I pull her a little closer and drift off to sleep.

Tomorrow is going to be fun.

Chapter 29

Ember

"WOULD YOU SIT STILL!" MY sister yells, throwing another Q-tip down on the kitchen table. "I swear to God, Ember, you act like you've never put eyeliner on before."

Blinking back some of the tears in my eyes, I look up at her and smile, or try to, but my nerves are going nuts in my gut and I'm too focused on trying not to puke.

"You're lucky I love you," she fumes.

Nate wisely left when the girls showed up earlier. I think he would have stuck around, but when his sister started talking about her night with Cohen, he gagged and left with the promise to be back in time to escort me to the gallery.

"When is Stella getting here?" Dani asks, twirling another lock of my hair around her flat iron. I've always wondered how she got those amazing curls to stay so long but never thought it would be a flat iron doing the trick.

"Dunno," Maddi hums, her breath hitting my face as she attempts to put my liner on—again—and I fight the urge to blink when she starts to come at me with the pointy end again.

"She had better hurry; she's got my dress," I mumble. When I realized that the fire had destroyed the one I had picked out, I knew Stella, or her father rather, was my only hope.

"What happened to the one you bought?"

I look over at Dani with a sad smile. "It was hanging on the molding in the doorway to my kitchen. I accidentally brought it in there with the groceries and just decided to leave it there." Even though I've come to terms with what I lost in the fire, it still hurts. My studio being the biggest of heartaches. But everything besides that room that had meant something to me was salvageable, so I need to focus on that and not on what I lost.

"Damn, sorry, Em," Dani mumbles.

"It's okay. Things are coming along with the construction, according to my dad. I've slowly started to rebuild my supplies, so I'll be fine."

"And luckily she kept a lot of her overflow in the guest room, so not all was lost, right Em?"

I smile at my sister and nod my head.

"That's good. You should take over a place here," Dani contemplates out loud.

It isn't something I haven't thought about, but I don't want to take over Nate's space with my stuff. He has a bonus room upstairs that has so much natural lighting and a huge picture window overlooking his backyard. When I first walked into the room, something that he had been using for a man cave type game room, I couldn't help but think of what a perfect space it would be to set up my easel and get lost.

His property is set away from the road, gated and secluded. When you stand in that room and look out the window, all you can see is the beautiful woods, the small creek, and the birds flying around. The trees aren't heavy back there, not like they are around the sides and front of his property, so the sun just gives a shadowed grayness to the land.

I've already decided that I would be painting it soon. My phone was quickly filling up with various angles and images from his woods and property in general.

"I'm here!"

All three of us turn when Stella comes bursting into the kitchen, where we have currently set up command central to get me ready for the show tonight. She rushes into the room and I notice that she's empty-handed, making what nerves I had been able to settle pick back up.

"Uh," I start.

"It's coming. I had a tagalong that I just couldn't shake when it was discovered where I was headed."

That's when I notice the heavy clicks of heels against the floor. There is only one person I know who takes that heavy of a step when in heels.

Sway.

Or Dilbert 'Sway' Harrison III.

He's not only one-half of Stella's fathers, as in plural, but he also owns the very popular salon, Sway's, that my sister, Dani, and Stella work at. He's gotten a lot of hype after the reality show aired a few years ago, *Sway All the Way*, and things just keep getting bigger and bigger for him and the girls at the salon.

But more importantly, he knows what he's talking about when it comes to fashion. I've known him my whole life and never thought anything but the best of the man who rocked designer fashions better than anyone else did. I've seen pictures of him from before all of our parents had kids, and this has always been him. Back then, he was always rocking a long blond wig, but these days, he has it shaped into a shoulder-length stylized mess of wavy curls.

Just because he's a gay man who prefers the tight clothing from the women's section doesn't mean he can't pull off jeans and a tee shirt from his husband's closet too. He just has it all.

"Looking good, Sway," Dani calls over my shoulder, and she isn't wrong.

He has on some tight flare-legged black pants with a white button-down shirt tucked into his trim waist. He used to be a little overweight, but nowadays, he's trimmed up and put on some muscle. Instead of his normal blond locks, though, he has his natural shaved black hair on display, something I know that even though he usually has covered up, he takes great pains to make sure his grays don't ever show.

"Of course, Sway does, darlin'. Would you expect any less?"

"I suppose not." She giggles.

"What are you wearing?" He gasps and continues to look at Dani.

"Uh … clothes?"

253

"Those," he puffs, "are not clothes and should be thrown out immediately. What have I told you about hiding that luscious body?"

"I know, I know, but give it a rest today. I was in a rush, and Owen spilled his breakfast on me, so I just threw something on. I'm going home to change when I finish her hair."

"You had better be," he fusses.

"And you," he says to me with a smile. "I have the best dress ever for you. Tight and black, but covers everything from shoulders to knees. I even have a gold shawl if you decide that bare arms aren't what you want. Finish that up with some gold heels that are just marvelous. I knew you wouldn't want something too flashy, even if flashy is my middle name, even though you should show off that body too. I'll let it pass tonight because you should flatter your art and not overshadow it with your beauty. So hurry up so Sway can get you all beautified for tonight."

I don't get a chance to talk because his face lights up and he starts bouncing in his spot.

"Oh! And now, tell me all about the hunky prince who owns this house. I always knew with parents as striking as Axel and Izzy that boy would be a jaw dropper. Even as a baby he was just the most handsome thing in the world, I tell you. Just the sweetest face, like his mama. But it was his daddy and those brawny, mouthwatering muscles that I knew would win out with his only son. That jaw, my lord. And his hair. I've been itching to get my hands on him for way too long, oh yes, I have. Tell Sway everything, if you know what I mean." He finishes with a dreamy sigh and drops into the seat in front of me, pushing Maddi out of the way. "I bet he is a dream in bed!"

"Oh my God, Sway! I'm going to puke!" Dani whines, making a gagging noise.

"Something is wrong with you," Maddi snaps and nudges him out of the way with her hip.

Sway continues to wag his brows at me, and I have to fight to keep my giggles in. I just give him a wink and hope that's enough to keep him quiet while Dani and Maddi finish my hair and makeup.

Chapter 30

Ember

AFTER BEING FUSSED OVER, BUFFED, and stuffed, the girls—and Sway—deemed me 'perfect' and left shortly after to get ready themselves. I still have another three hours before the gallery doors open, but I hope Nate gets back soon so I can get over there. The anxious anticipation for tonight hit a fever pitch when I took my first look in the mirror after getting dressed.

Sway wasn't wrong about the dress. It's perfect, understated, and classy.

It's also skintight, and because of that, I had to forgo any undergarments. Every step I take on the tall heels has me fighting the urge to look and see if my big boobs are swaying around. Sway assured me that it was designed to 'hug the girls tightly,' and even if I decided to jump up and down, they would stay put. Now, I just need to make sure Nate doesn't make my nipples hard, and I should be good to go.

The black fabric has a high neck, covering me as promised from my collarbone to the end of the pencil skirt at my knees. My arms are bare, which is perfect to keep me cool if I start to get the nervous sweats. My hips are outlined in a way that I look like the perfect model for an hourglass figure. That is until I turn to the side and you can't help but notice my butt. I've always thought it was one of my worst features, having more than a handful, but seeing how it's accented, I know it's probably one of my best. Lord knows, Nate can't keep his hands off it. Not quite a Kardashian butt, but close.

Dani took all my hair, curled loosely, and after twisting a few pieces at my temple, pinned one side back so all it hangs over my right shoulder.

My makeup is light, except for the light smoky effect that Maddi had created around my eyes. The normally dull brown color looks more like melted chocolate with the outline of black.

I look good. No, I look damn good. Just standing in front of the mirror in Nate's room has helped to ease a little of my tension about tonight because of the confidence my appearance brings forth.

"Fuck me," a deep voice moans, breaking through my thoughts.

I turn, my red lips smiling as Nate stands in the doorway breathing heavily.

"Well, hello to you too," I joke.

"How long is the show again?"

"A few hours. Why?"

"I just need to know how long I'm going to have to wait before I can peel that skirt over your ass and bend you over. Fuck, Ember. I'm going to be tenting my pants all night."

I laugh, walking over to him, and his eyes zero in on my heels.

"Those will stay on. All night. I have plans for those." He adjusts his crotch, moving the very noticeable erection around with a groan before holding his hand up to stop my movements. "Don't get near me. If you do, we'll never get out of here. Be a good girl and go wait for me downstairs while I get dressed."

He shifts, jumping away from the doorway when I take another step, making me throw back my head with a laugh as I walk out of the bedroom and down to let Bam outside to take care of his business before we leave for the night.

Thirty minutes later, he comes downstairs and gives me a narrowed eye look full of accusations.

"What?" I ask, tossing the magazine I had been thumbing through down on the couch next to me.

"What, she says," he grumbles. "Acting like you didn't plan this with your tempting body on display for me." He points at his crotch, and I can just see the outline of his hard cock still tenting the fabric.

My giggles bubble out and he puts his hands on his hips, the fabric of his black dress shirt pulling tight on the muscles in his arm. I lick my lips as my eyes travel back to the black slacks hiding—or rather, not hiding—his erection.

"Not helping, Ember," he says through clenched teeth.

I hold up my hands and have to stifle the bubble of laughter that is threatening to burst out. "I didn't plan anything. Promise. This is all thanks to Sway." I point at my dress.

"Sway did this?"

I nod.

"Hmm. Remind me to send him a thank-you note then," he mutters under his breath.

"Just a second ago, you were ready to spank me for having the nerve to wear this dress! Now, you're talking about sending thank-you notes?"

"Oh, I'm still spanking your ass, but I'm going to make sure and thank him for giving me a whole new list of fantasies when it comes to how I want to fuck you."

My jaw drops. "I think that's an inappropriate thank-you note, Nate."

"You're right. I should send him an edible arrangement and mention how he's should enjoy eating something delicious as fuck for giving me my own mouthwatering treat."

"You're incorrigible."

"I'm horny! You have no idea what that dress is doing to me. In fact, after I fuck you in it tonight, I might have the damn thing bronzed."

Speechless, I just shake my head and turn to gather my clutch and phone, smiling to myself when he makes a noise low in his throat.

Maybe I'll send Sway a thank-you note of my own.

"I'm so proud of you, sweetheart," my mom praises and gives me a big hug.

I look over her shoulder and let her admiration sink in. The nerves I had been fighting leading up to this moment had left the second Annabelle's gallery filled to the point of bursting earlier, and I haven't been able to stop smiling since.

When I got here, she had everything already set up, and with nothing to do but wait, I spent the quiet time I had walking the room with Nate, showing him all of my work.

The catering company Annabelle had hired had been working the room, passing out champagne flutes and light canapés. I've been enjoying a glorious buzz thanks to that. The low hum of classical music that was playing through the speakers earlier can't even be heard over the light babble of this many people filling the room.

She had sent out something like two hundred invitations, not counting the huge crowd that came from my personal guest list, and it looked as if almost every single person had shown up.

The only thing I was still anxious about was hearing what ended up selling at the end of the night. Optimistically, I was hoping for at least half of my collection to sell, but I really would be happy with anything. Just being here and seeing my work on display as everyone visibly appreciates my pieces is the most wonderful gift to my soul.

"Thank you, Mom. It's a little overwhelming but so exciting to see everyone loving my work."

"What's not to love?" my dad says from behind me, and I turn to smile up at him. "Except that woman wouldn't let me buy one."

My brow furrows. "Annabelle?"

"Snotty blond woman who looks like a stick is permanently wedged up her-"

My mom slaps her hand over his mouth, not letting him continue to complain, and gives me an apologetic look.

"That's Annabelle. Did she give you a reason?" My mind races with reasons why she would deny a sale, to my own father of all people.

"Sure as hell did," he answers against my mom's hand, his lips turning up as he smiles brightly at me.

When my mom feels his smile, she drops her hand immediately and looks up at him with one of her own. It's rare that he gives us this look, especially in public, so to see his stoic mask slip I know she is soaking it in too.

"Okay?"

"Sold out, my sweet girl. Every single fucking piece is sold." His smile gets even larger as his chest puffs with pride.

"What?" I gasp.

"Oh my God, Emberlyn!" my mom exclaims, pulling me back into her arms with a bruising hug.

My dad wraps his arms around us both and hoarsely gives me the words that make my eyes prick with emotion. "Proud of you, honey. So damn proud."

I've never doubted his pride, but I know he's always worried about me since my career started out so quick. I had so much success with my work before I even left my teenage years behind, and when I left art school after two years to pursue my dreams, his worrying didn't ease up. But this, tonight, goes a long way to extinguishing those thoughts in his mind.

"I need to go tell Nate," I tell them, pulling out of her embrace.

My dad, shockingly, gives a nod of agreement. "You did good," he states low and slowly follows with a smile that almost looks sad.

"Thank you?" I respond a little confused. He just said he was proud of me, so I'm not sure why he now looks sad about it.

"Talking about the man, not your night."

"Oh."

"Like I said, you did good. He did better, but you still did good. And if he makes you cry again, I'll kill him."

My nose tingles, and I look up at my big, strong father as I fight not to start crying. Maddi would kill me if I messed up my makeup, but I know my father would be upset if he was the reason I shed a tear ... even if they were happy ones.

"I did do better, didn't I?" I give a wobbly laugh when he winks, taking my mom's hand and pulling her into the crowd over to where the Reids are—well, one-half of them since I don't see Nate's dad, Axel. The Becketts, Coopers, and Cages are laughing and smiling in the back corner.

Their children scattered around the room, as well, but I only have eyes for the long-haired man in black standing in front of *A Beautiful War* with his father at his side.

I'm stopped a few times on the way to him. A few critics from the local paper and the *Atlanta Journal-Constitution* stop me for a few quick questions, making my high for the night climb even higher. The *AJC*? Holy crap. That's huge for them to feature an Atlanta artist! By the time I'm stepping up behind the Reid men, I might as well be walking on clouds I'm so happy.

"You going to tell her tonight?" I hear Axel ask his son.

"Yeah. I can't wait any longer. It's killing me to keep it from her."

My heart seizes in my chest, and I drop the hand that had been reaching for Nate's shoulder as I wait to hear what else they have to say. If they wanted privacy, well, then they should have had this conversation somewhere else.

"Good you don't wait any longer. Women don't appreciate that shit."

Nate nods, still looking at the canvas in front of him.

"Didn't want it to come to this, but I can't keep it in any-more."

This time Axel bobs his head, taking a swallow of the champagne in his hand. After a few seconds—minutes maybe—Axel gives him a slap on his shoulder and turns. He stumbles a little in his step when he sees me behind them but just bends to kiss my temple, covering his misstep.

"Congratulations, Ember," he acknowledges softly.

Nate's shoulders tense, but he doesn't turn. After his father walks away, I wait for it, but he still doesn't give me his eyes. Their words run through my mind and instead of feeling the over-whelming desolation I would have expected to feel, I have too much faith in him to just walk away without demanding an ex-planation.

I haven't come this far to just give up. If he's going to end it, he's going to tell me right now to my face.

Squaring my shoulders and taking a deep breath, I step around him, standing between him and the wall holding *A Beautiful War.* A fitting place, if there ever was one. Even if the crowd is milling about just a few feet away.

"Nate?" His eyes roam over the piece behind me for a second before looking at me, giving me his attention, and the fierceness in his gaze almost makes my knees buckle. "What is it?"

He studies my face before looking back over my shoulder. "That's us."

Not a question.

"That *was* us," I correct.

"And what changed?" he continues as his attention stays focused on the painting.

"Everything," I breathe.

With a deep inhale, I finally get his stunning green eyes. "Give me more than that, Emberlyn. What changed to end our *beautiful war*?"

Time to go for broke. We've been leading up to this for weeks now, and after everything that we've been through to get to this point, I just need to take a leap and pray this time things will end differently than it did the last time I told him how I felt.

"My head collided with my heart."

His pupils dilate, his eyes getting stormy as his nostrils flare. "Give me more," he demands, taking a step toward me until just the smallest of space separates us from touching.

"Love won."

His chest heaves, jolting at my words, and he dips until we're nose to nose. "*More.*"

"I love you." I softly comply with his demand, my voice steady, strong, and true. "I love you. And even though that has never changed through the years, regardless of my fears and hurt, what made everything change was when I realized you not only wanted my heart, but you would also protect it when I took the last step toward you and asked for yours in return again."

"I have all of you?"

"I think you always have."

His hand snakes out, going around my middle to pull me to him as he straightens to stand, my feet lifting to dangle above the ground. I reach up, curling my fingers over his shoulders as our breath mingles between us.

"Tell me again." The hunger in his eyes betrays the calmness in his voice.

"I love you."

His eyes close, and he presses his forehead against mine.

"Nate?" I whisper when he doesn't move.

"I had it all planned." His words just barely a whisper. "Everything I wanted to say to you, show you, and give you … all planned. It was getting so hard to keep it from you, though. I took one look at this painting, and I knew I couldn't wait any longer. It was killing me to keep those plans from you, but I just had to be patient."

I think back to the conversation I had overheard between him and his father when he finishes talking, and my body jolts when I realize what had really been going on.

"I knew that tonight I had to tell you, regardless if I had proven myself worthy of getting it in return, and I had to take a chance that you were ready to give that back to me. Then I see this and I knew that even if you weren't ready, I was more than prepared to give you enough to last for the both of us until you were."

Finally opening his eyes, I gasp when I see the blazing brightness illuminated by the slight dampness in them.

"My God," I wheeze when his arms tighten around me, wishing we were alone so that I could wrap my legs around him and never let go.

"I love you, Emberlyn Locke. I can't change that we lost us for a while, but I can promise you with everything that I am that you will never, not for one second for the rest of our lives, know another day without that love."

"Oh, Nate."

His mouth presses against mine. Not in a deep kiss, but the soft touch of his lips against mine is all I need to feel like we're the only ones in a crowded room. Taking my hands from his shoulders, I wrap them around his neck and take a deep pull of air through my nose, my eyes watering as every single crack I had ever had in my heart repairs itself with the power of us winning our beautiful war.

In his arms, I know that no matter what, as long as I'm with him, we can win any fight that is in our path.

Chapter 31

Ember

"I DON'T UNDERSTAND."

Annabelle gives me a sly smile before looking over my shoulder. I turn and follow the path to see Nate standing with our group, and Dani and Cohen laughing at something he's said. Maddi is standing with Cohen's sisters as they talk to Liam and Megan. The rest of our group—Stella, Zac, and Jax, as well as Cohen's brothers—left when the doors locked.

Turning back to Annabelle, I try to make sense of her last words.

"It is quite unorthodox but not unheard of."

"You're telling me, and not joking, that every single one of my paintings was sold before anyone arrived?"

There's no way. I mean sure we had sent out a little teaser to the guests before the show, but there is no way that someone would have even had time to see the whole collection, let alone enough people to buy the whole damn thing.

"I didn't say no one had arrived, just that every piece was paid for before the show started."

"Can you please stop talking in riddles and just let me see the purchase orders."

Her smile grows, and I look behind me when I feel Nate press against my back.

"What's going on?"

I turn slightly to look up at him while I sink into his hold, loving the way his hard muscles feel against my body.

"I'm trying to get Annabelle to tell me why, when my dad tried to buy a painting earlier, he was denied. She said that was because everything was sold, but Nate"—I take a deep breath after rushing that out quickly—"he tried to make a purchase less than thirty minutes after people started arriving."

"I see," he responds, his eyes alive with mirth. "Well, Annabelle?"

Pulling my attention back to her, I watch in confusion as she throws her head back and laughs.

"You," she says and points at him. "Are trouble."

"You might as well just show her the purchase order, so I can get my girl home to celebrate."

"Trouble," she huffs under her breath, shifting some things around on her desk before handing me the purchase orders.

Expecting to see a spreadsheet of orders or, at the very least, more than one single sheet of paper, my brain freezes.

"Oh my God," I stutter, seeing the words but not really understanding them.

"I told you I wanted every piece of you, and I'll be damned if I share this part of your stunning mind with anyone else."

"What have you done?" Still mumbling, my eyes rake over every word. It really isn't a question since not only can I see it with my own eyes, but also the only thing I'm capable of getting past the huge lump of emotion burning my throat.

"I have all of you now, Ember."

"Oh, my God."

Tears burn my eyes and I look up to an elated Annabelle. I'm sure she's thrilled that she sold every piece. After all, her commission alone is worth being excited about, but she looks like my reaction alone is worth more to her than any money she made tonight.

His deep chuckles at my shock vibrate against my back, and with a hitch in my breath, I turn with a leap and bury my head in the crook of his neck and cry the happiest tears I've ever shed.

"You're crazy," I tell him.

"Crazy for you."

"That … God, Nate. Do you have any idea how much money you just spent?"

He shrugs.

"Where are you even planning to put all of these?" My question is a hushed whisper against his smiling lips.

"I guess we can give one to your dad," he answers in complete seriousness. "But *our* war is going home with us. That's mine."

"There are still over thirty paintings that you now own, Nate."

His lips part, his teeth showing as he smiles big. "Looks like we're about to have some full walls then."

"I love you, you crazy man."

"I know."

I raise a brow, his laughter booming around us. "I love you, too."

"Nate!" I scream when his hand smacks against my exposed ass. "Please," I beg.

"If I would have known you were walking around bare under this dress." His words come out so deep and full of lust that he sounds animalistic.

My fingers flex against the wall in front of me, wishing he had, at least, pushed me against the couch instead so I would have something to grip. We didn't even make it a step inside the door before he was pushing me against the wall and making true to his promise earlier when he pulled my dress's tight skirt over my hips.

Then he discovered just what I had on underneath. Or, rather, what I didn't.

And that is where we are now. He's standing behind me panting while one palm between my shoulders pins me against the wall as his other continues to spank each of my naked cheeks.

He takes a handful of my flesh and gives me a painful squeeze, the feeling shooting something so heavenly between my legs. He lets go, brings his hand down again over the heated skin, and shifts so I can feel his pants-covered erection between my cheeks.

"You look so fucking hot wearing my marks," he utters against my shoulder before his teeth take a hard nip.

"Oh, God." I gasp.

He continues to play with me, nipping and licking at my shoulder and neck while rocking against me.

"Please. I need you, Nate," I whine, pushing against him.

"My mouth or my cock?"

My mouth moves, and between pants and incoherent mumbling, I try to answer. My legs are shaking so violently; the release I so desperately need is just within reach, rendering me incapable of conscious thought, let alone speech.

"You're soaking my pants, Ember. You need me, baby?"

I give him a nod, my forehead hitting the wall softly. With no strength left, I leave it there and sigh.

Nate continues his tantalizing movements with hips rocking against my backside. The burn of his pants against my heated flesh only spikes my growing need for him with each rub. His hands come up to roughly grab my breasts through the dress, pinching my nipples harshly. I whine and he answers with a coarse laugh.

With quick movements, he has me turned. My back hits the wall as my legs come up to hook behind his back. The second his hips connect with my core, I notice that at some point he had shed his pants, the hard heat of his bare erection hitting the spot that needs him the most, and I whimper shamelessly.

With our faces level, noses touching with each deep inhale, it's as if we both feel the need to be as close as possible and our hands move. Mine slowly travel up his chest until the tips of my fingers are in his silky hair and my thumbs are at his cheekbones. He moves slower, stabilizing our weight with his body before framing my face, his thumbs sweeping over my cheek slowly.

His luminous eyes burn their gaze into mine as he stares at me with raw hunger. Our mingled breaths rush between parted lips, just inches from touching, as we continue to gaze at each other. What had started as a desperate desire to feel each other changes in that instant; it's no longer about the hunger to find our releases, but to share something more intense than we ever had before.

I gasp when he lifts his body from mine; taking his cock from the hug my lips had been giving it, I mourn the loss. With our faces so close, I see his hooded eyes darken to a mossy green that burns brightly, reminding me of a rain-soaked field after a hard downpour.

Hypnotizing.

Alluring.

All-consuming.

The second he enters my body, we both call out. His fingers flex on my neck and pull my forehead to his without breaking eye contact.

He moves slowly, each inch entering my body with unhurried measured thrusts that have a new burn crawling up my skin, leaving goose bumps in its wake. I tighten my thighs, trying to bring him closer, or speed him up, but he ignores me. Even as my whimpers turn to an aroused whine, he doesn't take me harder than the slow glide he had created. The sounds of our breaths echoing around us mingle with the wet sounds of him entering and exiting my body.

"More," I say breathily.

His forehead rocks against mine as that mossy green bright-ness takes on a blaze from within. His nostrils flaring and his breathing labored.

"More," I beg.

His movements still with his cock buried deep. I whimper, the fullness stretching me. He twitches but still doesn't move. Just bores into me with an expression that causes my heart to gallop at dangerous speeds.

"I love you." His voice is guttural, hoarse from the intense moment we're sharing.

"I love you, too. So much."

Not breaking eye contact and his cock still deep inside me, he closes the small distance to my lips. Only when our tongues make contact does he start to move again. The same slow—painfully slow—infiltration of mind, body, heart, and soul.

I pull my mouth from his when the intimacy becomes too much. My hands fall from his face to his neck, and I feel my eyes wet when I realize that, at this moment, we're as close as anyone could ever get to experience paradise.

Not even completely nude and with me against the wall, Nate makes love to my body. And if there was any doubt about him owning all of me before now, it was obliterated the second I clamped down on him with a scream as his own grunt of comple-tion rumbled from deep in his chest.

Chapter 32

Nate

I T'S BEEN TWO WEEKS SINCE Ember's art show. Two weeks since I earned the right to have her heart back and gave her mine in return. Sometimes, I feel like the biggest pussy-whipped bastard around because all it takes is one sly smile from her and I'm ready to drop to my knees and promise her the fucking world.

And I love every single second of it.

She's still at my house, and honestly, I wasn't kidding when I had told her that it was where I wanted her. Fuck rushed. I don't see the point in changing the way things are now just because society has some misconception on how fast two people in love should move. Ember and me, we aren't conventional. Our past proves that, and just because we haven't been together that long—almost two months—we've known each other our whole lives. We're closer than most couples who have been married for years.

So if I want my girl with me, I'm going to make sure I do whatever it takes to convince her to stay.

However, judging by how quick her dad is moving the construction on her house along, I have a feeling that *he* isn't too happy with his daughter 'living in sin.'

I make a mental note to have a conversation with him tonight at our first family dinner together as a couple. I would be a fool if I weren't a little worried that he might kick my ass just for suggesting it.

But it's a chance I'm willing to take.

Even though everyone had come out to her show, our parents knew that we were together now, but they haven't actually come face-to-face with just how together we really are. There hasn't been time before tonight. She's been busy working in my guest room on some more pieces Annabelle had commissioned out, and I've been busy with Dirty.

Thankfully, Dirty is running so smoothly with Shane and Dent managing the club that I've been able to really take a step back. I still go in every day, but I trust my team, and I've been able to be home early more often than not. My girl got the dates she deserved, and it's rare that I miss one of her home-cooked meals. Sometimes, she comes with me when I go over at night, and sometimes, she doesn't. All that matters is that we found our stride and it's fucking perfect.

"Hey, handsome," I hear and look up from the socks I had been pulling on to see Ember standing in the bedroom doorway, Bam panting at her side.

Pulling my jeans legs down, I grab my shoes and slip them on before standing to get my hands on her. She laughs when I bend and grab her ass to pull her up so that I can take her mouth. The sound muffles against my lips, and I smile, breaking the kiss to look at her.

"Hey baby, you ready?" Her face heats and she pulls one plump lip between her teeth. Well, shit. I thought she had gotten over her nerves about tonight, but apparently not. "What is it?"

"Nothing really. I just stupidly let some nerves take root."

"I told you, Ember, you have nothing to feel uneasy about."

She gives me an adorable pout, and I have to remind myself that we really don't have time for me to fuck her. Even if we did, I'm pretty sure her father *would* kill me if we show up smelling like sex, regardless of me having his blessing to be with his little girl.

"I know, logically. I just can't help it."

"What are you really worried about?"

She sighs. "I don't know. Maybe that they won't agree with our relationship. Or that it will be awkward."

"And would it be a problem if someone did have an issue with us being together?" I ask. To me, fuck no, but Ember has always been treated a little differently as the baby of the group. The overprotective father acting like a giant guard more often than not, and I understand where she is coming from because of that. After all, I did use that as a reason for us not to be together in the past.

"Not even a little, to me, but like I said … it would be awkward."

"Good thing for you, awkward is my middle name."

She laughs, the mood lifting, and I give her another brief kiss before placing her on her feet.

"I love you, Ember, but so does every single other person who will be there tonight. They won't even think twice because they can see with their own eyes that not only do you have my love, but I have yours. Give them the benefit of the doubt until they prove otherwise, and if they do, then we will deal. Together."

"Together," she echoes.

"You're stuck with me, baby. If they give you any lip, then just light the fuse on that little firecracker temper of yours and put them in their place."

She barks out a laugh, the heaviness of her mood dissipating instantly.

"I'll go take Bam out. Come get me when you're ready to leave."

"Okay, Nate."

The second her body passes by mine when she walks into the room, I let my hand fall back and give her ass a loud smack. She jumps and turns quickly. I wag my finger at her.

"Not fair, Nate!" she whines, the sound falling on my back as I walk out of the room.

"Foreplay is a good thing," I call back, laughing to myself as I walk through the house and start tossing Bam his ball in the backyard.

"Everyone is already here," she softly observes, looking through the windshield of my truck at the vehicles that line my parents' driveway.

"Well, that's what happens when your beast of a dog decides that he would rather hunt his own dinner than have that bag shit."

She laughs nervously.

"Calm down. It's going to be fine."

Her head moves, but her eyes stay focused on the driveway.

"How many times do I have to remind you that this isn't the first time they've seen us together?"

"My show doesn't count. I hardly had time away from Anna-belle parading me around to even be at your side."

I hum, not responding. She has to work this out on her own, and nothing I say will ease her mind.

"Plus, this is so much different. This is our *family,* Nate. Someone is bound to say something. I just don't want to cause any issues."

Again, I just nod and make a noise in my throat.

"Then again, our parents are the only ones who it could cause issues with and they know about us, so it will probably be fine. I mean we've had the group over to the house and they've seen us together, so it's not as if this is going to be shocking. But all of our parents, I mean … yeah, they haven't really seen us together. But you know what, you're right. We love each other and that's all that matters. If someone has a problem with it, then screw them."

Her head finally turns as she slides her hand into mine.

"Firecracker."

She smiles brightly, happiness clear on her face, and I know she's ready.

We walk up the driveway, having parked all the way at the end, hand in hand. I give her one more look before pushing the door open and stepping into my parents' house. She follows behind; I'm not sure if she's using me to hide behind or if I'm just too pumped to be here *with* her that I'm rushing, but when I stop walking a few feet in to shut the door behind us, she crashes into my back with an oomph.

I turn and look down at her. She looks up with a glare.

"Would you rather I just jump on your back so that you don't have to drag me around?" she says sarcastically.

I drop her hand and bend to hold her face between my palms. "The only time I want you jumping on me is when you're taking my cock in your tight cunt." My voice is low, for her ears only. When her cheeks pink and eyes darken, I drop my mouth to hers for a deep, wet kiss. Her hands grab onto my tee shirt and I feel her try to pull me closer, completely forgetting where we are.

That is until a tiny little angelic voice screams out.

"OH! Mommy! Nate has his tongue in Ember's mouth! That's *bad*. Mommy *and* Daddy said so. You have to keep your tongue in your mouth and only when you are married can you do *that*! Oh, boy. You're in trouble! Mommy!"

I regrettably break away from Ember and give her shocked eyes a wink before looking down at Molly. I've loved this kid since the day I met her, but right now, I'm having a hard time remembering why. I give her a smile before bending down. Not willing to give Ember a chance to freak out again, I grab her hand and pull her to my side. She almost stumbles but keeps her hand in mine while standing next to my crouched form. Molly's eyes move from my face to our joined hands. Her mischievous expression gets a little wonky before she replaces it with a sickeningly sweet smile. Her little angelic act isn't fooling me, though; I know she's up to something.

"You have spit germs in your mouth now," she scolds. "You could be sick."

"I'm used to spit germs in my mouth."

"You had your hand on her booty. That's a no-touch place. Daddy said so."

"I can touch her booty."

"You might put a baby in her belly if you keep putting your tongue in her mouth, and Mommy said you have to be married to tongue touch spit germs and put babies in bellies. That's how I got my baby Jack. Daddy told me so."

"I think we're going to be okay, Molly-Wolly."

She tilts her head and studies my face. "I don't like that lipstick on you."

I look up at Ember at that, confused, and see her giggling. She points to her own dark pink lips before I realize what Molly means.

"My apologies, your highness. I vow to never wear another woman's lipstick other than the one you deem worthy of my complexion."

Molly giggles.

"Molly? Why don't you let Nate and Ember come in now?"

I look up and see Molly's mom, Megan, a few feet away. Behind her, I see my sister, Cohen, and Molly's dad, Lee, losing the fight to keep their laughter in.

Assholes.

"It's not that funny," I tell them after Megan had taken Molly away from the group.

"It's freaking hilarious," Dani wheezes through her laughter. "Oh, Nate, I sure hope you didn't tongue a baby into Ember." She doubles over, and I narrow my eyes at her.

"Danielle Cage."

She still doesn't stop.

"I mean maybe you could keep wearing that pretty lipstick and your 'tongue spit germ baby' can call you mommy too."

My jaw ticks.

"Mommy Nate," she snorts.

Cohen backs up with one look at me, knowing that if he sticks behind his wife, he's going to take a foot to the balls when I pick her bratty ass up. Ember lets my hand go, and I make a mental note to spank her ass later for laughing along with Dani. The second my shoulder goes into her stomach, she lets out one ungodly loud scream, but I just stomp through the entryway and into the kitchen before turning and depositing her on her feet right inside the living room. Her shoulders are turned first, and then I push her nose against the wall.

"Five minutes. Time-out, brat."

Turning from my sister, I see Ember standing behind me with her chest still moving in silent laughter.

"Keep laughing. You've earned my palm later, Emberlyn."

Her jaw drops at my growled words, and I take way too much satisfaction in seeing the blush that crawls up her chest. The minimal coverage of her sundress is not hiding how much she loves my words.

"Hey, you guys," Maddi calls, walking from the back porch into the kitchen. "Why is Dani in the corner?"

"Because she doesn't know how to keep her damn mouth shut," I respond, still looking at Ember as she licks her lips. I have to bite my tongue to keep my cock in line.

"Rightttt." Maddi laughs. "Well, I was sent to drag you outside before Molly had a chance to tell anyone other than Lyn and Lila that you two were in here making spit germ babies."

"Oh my God," Ember gasps in embarrassment. I, with no other option, throw my head back and laugh.

"Let's go," I tell her, taking her hand in mine and walking out the door.

We stand on the deck, overlooking the backyard, and I give her a reassuring squeeze. Her smile comes instantly, even if she still looks slightly self-conscious from her sister's comment.

"I love you," I express, offering her that reassurance to *us* if she needs it.

With a deep breath, her plump lips spread and she gives me one hell of a blinding smile. "I love you, too."

"Yeah, yeah … everyone loves each other. Jerk." Dani brushes past me with a shoulder bump meant to knock me off balance, but she stumbles against my unmoving body.

We walk down the steps, together, hand in hand.

Chelcie and Asher give us both a wave when we walk past them. Their boys, Zac and Jax, stop tossing the football around to call out a greeting before returning to their game.

Dani, now standing next to her husband and in-laws, is still glaring at me. I ignore her and give Cohen a lift of my chin.

"Hey, Melissa." I address his mom, bending down to kiss her cheek.

"Hey, honey." She grins at me before looking at Ember, her happiness spreading to her eyes, which squint slightly. She steps away from her husband and I'm forced to let Ember's hand go when Melissa wraps her in a hug.

Looking over at her husband, I give Greg the same lift of my chin that his son got.

"Give me a damn hug, boy."

I shake my head but give him the hug he demanded with a slap of my hand against his back.

"I'm sure her father already told you, but you make her cry and I'll kill you," he says before pulling away, giving me a stern smile to cover up the fact he just threatened my life. "Good to see you, Nate."

"Yeah, likewise, Greg." My chest moves with my silent laughter.

Ember pulls from Melissa, and I see a slight wobble to her chin. Melissa cups her cheek. "You wear love beautifully, honey." Her words are low, and I know she didn't mean for anyone to overhear them, so I just wait for Ember to step away before taking her hand back in mine.

When we turn, Beck and his wife, Dee, are right behind us. They give their hellos much like Greg and Melissa did. By the time we step away from them and walk to where Liam is standing, I've already had two men threaten to kill me if I hurt Ember.

I wouldn't have it any other way. If I somehow hurt her, I would welcome their anger.

Lyn, Lila, Stella, and Maddi are laughing with Megan and Molly. By the glances they keep sending my way, I'm sure there is still talk about spit babies by that girl.

"You sure do know how to make an entrance." Lee laughs. "Hey, Em." He gives her a hug.

"Yeah, seems so."

I look around and see Cohen's brothers have now joined the Cooper boys with the football; they're too wrapped up in their game, so I skirt my eyes around them to see my and Ember's parents standing by the grill looking at us. Both our moms have big smiles on their faces, and if I'm not mistaken, tears in their eyes.

"Well, aren't you looking handsome today?"

I look away from our parents and laugh at Sway.

"I always look handsome."

"Just as cocky as your father. Come wrap those big strong arms of yours around Sway and give me a proper hello."

I bend, giving him the hug he wants. "Hey, Davey," I tell his husband over his shoulder and wait for him to finally let go.

Finally, he does, but not before I get a kiss on my cheek. Ember is at my side laughing at his antics, and I would gladly let that man kiss me again if it means she's no longer feeling unsure about how we will be received today.

"I think we should probably go finish the rounds," I whisper in her ear after stepping away from Sway.

She looks up before following my eyes to our parents and gives me a nod. This time, she takes my hand before leading the way. You couldn't have stopped the grin that came over me at her claim of ownership. My mom passes my nephew, Owen, to my father before walking from their foursome and meeting us half-way. Instead of giving her baby boy a hug, though, she approaches Ember.

She places her hands on Ember's biceps and says, "Hey, sweetheart. You look beautiful." I clear my throat and raise my brow when she looks up at me. "What? Do you want me to tell you that you look beautiful too, son?"

"That would be lovely. Yes, you can tell me how beautiful I am."

She shakes her head and looks back at my girl. "I'm so happy for you two."

I don't need to look at Ember to know that her happiness does, in fact, make her look beautiful.

"Thanks, Izzy," she says softly. "You have no idea how much it means to hear you say that."

I give a mock gasp. "You mean you doubted my own mother thought her baby boy was beautiful?"

Ember pulls her hand from mine to give me a playful smack against my chest at the same time my mother does, and we all three laugh.

"Go on," she tells us before turning and calling Owen's name. He jumps from my dad's arms and starts rushing to his grandma. "Don't let those big men intimidate you," she warns before walking away.

"Let's go, baby."

We move until we're standing in front of them. My dad reaches out and hooks my shoulder before pulling me to his body. With just a few inches separating our height, his mouth turns to my ear. "Don't make me hurt my own boy by doing something stupid as fuck to his woman. Got it?"

"Yes, sir," I lament, shoving off him playfully and turning to Ember's dad.

He has his arms crossed over his chest and his face gives nothing away as to what he is thinking. It doesn't matter that he knows about us. It doesn't even matter that I have his blessing to be with his daughter. Right now, he's playing the part of a father that is, in a sense, letting go of the daughter he has loved and raised for twenty-one years and giving her to the man who will spend the rest of her life being the one to make sure no harm comes to her heart.

"Maddox." I nod.

"Nate." He doesn't move.

"Mind if I have a word?"

His nostrils flare; the only tell he gives me before nodding. I step back and watch him wrap his arms around Ember before giving both her and Emmy a kiss on their foreheads. Ember looks up at me, worried, but I just smile. Then enjoy the fuck out of the growl that I hear from her dad when I pull her into my arms and give her a deep kiss.

"Be right back, baby."

Chapter 33

Nate

WE WALK TO THE SIDE of my parents' house, out of view and earshot, and I turn to stand tall in front of her frowning father.

"I love her," I blurt without any lead-up.

I wait for him to speak, but he doesn't.

"You gave me your blessing once, but I need you to understand just what you were giving me when you did. I love your daughter with every fiber in my body. Her happiness is the only thing that matters to me. Her smile will never die again if I have anything to do with it. I promised myself that I would prove to her that I was worthy of her love, and even though her opinion is really the only one that matters, I'm asking you again to respect the love we share and let me have her."

"What exactly are you trying to say, Nate?"

I take a deep breath. "I don't want to spend another day with-

out her by my side. The same goes for her. I will be her sup-
porter in every aspect of her life personally and professionally.
No cheerleader in her corner will yell louder. I will make sure
she never doubts the love we share and her choice to give me a
chance. I would give my life for her, Maddox. One day soon, I
pray to God that I'm lucky enough to have you walking her down
the aisle. But most importantly, I want all of that to happen with
you not only giving me your blessing to make sure it does but with
you being happy that you did."

"If I told you I would cut your arm from your body if you
caused her a second of pain, what would you say?"

I stand a little straighter and keep my face as impassive as his.
"I would hand you the knife."

"If I told you that you didn't deserve her?"

"I would agree. She deserves the world, but she's just getting
me, and with me, she's going to get a man who works his ass off
to hand the world to her."

He continues his stare down when I finish speaking, and then
he gives me something that not once in my damn life have I been
on the receiving end of.

His smile.

"I always knew this day would come. Out of my two girls,
Ember was the one I always knew would use her head and find
a good man. Still, I thought I would hate the bastard. You're a
good kid, Nate. You always have been. I can't say I'm happy that
you're asking to take my girl from me, but I am happy that she's
found a man who will always make sure she comes first daily and
goes to sleep knowing that she's got a blessed life. The only thing

I've ever wanted for her."

My shoulders drop some when I let out the breath I had been holding.

"I'm going to marry her," I declare and raise my hand to stop him when he opens his mouth, smile gone. "Don't tell me I couldn't possibly know that after only having her love for just under two months. I just want you to know that this is where it's heading, and it's heading there real fast."

"I wasn't going to say that." I raise a brow and he gruffs out a chuckle. "Time is a fickle motherfucker, Nate. I had my own experience with it before I made Emmy mine, so if anyone gets you, it's me. I realized not too long ago that this—you and Ember—has been a long time coming. You had your reasons for pushing her away the first time, and I can respect the hell out of them, but now, you know what you've spent years missing out and you would be an idiot to waste a second more now. That being said, if you think I'm happy about my girl being under your roof without you taking the steps to make her yours completely, you might actually be a dumb shit."

I shake my head. "No, sir. She's an independent woman, but I hope that I can rectify this situation by the time her house is done. If I have it my way, her storage unit full of belongings will just be making one stop, and that's to my house."

"I've enjoyed watching you turn into the man standing in front of me, Nate. You have a good head on your shoulders and your heart's in the right place. You want my blessing, all the cards now on the table, well … you've got it."

Hearing those words from him and knowing that he means it

fills my chest with happiness. "So do we hug now?"

"Jesus Christ," he grumbles. "Seems like her sass is wearing the fuck off." He uncrosses his arms and tags the back of my neck, and shockingly, Maddox Locke gives me a hug. "Welcome to the family," he rumbles and lets go.

"Thank you," I tell him after pulling back. "Thank you for letting her go and trusting that I'm going to make sure you never regret that."

His throat moves, but he doesn't speak. With a look demanding I follow and a small smile on his face, he starts walking.

When we walk around the side of the house, I see Ember standing with our mothers and wringing her hands in front of her. The second she sees the looks on our faces, though, she drops her hands to her side and starts running. Maddox stops and I move to the side so she can go to him.

But to my utter shock, and everyone else watching, she passes him with a huge smile and leaps into my arms. I curl my arms around her back as her legs wrap tight around me and contentment like I've never known settles over me.

"I love you," she repeats over and over, not giving me a chance to say a word.

I look at her dad, expecting to see his fury, but instead, I once again find myself on the receiving end of his smile.

Chapter 34

Ember

"I'M SO EXCITED TO GO to Dirty with you!" I exclaim, pulling one of my black heels on and jumping off the bench in front of Nate's bed.

He takes a long sweep of my body, spending a little time on my dress, before looking back up at me, the hunger in his eyes shining brightly.

"You can't wear that."

I look down and try to see what about my simple black lace dress is so offensive, but I come up blank, so I look back up at him.

"You really can't wear that."

"Why?"

"Because if you wear that, the only thing that is going to get done tonight will be you, and as much as it pains me to say this, I really have to get some work done."

I toss my head back and laugh loudly. When I look back at him, he's licking his lips and staring at my legs. "You're crazy."

"Baby," he groans, adjusting himself. "You can wear that any other night, but please not tonight. If I can get all my shit done, that means I don't work all weekend and I have plans to lock you in this room and not leave for forty-eight long, sweaty hours."

"Oh."

"Yeah," he gulps. "Please change?"

"All right, honey." I walk over and stand on my toes to give him a kiss before walking to the closet and looking through what clothes I have here. I settle on a pair of leather leggings and a black halter-style top. Surely, he can't complain about every inch of skin except for the top of my back being covered.

Hobbling on one foot, I pull on the other black heel I had discarded to change and step back into the bedroom. He groans again, and I snap my head up to see what his problem is now.

"Now you look like a sexy dominatrix."

"You going to let me tie you up later?" I joke.

"Not a fucking chance, but if you want some rope play, I'll make sure you get it. Come on, we need to leave."

"Take Bam out, please!" I call after him. "I just need to finish my hair."

He calls out to Bam, and I walk into the bathroom, pulling my hair into a high ponytail as I go. I add a little dark shadow to my eyes to give them more of a smoky look to what had been subtle before when I was wearing the dress. These leather pants have always made me feel like a different person. One who wears her self-assurance. Before now, I had worn that confidence and faked the hell out of it, but now, I don't need to fake a thing. And I have Nate to thank for that. The way he looks at me added with the way he worships my body—all of that has turned me into a whole new person.

I love it.

He is unsure, on a good day, if he's going to let me leave the house because of it. Something about not sharing what's his.

Again, I love it.

Ever since what our families refer to as our 'coming out dinner' a month ago, we've grown even closer. We've even had both of our families over for dinner a few times. Once again, I was nervous about that, but each time, we all ended the evening with loud laughter filling the house.

The only thing that we've disagreed on lately is if I'll be returning to my house in two weeks when it's done. Nate seems to think my moving in permanently is a done deal, but I'm not so sure. I figure we would address it when it became a reality; until then, there was no sense in fighting about it.

That being said, a big part of me doesn't want to leave, and I have a feeling when it comes down to it, I won't be able to. Not when I've come to think of his house as *our* home.

"Ember!"

Rolling my eyes, I give my red lips a pucker and smile at my reflection.

The crowd is thick and the music is loud.

Like every other time I've been to Dirty, things are` a flurry of activity. Each of the dance floors is crammed with bodies, no room between them, as they move with the music. With the view I have from Nate's office, I'm able to see just how crazy everyone gets each time there is a bar dance from the bartenders. It's like watching ants move, but the second one of the guys jumps on the glossy wood, they all move as one to try and get a front-row spot.

Dirty Dog is a beast.

"Things are crazy, honey," I call over my shoulder to Nate.

We got here a few hours ago, and he's been at his desk pretty much the whole time. I've been content watching the madness below because I know he's not only catching up on some paperwork but making sure all the orders and inventory is squared away for the next week to ensure we have more time together at home.

"Hmm?"

Turning, I look over at him as his brow pulls in. He looks at some of the papers beside his computer before punching a few more keys. He looks so hot right now. The glasses that he put on before starting to look over the paperwork have had me hot for him since he started.

I'm tired of waiting.

He doesn't notice as I kick off my shoes and kneel. His desk, a sleek black design with no back, puts his legs in view when I drop to my hands and crawl under. His scent is strong down here, and it just bumps my desire for him higher.

I crouch, keeping my back bent so I don't bump my head, and reach out to place both hands on the inside of his thighs.

He jolts. "What the hell?"

"Sit back and let me give you something to help you relax."

"Fuck me."

He shifts, coming down a little more, but just enough for me to be able to undo his belt and pants. I take his velvety smooth cock in my hands, licking my lips when the tip juts out toward my mouth.

I take him deep in my mouth and smile around his flesh when I hear something slam on the desk above me. Because of my position, I can't do more than fist the base of his cock and swallow a few inches of him, but I work him with my hand and mouth until he's cursing and tensing.

"Come up here and let me fuck your pussy."

I ignore the command, hitting my head on the top of his desk when I pick up my speed. My saliva runs down his shaft until my fist is slick. When I graze him softly with my teeth, he lets out a groan as his legs straighten and I feel him clench his ass.

If I were in a better position, I would push my hand down my pants, but I know he would be pissed if I took my 'sweetness' from him. Instead, I just shift a little and enjoy the way my pants rub against my swollen clit.

Humming my pleasure, I speed up and grip him tighter.

He starts making rough sounds above the desk, and I know he's close. Pulling back, I kiss the tip and blow against the skin. He hisses loudly, causing me to smile.

"Suck my cock, Ember."

Not one to disobey—much—I do as I'm told and take him back in my mouth.

It doesn't take long before my jaw relaxes as I sense him close to the edge before I take him as deep as I can and use my throat muscles to constrict against his cock.

He shouts out my name and then bathes the back of my throat with his come. I pull back slightly when he keeps coming so I don't choke. I continue to slowly move my mouth up and down his shaft, waiting for the last twitch before licking the tip once more and pulling him from my mouth.

He doesn't move when I back up and crawl out from under his desk. When I stand, I look down at him and feel a rush of power from what I've done. He's slouched in his chair, his head resting against the back and his eyes closed.

I turn and walk to the bathroom in the corner to wash my hands and fix my hair and makeup before returning to his office, finding him standing and tucking his semi-hard cock back into his pants.

"Not that I'm complaining, but what was that for?" he questions, color still high on his cheeks.

"No reason. You looked tense, and I couldn't have that."

He laughs, the sound like a low rumble of thunder, and walks toward me. "Next time you're in deep concentration on one of your paintings, I'm going to have a lot of fucking fun returning the favor, baby."

I sway in his arms and lick my lips, his eyes following the movement of my tongue.

"I just have to get payroll submitted and then we're out of here. I'm going to fuck you hard all night."

"Promises, promises."

He kisses my forehead, and after another moment of searching my eyes, he walks back to the desk.

"Do you mind if I head down to get a drink at the bar?"

He pauses, half down in his seat before nodding. "Let me text Shane and have him send someone up to escort you. I don't want you fighting through that crowd on your own."

I nod. "Thanks, love."

He presses a few buttons on his phone, and I wait for someone, who is security I'm assuming, to come up. It takes almost ten minutes, but finally a mountain of a man enters the office after a brief knock. His black shirt says SECURITY in bold white letters.

"Sir?"

Nate looks up and frowns slightly. "Are you new?"

"Yes, sir," he replies, his tone dark.

"Joe, right?"

The huge man gives a grunt in response.

"Right, well, Joe, this is my girl, and she wants to head down for a drink. Make sure she gets to the bar without any trouble. Shane knows you're coming and is waiting for her at the main bar."

Another noise from Joe.

"Love you, honey," I call to Nate and walk over to the scary-as-hell Joe.

"Love you too, Ember."

Joe doesn't speak. He gives me about two seconds of attention, his ice-blue eyes sweeping my whole body in about a second, before turning to open the door. I step out with one last wave to Nate and wait for Joe to close the door and lead the way. If I know Nate, he's now standing behind that wall of black windows, watching our every move.

The crowd might have looked crazy from his office, but being down here and trying to move around takes it to a whole new level. I keep my eyes trained on Joe as he seems to part the sea of people with no effort at all. It's as if they sense the danger coming toward them and want to get as far away as possible.

We make it to the bar with no issue, and after a nod to Shane, Joe walks away and over to the entrance to the holding room. His back goes to the wall as his massive arms cross over his chest. Whoever hired him did one hell of a job on making sure they had not only the muscle but the fear factor as well.

"Hey, Ember," Shane yells over the music.

"Hey!"

"What can I make you?"

With a smile, hoping Nate is still watching, I point up to the sign where *my* drink is still written above the bar. Shane laughs, shakes his head, and turns to get everything he needs.

Once the flames stop, I take the drink down quickly, and this time, ask Shane to just make me something fruity. He gets busy and I turn around to survey the crowd. I smile when I take in everything around me. I still think it's a beast, but this beast is just proof of how successful my man is and I couldn't be more proud of him.

The music changes and my eyes widen when the dance floor I just walked around seems to come alive and not in a good way. Bodies start colliding, and it isn't long before I hear someone screams something about a fight. I look around, seeing Joe start stalking into the fury, but I lose him the second he enters the tangling bodies.

I was just about to turn around and ask Shane to get me back up to Nate when I feel someone bump my side. I jump when something pokes me in the ribs and turn to look up at the man next to me.

What I see has my heart seizing in raw fear.

He bends, making it look like he's about to call over a bartender. The shift digs whatever is at my side deeper until I cry out slightly. Then he turns his head and looks at me sinisterly.

"Get up and walk to that back hallway. Don't even think of doing shit to make anyone get curious."

My blood runs cold, and I risk a glance toward Nate's black wall of windows, hoping that he still has his eyes on me, but I feel a palm shove between my bare shoulders and the movement pulls my eyes away when I almost fall to the ground.

With each step I take toward the hallway, my panic starts to take over until I feel like I'm going to pass out from the fear alone. I know nothing good can come of this, but when one bruising hard hand wraps around my bicep, I fear there is nothing I can do but follow.

I stumble down the hallway as he drags me with him. He moves me around like a ragdoll, my arm aching from his hold, until he slams open the back door and the cool night air hits my tear-streaked face.

Then with a rough shove, he pushes me until I tumble to my knees with a cry of pain.

"Levi, you don't want to do this," I weep, my words hitching as my sobs grow. I fall on my ass when he takes a step toward me and I start to crab crawl backward.

"Wrong move, bitch."

He reaches down and pulls me off the pavement with a rough hold of his hand at my throat. I claw at his arm when the air to my lungs cuts off instantly, but I'm no match for him. Before I know what's happening, he's holding me up off the ground with just his hand squeezing tightly around my throat. Tears fall and I kick my legs frantically as I fight to take a breath.

He grunts when my legs connect with his body and throws me back with all his strength. My back scrapes roughly against the pavement and my head hits the unforgiving surface with teeth-rattling force. My vision goes black for a second, but I struggle until I can see him again, fighting against the dizziness.

"All you had to do was listen, Emberlyn. I gave you plenty of chances to come running back. You just kept ignoring them. Cleaning up my *presents* instead of being scared and calling *me* for help! You called him, though. Spread your whore legs for him without a second glance at ME!"

Oh, my God. All those things that I thought were just weird accidents. It had been Levi the whole time.

"I should have killed that fucking mutt of yours the night you used a headache as an excuse to go home. I still have his teeth marks on my ass from when I brought you back. I couldn't even fuck you because he took that away from me."

"Levi," I moan in pain when I try to move from the pavement. Not wanting to have him this close now that I see he's holding a knife in his hand. "You don't want to do this. Let's talk?"

"You're fucking wrong. I'm going to fuck you right here under his nose, and by the time he finds you, he's not going to want you. You're going to be used up, and if you're lucky, you might be alive."

"Please," I beg, holding my hands up when he stands above me and bends over my body. I keep fighting with the blurred darkness that is trying to suck me under, blinking rapidly as my head swims.

"You were supposed to run into my arms after I made sure your old ass house had some wires cross. That was my chance to come to save you!" His spit hits my face and mixes with the tears running down my cheeks. "I had just enough time to start that fucking shit and rush over to the station so I could be in the right place at the right fucking time, but you still didn't listen, and I'm done waiting. If I can't have you, bitch, no one can!"

His hand comes up, the one with the knife, and I sob louder knowing that this is how it's all going to end. I bring my hands and arms up to shield my face from the knife that is shining in the moonlight, and I pray.

"You mother*fucker*!" I hear roared. It takes me a second to realize that the blow I had been waiting for didn't come, and I try to blink back some of the darkness that had been edging in my vision.

But once I hear Nate, it's as if that was all my mind needed to give up, and with a rushed exhale of relief, I pass out.

Chapter 35

Nate

I STAND IN THE DARK HOSPITAL room and keep my eyes on Ember. I haven't looked away since the doctor assured me that she was going to be okay. Other than the handprint to her throat and the few scrapes and redness on her back, she has no outward signs of what happened earlier.

But the blow to her head left her with one hell of a concussion.

She's been sleeping peacefully under my watchful eyes for the last three hours, and all I've been able to do is pass the time by planning.

When I saw him leading her away from the bar, I rushed after her. The fight had kept me from getting through the club floor quickly, and all I could do was pray as the dread consumed me and I worried I wouldn't make it in time.

I can still feel the jolts shooting up my legs as I ran as fast as I fucking could through the crowd and then down the hallway. When I finally got to her, seeing that motherfucker she used to date standing over her with a knife, I saw red. I was ready to kill him with my bare hands.

But when he took off running, I had to pick between him and my sweet girl and *that* had been an easy pick.

And now, I'm left with the need for vengeance that rivals the hunger of a starved man. Now that I know she's going to be okay, all I've been able to do is plan for that vengeance and thank God she wasn't taken from me.

"Son? Why don't you go get something to eat?"

I don't look at my mom.

"Nate, we won't leave her side."

I blink at my father's tone but keep my eyes on Ember's face.

"Leave him be."

That voice gets my attention, and I look up to see Ember's father standing on the other side of her bed. Emmy's in Maddox's arms as she cries silently, but what I see in his eyes lets me breathe for the first time since I picked her up and rushed her to the hospital. Some of the fear made tension easing off my chest when I realize he isn't trying to get me to leave or to calm down. He's accepting my need for blood, and if anything, giving me his silent support. I give him a nod but look back at Ember.

Our sisters are sitting behind me on the bench by the window, but they've been silent since they arrived.

Meanwhile, I wait.

It isn't for another hour that I know it's time. My parents had stepped out to get me some food since I refused to leave, and Dani had left to call her husband and check on her kids.

I waited for the nurse to check her and give us a small nod. I heard her tell me that she still had stable vitals and was just sleeping. I stayed put with my eyes on her until the doctor came in to say that as long as everything was clear on her scans later, she would be released in the morning.

Then I made my move.

I stood, silently, and bent to kiss her slack lips. Without a word or a glance to the people around me, I started to stalk down the hallway. I had one thing on my mind, and I wasn't going to rest until I had retribution for every scrape and bump on her body.

I knew from the background check I had run on him after the fire that the sorry fuck only spent time in three places—the station, the gym, or his house—and seeing that it was three in the goddamn morning, I was going with the last option.

Lucky for me, his house butted up to a road so I parked my truck on the shoulder and moved through the woods separating me from my prey. I tagged his SUV in the driveway first. Walking around the side, I felt nothing but hatred as I moved to the back of his house. His back door was older, and with a solid kick at the knob, it gave and crashed open.

I hunted inside. My eyes searched through the darkness as I moved. When I rounded the corner, entering what looked like his living room, I found him jacking off. The porn was turned up so loud that it's no wonder the motherfucker didn't hear me enter.

"Get up!" I thunder and watch him jump.

The lube he had been about to squirt on his small ass dick came out with a rush when his startled movements made his fist tighten.

He moves to stand, getting hung up on the pants around his ankles, and I wait for him to stand completely, pulling his pants up roughly as he goes.

"I'm going to kill you," I fume through clenched teeth. When he doesn't move, I feel my rage spike even higher. "Can't hold your own against a man?"

"What the fuck are you doing in my house?" he screams, but I see the fear in his eyes, and I let it fuel me.

"I'm here to show you what it feels like when you mess with the wrong man's woman. I'm here to make sure that you feel the pain she did, but the difference is, I'm going to fucking kill you."

I stomp toward him, and he finally gets with the program and tries to rush me. But I have the power of a man set to avenge his love right now because as I crack my fist against his nose, he tries to fight back, but I keep pounding into him with an inhuman speed. Each blow to his body makes him stumble until I have him flat against the wall, holding him up for me as I use him as a punching bag for every second of panic, fear, and pain that Ember felt.

"Stop."

At the voice behind me, I halt and let this sorry fuck slide to the ground.

"Why are you here?" I ask, my chest heaving with exertion.

He ignores me. "You do my daughter no good if you end up in prison for murder. Get the fuck out of here, clean yourself up, and get back to her."

When I hesitate, he moves forward, and with a meaty hand to

my neck, he shoves me toward the back of the house.

"You got what you needed; now, get the fuck back to your girl before she wakes up needing the one person not there!"

With one last look at the passed out man on the floor, I give Maddox a nod and walk out of the house.

My first stop is my house. I let Bam out quickly before I rush to wipe the sweat and fear from my skin with a damp washcloth. I run to my closet and move some shit around before I grab what I need. I change my clothes quickly before rushing to the laundry room and throwing the ones I had on in the washer. After making sure Bam is back inside with a full bowl of water, I'm on my way out of the house with a squeal of my tires as I head back to the hospital.

No one says a word when I walk back into Ember's hospital room two hours after I had left. Not one mention of my new clothes or the fact that two knuckles are now split with dry blood. And not one damn word is said when I stop on the opposite side of the bed from my chair to take her hand in mine, slipping the diamond ring on her finger before placing a kiss on her hand and laying it gently back down.

Not one word.

I sit back in the chair I had left earlier, and with my eyes back on her sleeping face, I take my first deep breath of the night.

Nothing will ever take her from me.

Not one damn thing.

Chapter 36

Ember

"I'M OKAY," I TELL MY fussing mother as she pulls the covers up to my chin.

"Yes. You're okay, sweetheart." Her voice wobbles, and I just sigh, letting her fret if that's what she needs to assure herself that I'm okay.

"Emmy, leave her alone." I look over her bent head and smile at my dad.

"I'm not going to leave her alone. She's been through something traumatic and then had to sit there while the police questioned her as if she had done something wrong. She is not *okay*!"

I whine when her voice gets louder; the slight headache that I've felt since I woke up this morning had followed me all the way to where I am now in Nate's bed.

Dad walks over to the side of the bed, and I follow his movements. I lose his eyes when he bends to place a soft kiss on the top of my head.

"It's time to go, Emmy. Let Nate take over. He's what she needs now."

My heart flips at his words and the bigger meaning behind them, and I feel my chin quiver with emotion.

He's letting me go. Completely letting me go to give me to another man.

And … he's happy about it.

I watch in awe as he pulls my mom away and walks to where Nate is leaning against the doorframe with his arms over his chest. He pulls him in for a quick hug before letting go and looking into his eyes. The flipping in my heart starts to turn into summersaults as I watch something heavy move between them.

They leave with one last look over their shoulder, and I watch as Nate moves over to sit at my side.

"Are you going to cry?"

I blink a few times but don't answer. I'm sure, without a doubt, that if I were to open my mouth to speak, I *would* cry.

"Are you really okay?"

I clear my throat. "I am now. Thanks to you."

He looks down, holding my hand in his. "I've never felt the kind of fear that I did when I thought I was too late, Ember. Just the thought of spending one second without you is more pain than I care to ever feel."

"Nate, baby, I'm here. I'm *okay*."

"I can't, Ember. Not one second or any day. I can't be without you."

I can't see his face with his hair hanging like a curtain shielding him from me, but I don't miss the tear that falls down from his eyes to his lap.

"Get up, Nate."

I shift to the side and wait for him to stand. He doesn't argue with me; instead, he climbs to his feet and looks down at me. My heart clenches when I see the expression on his face. Eyes wet with unshed tears and full of fear as they look down at me. His strong chest is moving with the force of his harsh breathing. I see his hands shake before he clenches them into a tight, white-knuckled fist.

"Come."

I make sure my tone is hard and unbending, giving him no doubts that I mean what I'm telling him.

His fists release, and with shaky movements, he pulls his pants off and his shirt over his head. With just his black boxers on, he lifts the corner of the sheet and folds his tall body down next to me. I move to my side, facing him, and with the hand that is against the bed, I slide it up until I'm holding one of his. My other hand moves up his arm until I can curl it around his neck and focus on his face.

I stare into his eyes. "I'm not going anywhere."

His breath hitches.

"You saved me, Nate. You saved me long before last night when you showed me just how much your love completed me. I won't lie to you and brush last night under the rug. I was scared out of my mind, but I'm going to look at it as the last battle in our beautiful war. It's fought, now over, and we won. It's up to us how we move on and turn that beautiful war won into a beautiful love."

"God, Ember. I mean it, baby. Not one more day can I spend without you."

I smile, feeling the ring on my left finger move when my hand shifts against the mattress, and I know in an instant what it will take to get him to realize that no matter how horrible last night was, I'm still here and never leaving.

"So here's what we do. I apparently gained a fiancé last night, so he's going to sit with me as I plan a wedding. I'll have my dad put my house on the market and you make sure all my stuff stuck in storage is filling this house. I'm going to take over your man cave and you're going to turn Dirty into the biggest club the South has ever seen. Then, the way I see it, we spend the next ten years making babies or practicing to make babies. I'll let you know when I decide how we're going to spend the next fifty plus years after that. Is *that* enough to convince you that you won't have to spend another day without me?"

His eyes change and he looks at me with wonderment instead of sad trepidation.

"Is that all?" His voice is thick with emotion.

I shrug. "All for now."

"I think that's a great start, baby."

He pulls me into his arms, and with a deep breath from us both, we fall asleep knowing that as long as we're together, in each other's arms, we will feel the beauty of our beautiful war won.

I woke up the next morning feeling a lot better than I had the day before. My headache was gone and my back no longer hurt. The scrapes I had were small and the slight redness was the only thing left. My neck looked bad, the bruising something that I would have to face for days before it faded away, but at least I could move without pain.

True to my word, when we woke up this morning, I had my dad contact a realtor. He didn't question my decision, and I had a feeling that he was proud of the choice I had made.

I look down at the huge diamond on my hand and smile. Leave it to Nate to not even ask, but to slide the ring on and not mention it. He's crazy, but I love him for it.

"Hey, Nate," I call over to him. He turns, looking at me from the kitchen as I stay sitting on the couch, curled in the softest blanket I've ever felt. "Just in case our kids ask one day, I said yes."

He tips his head to the side and looks at me as if I'm the crazy one. I hold my hand up and enjoy the hell out of seeing his face get soft when he looks at the engagement ring on my hand.

"But just out of curiosity, were you even going to ask me?"

He pauses in his dinner preparations and leans both hands down on the island. "There was no doubt in my mind, Ember, so I figured asking was just a formality. I'm sure I could have thought of something romantic, spent an hour after trying to dry your tears when you were overcome with happiness, and then taken you home and fucked you until you passed out with nothing but bliss in your eyes. But I didn't want to see you cry any kind of tears, so I went with my gut and just took what's mine."

I laugh, the sound making him smile. "I love you, you crazy

man."

"I know; I'm easy to love."

"I wouldn't have cried for an hour," I add a few minutes later.

He looks up from his chopping with a face that tells me he knows I'm lying through my teeth, his eyes sparkling with mirth. "You're right, baby. It would have probably been more like two."

I open my mouth to respond but stop when the doorbell sounds, waving him off and standing from the couch.

My parents come in and greet me with a hug, followed by Nate's.

"How are you, honey?" Izzy asks after we move to sit around the kitchen table.

"I really am okay. It happened and it sucked, but I have to move on."

Nate gives me a hard look

"Have the police found that man yet?" I look over at my mom and shrug.

"They won't be bringing him in."

Everyone looks over at Axel after his comment, and I feel a little spark of worry.

"And why the hell not?" His wife gasps.

I look over at Nate, terrified for what this might mean, and wait for him to take the lead, but he isn't looking at me.

"He died last night. Lost control of his car and hit a tree head-on," Axel answers.

"Good riddance," my mom mumbles.

"I hope he suffered," Izzy adds, nodding at her.

"Oh, I'm sure he did since his engine caught fire. From what the ME says, he didn't die until after that." Axel finishes talking, and I can see from his face that he's happy that Levi didn't die instantly.

I move my attention to Nate. He's stopped his hands completely, hovering over the cutting board. I would have missed it had I not been looking at him, but he struggles slightly to keep his face blank before lifting one brow slowly. I follow his eyes and see my father looking at him with the same intensity. And then, to my utter confusion, he winks, causing Nate to let out a rushed breath. I snap my eyes back and see him nod with a small grin on his lips.

"Accidents happen," my dad grumbles under his breath, still looking at Nate. He turns his head and looks over at me. "He can rot six feet under now instead of in prison. Ember's safe from him, and that's all that matters."

What the hell was that? I look back at Nate, but he's not looking up. He's also not moving, just focusing on the vegetables he had been chopping with his chest moving with harsh deep breaths.

"Ember?"

Nate looks up when my mom calls my name, carefully masking his expression before giving me a look of pure adoration. Whatever just passed between him and my father is gone, and all I see now is that love he has for me shining brightly.

I shake off whatever I just witnessed. If he wants me to know, he'll tell me, but all I care about in this instant is that we really can move on from this moment and put it behind us. Move on and spend the rest of our lives with this being a tiny little black dot in our past.

"You know what? I'm starved." I stand from the table and walk over to him. He lifts one arm and I curl into his side. "What can I do to help, Nate?"

"I've got it," he answers in a deep rumble, looking down at me with a smile.

"I love you."

He swallows thickly. "Right back at you, baby."

Chapter 37

Ember

"DID MY DAD SAY ANYTHING to you about my call this morning?" I ask, thinking about the fleeting comment my dad made about needing to get my stuff moved over from storage since I had finally decided where I wanted to be. A weird comment from him, but one Nate took with a huge smile.

He pauses, his fingers stopping the soothing brushing of them through my hair. "Not exactly."

I turn my head in his lap, looking away from the episode of *Chopped* we had been watching, and smirk at him. "Oh, really? What does that mean?"

His eyes dance. "He just pointed out a few things."

He grunts when I shift and my head brushes against the bulge in his sweats, and he moves his arm away when I lift my body off the couch. I have to pause to pull the shirt I had changed into after our parents left down as it starts to ride up. His eyes follow my hands, and I just roll mine when he lets out a sound of complaint when my panties are covered up.

When I turn and climb into his lap, this time with my legs straddling his thick thighs, his muffled complaint turns into a noise of pleasure the second my lap settles against his.

"Let's try that again," I start, placing my hands on his shoulders as his hooded eyes darken. "What did my dad say to you about my call to him this morning?"

He shifts, his erection rubbing against me, and I have to fight back a moan.

"Nate?" I question when his attention strays to my now exposed again lace panties.

"Uh." He clears his throat. "He might have said something about a ring not making an honest woman out of you."

My jaw drops. "Focus, honey."

He snaps his eyes up and his full lips tip up slightly. "I might have said something about not giving a shit because you were where you belonged, honest woman or not, and that I would make sure to rectify that before I put babies in you."

"You didn't!" I tease.

"Like I said, that *might* have happened."

"You are a crazy man," I joke.

"Not a surprise, Ember." His lighthearted expression is full of unmasked happiness.

"I *am* surprised, however, that you didn't get your ass kicked for talking about *putting babies in me*."

He shrugs. "In all seriousness, he knows you're happy and

that I will do everything in my power to make sure you stay that way. He's a smart man, baby, and he knows where you belong."

"I guess I expected more of a show from him. He didn't even blink an eye when I called to tell him to get my house on the market because I was officially moving in."

Nate's shoulders shake. "Oh, trust me, the show happened. It just happened long before I put my ring on your finger."

"Want to explain *that*?"

"Not really. We had a few man-to-man chats. He's known where this was headed for a while now. Hell, I'm pretty sure he knew well before we did."

I study his face and think about his words. My dad has always been ten feet ahead of everything, so that's not far off the mark.

"Ember," Nate says, breaking through my thoughts, and I concentrate back on him. "He really is okay with it. All joking aside, he understands that it's time to let you go. You've been on your own since you graduated and have accomplished more success at your age than some people ever will. He knows that you have one hell of a good head on your shoulders and nothing you do will ever be without the knowledge that it's the right move for you."

"Don't make me cry," I warn, sniffing a few times.

"It's true. I've given him everything he needs to witness with his own eyes and hear with his own ears. He *knows* that we're ready to start living our lives together."

I drop my head, our foreheads touching, and breathe deeply through my nose.

"I'm still not going to waste any time making an honest woman out of you. Even with his acceptance of us—blessing given or not—I'm not going to risk him cutting off my dick for dragging my feet a second longer. We lost years, Ember, a fact I don't have to remind you of, and now, *this* is our time."

"If we have a shotgun wedding, people will think you knocked me up."

His eyes flare and I suck in a breath. "I do not really see how that would be a problem."

"Nate," I breathe. "It's way too soon for that kind of talk."

When our eyes connect, I almost gasp when I see the seriousness in his. "Ember, I'm almost thirty years old. I want a house full of kids with you, and I really don't want to have to wait to make that happen."

"We just got engaged, Nate. Besides that, we've been together for only a few months."

"If you need my last name before you let me put babies in here"—his big hands move from my hips to press lightly on my belly—"then that's going to happen sooner than later."

"You're stuck on this?"

He nods.

"Let's revisit this conversation in six months, okay?" I can tell that isn't what he wants to hear, so I rush to finish. "Give me six months, Nate. We have time to get settled in *our* home and with each other. I want to have that time to show you how much I love you this time."

His eyes flare. "Six months and not a day longer. You have that long to make my house our home and then I'm going to start doing my best to put babies in you."

"We'll see," I hum, kissing his lips softly before bending to rest my head on his shoulder.

His arms curl around me, the strength of him soaking into my skin. We stay like that for a while, him just holding me tightly.

When he pulls one arm up and his hand gently grips the back of my head, I feel him take a deep breath. "How are you with what we found out before dinner?"

I think about what he's asking and answer him honestly. "I'm okay, I think. A man lost his life, and as much as I hate to think it, let alone say it, he deserved the karma that he got. Would I have wished death on him for what he did? Probably not, but it happened and we both know he made his own path of destruction."

"Hmm." He doesn't say more, and I lift up to look at him, his hand falling from my head to rest back at my hips.

"You heard what I told the police at the hospital. The things he had done even before setting the fire proved he wasn't right in the head, but even if you and I hadn't gotten together, I would never have gone back to Levi." His expression turns hard when I bring up his name. "I know he knew that too. We weren't together long, but I feel like, had he not died, he wouldn't have given up, and I realize now that nothing I could have done differently would have changed things in his head."

"I'm not sorry that he died. I just wish I would have been the one to end his life."

I smile sadly. "Yeah, then he would have taken you away from me anyway."

"Never," he says heatedly.

"It could have been worse, Nate. I don't want to downplay

it, but I also don't want to give what he did any more power by continuing to let it affect me—us. His death means we get instant closure, and as we start this new chapter in our lives, we do it without anyone being able to taint it."

"God, you're one strong woman."

"Nate." I smile with a sigh. "Don't you see? When I'm with you, there isn't anything I can't overcome."

His eyes close at my words. When he opens them again, I feel a lump of emotion form in my throat. There is so much love hitting me from just that look alone.

"Promise me, Ember, that if you start to feel the darkness of what happened ever touch you, you'll tell me. I don't care how big or small those shadows might be; I want you to know that I'm here to shield you and protect you from anything."

He brushes a tear from my cheek and I nod. "I promise, honey."

When he pulls me forward, I brace myself with my palms to his chest and open my mouth to deepen our kiss the second our lips touch. He doesn't make any move to take things further than the intimacy of our kiss, but the second his tongue slides against mine, I know I need to feel all of him.

Breaking away from him with a small shove, both of our chests rising rapidly, I quickly pull the shirt up and over my head. The desperation I feel to be filled by him hits a fever pitch, and I shift my hips until I can place my feet on the ground to stand before him. I rip my panties down my legs at the same time he lifts off the back of the couch and silently pulls his shirt off. I rock on my feet while he pulls at the waistband of his sweatpants. The second his erection springs out, I pounce, not even giving him a chance to get his sweats past mid-thigh.

When I get back in his lap, his shaft hits my folds, and I moan deep in my chest. I thread my fingers into his hair and pull him to me as I restart our kiss. There is no slow speed for us right now. No need for a gentle buildup of seduction with our hands. We both need this, his hunger just as fierce as mine is.

I push off the couch with my knees, and he helps me with one hand at his cock. When I sink down on his length, we both cry out. My body welcomes his thickness with a tight hug as our lips feast on each other.

No words are needed. His normal control-fueled demands are silent. He lets my body set the pace only tightening his hold on my hips when my pleasure becomes too much to handle and I lose the ability to make love to him. He bottoms out with each thrust of his hips off the couch, hitting something so deep inside me that I swear I could pass out from the intensity of that alone.

This is so much more than just making love to each other. I've never imagined that our already powerful bond could grow, but as my body clamps around him with a hoarse cry from my lips, he thunders out his release as his heat fills me.

I know at that moment what we just shared was our souls colliding with the power of our love, solidifying our unbreakable and unshakable bond. A bond that guarantees we will only feel the beauty of it as long as we're together.

"I love you with everything I am, Ember."

"As do I, Nate. As do I."

Epilogue

Nate

Six months and sixteen days later

I CAN'T HAVE AN ERECTION AT the altar.

I can't have an erection at the altar.

I can't have an erection at the altar.

"I can't have an erection at the altar."

"Uh, I'm thinking you probably shouldn't think about having one at the altar, either."

I turn my head from where Ember will be walking at any second and give Cohen confused look. Shane, my other groomsman, is having a hard time holding in his laughter. Cohen, the bastard, laughs softly as he looks around the church, and shifts a little closer to me.

"You have been mumbling about not getting hard for the last five minutes. I figured you might want to shut up with all that before your bride-to-be makes her walk down the aisle or you'll be saying 'I'm hard' instead of 'I do.'"

"Fuck," I hiss.

"Yeah, probably shouldn't say that either."

Before I can think of a comeback, the soft music, which had been playing since I stepped out from some secret room on the side of the altar, changes.

"Get ready," Cohen whispers, straightening himself up.

I don't turn to look at him. Instead, I watch as Molly and Owen start walking down the aisle. Owen, giving no fucks whatsoever, starts some weird run waddle thing. Hell, I don't blame him. I don't even want to be wearing this damn monkey suit, so I can't imagine the little dude does either.

My mom, laughing softly, stands from her front-row seat and kneels at the end of the aisle. Owen runs right to her while laughing his ass off.

I look back at where Molly is still standing in the doorway to the sanctuary. Only this time, she looks annoyed that Owen doesn't know how to do his 'job.' Finally realizing that the attention is back on her, she wipes the snotty look off her face and her beautiful smile takes over. Never one to miss a moment to shine, she starts tossing the flower petals from her basket all fancy-like, almost falling on her ass because she's twirling with each toss. Hell, I'm shocked she didn't demand to wear the tiara she's been sporting since Ember showed her what her flower girl dress looked like.

She looks like a mini-bride. The white dress is puffed out around her with some shiny beads or something all over the top, straps, and skirt. But that smile alone is worth the ridiculous price Ember paid for that thing.

Molly's had a hard time adjusting to my and Ember's relationship. She's always loved Ember, but when she realized what Ember was to *me,* there was some weird jealousy for a while. Ember took it in stride, but I hated it. Molly might not be my blood niece, but I love her like she was. Luckily, she realized real quick that just because she isn't number one in my heart, she still has a big place.

It didn't hurt that I spent four hours letting her paint my face and nails with all that girly shit. And took her to the movies dressed like a goddamn princess.

"Nate! I look like a princess," she whisper-yells before standing next to Maddi and Dani on the other side of the little stage we're all on.

I give her a wink but look away the second I hear the music change again and the pastor asking everyone to stand.

I can't have an erection at the altar.

I can't have an erection at the altar.

I can't have an erection at the altar.

Then I see her.

The woman that, for almost a year, has shown me a love that almost brings me to my knees daily.

All previous thoughts disappear from my mind when I get my first good look at her. The skintight white dress fits her mouthwatering curves like a glove. The tiny straps at her shoulders look like they would snap with one tug by me.

Maybe with my teeth. I'll have to try that later.

The small flare that starts at her knees comes up slightly at the bottom when she takes her first step, and I can just see the tip of a sparkly shoe.

My eyes roam back up the white fabric, following the intricate lace design until I'm looking at her chest. She takes another step, and they bounce. I have to look away before I embarrass myself.

When I see her face, though, that's when I feel like my heart might stop. She's crying, and even though I know it's because she's over the moon happy right now, I hate seeing her tears. But it's the look of pure fucking love, for me, that has my heart restarting and thumping wildly in my chest. Each step she takes makes the rhythm crank up until I feel like I can't breathe.

I swat at my cheeks when I feel my own emotion trickling from my eyes. I have no shame in my tears, not one fucking ounce. I want the world to see what this woman does to me.

When she takes her next step, bringing her to my side, I have to swallow the huge lump in my throat. The pastor says something, I couldn't tell you what, and she continues to smile through her tears at me.

"Her mother and I do," I hear.

I lose her beautiful face when she turns, and for the first time since she walked through that doorway, I see her father. He kisses her temple and pulls her into a hug while looking over her shoulder at me. I'm not sure what I expected from him right now, but seeing his own eyes wet wasn't even in the realm of possibilities. Hell, I was still anticipating him coming down the aisle guns blazing and refusing to give her away.

Ember steps back and he straightens. Instead of turning to go sit next to his wife, he reaches his hand out. I close mine around his and almost fall on my face when he pulls me forward. His hand tightens as he pulls his other around me with a strong smack against my back.

Then his head turns slightly. "I couldn't be more proud that my girl found a man worthy of her. You're a great man, Nate. Enjoy this blessed life."

He steps away, and I watch his back until he sits next to Emmy. She hands him a tissue and he wipes at his eyes, eyes that I notice are now letting those tears fall freely.

I give him a nod and then … then I turn.

"Hey," she whispers.

My mouth twitches, and I whisper back, "You look hot."

Her eyes widen, and I notice my mistake instantly when I hear the pastor clear his throat into the mic. I just shrug, not ashamed at all because she does look hot.

With her hand in mine, not even hearing a damn thing that is said, I follow the cues and speak when I'm told. The whole time my heart grows a little bigger, filling my chest until I'm convinced it will burst.

"And I now pronounce you man and wife. Nate, you may kiss your bride."

She's in my arms before he finishes. I get an ear full of flowers when she wraps her arms around my neck, and I tighten my hold around her waist to bring her up off her feet.

And I kiss my wife deeply and thoroughly.

I would have kept kissing her, had I not gotten a nudge on

my back. I make a mental note to kill Cohen later, then place her gently back down on the ground. Her lipstick is slightly smudged, and when her free hand comes up to wipe at my lips, I'm sure I'm wearing some now too.

Her eyes dance, and she smiles up at me before crooking a finger at me.

She turns obviously wiser than I am when it comes to the damn mic and I feel her breath against my ear. "You said not a day over six months and I should have believed you … Daddy."

I can't move.

I'm not even sure I'm breathing.

Nope, I'm lightheaded, definitely not breathing.

"It's my pleasure to now introduce to you, Mr. and Mrs. Nathaniel Gregory Reid."

I hear the pastor talk, but fuck if I'm not dumbstruck.

Her giggles bring me back to my senses, and I have to choke back a sob as I stand to my full height to look down at her. She's smiling through her tears as she wipes my own away with her finger.

"Come on, husband."

"I didn't think I could ever love you more, but you proved me wrong, wife."

I turn, the tears still falling, and after her arm loops through the crook of my waiting elbow, we walk down the aisle. This isn't the first time I've felt the intoxicating power that loving her brings me, and it damn well won't be the last.

Epilogue Two

Nate

Eight Months and Seven Days Later

"**I**'M NEVER LETTING YOU *PUT a baby in me* again!*"

I bite my tongue when her hand clamps down on mine with the strength of ten men. Fucking hell, I think she might actually break my hand before she gives birth.

"Okay, firecracker. No more babies."

Hell, I would agree with her if she told me the sky was purple and the grass was black at this point. Anything to get her to stop looking at me like the devil has possessed her body.

Her eyes tear, and her face changes. Instead of anger, she looks like I just told her that all the puppies in the world are dead. "You don't want more babies with me?"

I look over at the doctor between her legs when he snickers, and I try to figure out how to answer that without pissing her off more. Her hand tightens as another contraction hits, and the doctor tells her to push. I welcome the pain of my crushing bones since they just saved me from potentially saying something to make her head start spinning.

"That's great, Ember. One more just like that."

"Good job, baby," I soothingly say. "Just a few more."

I hope.

Almost thirty minutes later, Ember is worn out and still pushing like a champ. I know everyone warned us that this takes time, but seeing her in so much pain is killing me.

"One more, Ember. One more strong push."

I tighten the hold I have on one of her legs. She takes a deep breath and lifts her back off the hospital bed, curling into her round stomach. Her face reddens and she clamps her eyes tight as she pushes with every ounce of strength she has left. I count like I was told to and push her sweat-dampened hair out of her face with my free hand.

She falls back the second a loud cry starts to fill the room. She looks up, a tired smile on her face, and I bend to kiss her lips.

"It's a girl!" the doctor announces and then places our baby on Ember's chest.

I blink a few times to clear the emotion out of my eyes and give her another kiss before looking down at our child.

For the second time in my life, I gave my heart away. When I looked down at the cone-headed, blood-and-white-goo-covered, scrunched-in-anger face … I fell head over heels in love with our daughter.

I'm not sure who was crying more by the time the nurses took her off Ember's chest to clean her up—Ember, me, or the baby. When I looked down, torn with staying at her side or going with the baby, Ember just reached out and gave me a shove.

One more kiss to my wife's lips, and I stumbled like I was drunk over to where the nurses were working on my still very angry daughter. I stood by, my heart in my chest, and watched them. I feel powerless as she continues to cry, getting more pissed as they wipe her skin, and I have to clench my fists so I don't knock them all to the ground and steal my child back.

Then, finally, I hear the words I've been waiting to hear since Ember told me she was pregnant.

"Would you like to hold your daughter?"

I nod, I think, and hold my arms up as she places her into the safety of her daddy's arms. Her cries stop almost instantly as I make my way over to Ember. I got one glance at the doctor still working between her legs, and I quickly covered my shock at what I saw coming out of my wife before Ember noticed.

"Hey, Mommy," I say softly to Ember, bending down to place the baby in her arms.

"Oh, Nate," she coos. "She's so beautiful."

I run my fingertip over her satiny-smooth cheek. "Yeah," I weakly respond.

"So tiny," she muses.

I pull my eyes from our daughter and look at Ember. She's smiling down at her with pure wonderment. Once again, my chest swells with love as I see my woman holding our girl. The two most important ladies in my world are right in front of me.

"Thank you, Emberlyn." My voice wavers and she stops kissing our baby to look up at me. "You've once again made me the happiest man in the world. Thank you for providing me this kind of love and for giving us the most beautiful little girl."

"Oh, honey."

I bend over the bedrail and give her a deep kiss. When I pull away, I bend to bring my lips to our daughter's forehead.

"Quinnly Grace," I softly mummer. "We're going to love you so much, baby. Mommy and Daddy are so happy you're here."

Epilogue Three

Ember

SIX MONTHS AND TWO WEEKS LATER

"WHY ARE YOU LOOKING AT me like that?" I drop my brush and turn to look where Nate is standing in the doorway of our bathroom.

"What way?"

I roll my eyes. "Like you're starving."

He pushes off the door jam and starts to stalk toward where I'm standing in front of the vanity. "Quinnie is sleeping," he rasps. "I miss your belly round with my baby, Em. My little queen is growing too fast and she told me she wants a sister." The gravelly tone to his voice is working its magic on my body even though I'm determined not to give in.

I hold the brush between us like a weapon. "Oh, she did, huh?"

He nods.

"Our daughter, the one who can only babble and drool, told you she wants a sister?"

He nods, his smile turning wicked.

"She's just now crawling, Nate. We agreed, two years between children."

He takes another step, frowning now.

"I'm going to give her what she wants."

"You mean what *you* want." I laugh, dropping the brush when he pulls me into his arms.

"I don't see a difference here."

His mouth drops to mine in one hell of a toe-curling kiss. I find my protests falling on deaf ears when he pulls my sundress over my head and cups my naked breasts; the feel of his hands on me never fails to render me incapable of speech.

"Are you going to give us what we want?" he whispers against my neck, trailing his tongue down to my shoulder to give me a light nip of his teeth.

"Usually, it's the woman with the ticking biological clock, you know?"

His soft chuckles tickle my skin. "You knew I wanted a house full of babies, Em. The way you look when you're pregnant, I can't even put it into words. Just knowing that you're growing our love in there unmans me. Straight to my knees, baby."

"Quinnly is so little, Nate," I weakly add, and judging by the ear-splitting grin on his face, he knows I'm going to give him what he wants.

"Just think about how close she will be to her sister."

I laugh. "You can't guarantee her a sister, you know?"

His handsome face brightens instantly. He looks down at my naked chest and bites his lip, the bright teeth peeking out for a brief second before he releases it. When he looks back up at me, the look of rapture in his eyes makes me gasp softly.

"Watch me," he rumbles against my mouth before literally sweeping me off my feet when they give out in a rush of desire.

When he pulls me from the bathroom and pushes me down on the mattress, I look up at him and lick my lips as he pulls his sweats down and yanks his shirt off, blindly tossing them in the corner.

Ever since Quinnly was born, we've been using condoms. I didn't want to go back on the pill while breastfeeding, regardless of how safe it was. Call me weird, but I wasn't willing to take a chance that she got traces of that when I nursed. I had started to wean her two weeks ago when she started to prefer the formula that we had to supplement when I got the flu. I was heartbroken, but I knew it was time.

Nate's been dropping hints ever since about starting to try for another child. Hints that I've been ignoring, but judging by the hungry look on his face as he looks down at me, he's going to do his best to make sure I'm pregnant by the end of tonight.

He leans down, placing his hands on my knees before slowly dragging them up. The slow seduction of his touch makes me squirm, eager to feel him against me. He rubs his nose against my lace covered pussy, and I almost die of need when I hear him moan as if the smell of me alone is the best thing he's ever smelled.

"Nate," I whine.

"Hush," he scolds, looking up with a smirk. "I'm enjoying my wife."

He spends the next painfully long five minutes doing just that. I know because I whine every time the clock turns over a new number, my oversensitive skin burning with every touch of his fingers, mouth, and tongue. Each nip of his teeth causes me to cry out against the palm he placed over my mouth when it became obvious I wasn't going to be able to quiet my screams of pleasure.

And we learned the hard way over the last six months, babies seem to sense when the worst possible time to wake up will be. Which is usually the second he pushes his thick erection inside me.

"Please," I beg, muffled against his hand.

He looks up from the nipple he had been teasing, and he must sense how high my need is for him because the next second, he's holding my legs up by the back of my knees and pushing into my body with one powerful thrust.

I whimper, rolling my lips together and biting down on the flesh to keep from screaming as he pounds into me with deep, rough, measured drives. Of course, when he pulls out, grabs my hips, and flips me over, I let out a loud yelp. That yelp turns into a scream of ecstasy when he slaps my ass while pushing back into me, even deeper than before.

His balls slap against my aching clit as he continues to push into me; swiveling his hips each time, he bottoms out and only lets go of my hips to smack my ass.

The painful smart of his palm mixing and mingling with the frenzied rush of pleasure he's creating every time he hits that spot deep inside my body becomes overwhelming in its power. My fingers hurt from the grip I have on our sheets, and I start rocking back to slam into his hips, welcoming each thrust he makes. We both let out grunts and cries as we climb the peak, ready to tumble over the edge of what promises to be one hell of a powerful climax.

"Fuck, your pussy is so tight, baby. I can feel you hugging and pulling me deeper. You want me to fuck you harder?"

I make, what I hope, is a sound of agreement. I know words aren't going to cut it, not when I feel like I'm about to burst into a million tiny pieces.

"Hold on," he rumbles, tightening his hold on my hips with his fingers digging into the soft skin as he starts to piston into my body rapidly.

"Yes! Oh God, yes!"

He grows impossibly hard inside me, and the second his hand lifts off my hips to give me another one of those smacks that I love, I detonate. When he feels my walls start to flutter, he pushes in deep and even through the haze of my orgasm, I feel the delicious hot rush of him emptying inside me.

Hours later, after a quick late-night bottle to Quinnly and one delicious coupling, I rest my head on his sweaty chest and sigh contently.

"You know, I think I'm going to enjoy this whole practicing for another baby thing."

He huffs. "No practicing, baby. My baby is already in there."

I roll my eyes and curl into him more. "Whatever."

His chest moves and the arm around me tightens. "Go to

sleep, mama."

He doesn't have to tell me twice.

Epilogue Four

Ember

FOUR YEARS, SEVEN MONTHS, AND TWO DAYS LATER

"QUINNIE, BABY, WHERE IS MOMMY'S make-up bag?"

She turns and looks at me over her shoulder with a face that is so much like her father's, it's almost like looking in the mirror, and shrugs. Her chestnut ringlets dance around her face with the motion.

"Right dare," Brooklynn, our four-year-old, says and points at her sister. Her sweet little lips turn into a sassy grin before she sticks her tongue out at her big sister.

"Brookie!" Quinnly shouts and finally turns so I can see what she was trying her hardest to hide.

My mouth falls open as I look at the mess she's created.

"I made a princess."

Kaylee, our two-year-old, gives a little clap and looks back and forth between her two sisters and me with the happiest of expressions on her face.

I have no idea how Quinnly managed to cover so much of her baby sister, but I'm fairly confident some splattering of various colors covers every bit of her. My makeup bag is wide open in front of her with just about every item that was inside of it spread in Kaylee's lap.

"I see, Quinnie."

She beams, looking quite proud of herself.

"Kaykay," I coo, bending to pick up my messy daughter. "Want to take a bubble bath before Daddy gets home? He's going to want his *princess* all clean so he can give you tons of kisses."

She lets out a loud squeal of joy at the mention of her father. The blond curls bounce around her. We still don't know how she ended up with those beautiful locks, but they make her already angelic face look like she has a halo on when the sun hits her head. Of course, that wouldn't be the case right now since different shades of red and pink currently streak through it.

"Quinnie, honey?"

She smiles up at me.

"Did you put lipstick in your sister's hair?"

She nods and that smile grows huge and wonky. One little dimple coming out in her left cheek.

"And why did you think you should put it there?" I laugh because really, what else can I do?

"Because Uncle Sway taught me how to do highs lights."

Ah. And that will teach me to let my sister bring her niece to work with her. I thought it would be fun since Quinnly loves to play in my makeup, something that started during one of the many tea parties her daddy and little Molly Beckett had with her.

"Okay, sweet girl. You did a wonderful job, but let's get this all cleaned up before Daddy gets home from work, okay?"

She nods, her smile still huge, and with the help of Brooklynn, they start cleaning up my makeup.

It takes me almost thirty minutes to get everything off Kaylee, and she loved every second of it. Her laughter never stopping. By the time I finish with her bath, I'm just as wet as she is.

Just when I'm pulling a new shirt over her head, I hear Nate arrive home. His thunder of a greeting to the girls is something that never fails to bring a smile to my face.

"Where is your mom and sister, my beautiful, enchanted fair maidens?"

"Right here, honey."

"Goldilocks!" he booms and holds his hands out to Kaylee, who of course gives a loud scream before diving from my arms to his when he steps in front of us. She curls into his chest and sticks her thumb in her mouth, looking up at him as if he hung the moon.

I understand how she feels. There is no greater feeling than being in his arms. Which is probably how I ended up with three children in five years. I wouldn't change a thing, even though I give him a hard time about it.

He pulls me into his side and places a kiss on my head. "I missed you."

I snort, looking up. "You've only been gone a few hours."

"Yeah, but the last thing I want to do on a Saturday is spend a few hours doing payroll at Dirty when all my girls are at home having fun without me."

"Yeah, you could have been here almost an hour ago to see your daughter turn this one into a makeup experiment."

He looks down at Kaylee and gives her a wet kiss on her cheek, making her little Tinker Bell giggles erupt. "I bet she looked beautiful."

"She looked something, that's for sure." I yawn, and he brings his attention back to me.

"You look tired." I narrow my eyes, and he holds up his hands. "I just meant; shit, never mind."

"I *am* tired, but only because I had the paintings Annabelle commissioned two months ago to finish. I'm lucky she's so under-standing. I just hope she continues to be that way."

He frowns in confusion. "I thought you didn't have anything else due after you finished this last painting? We have the Disney trip coming up this summer."

I turn when Brooklynn screams at her sister, telling them to stop running around the living room. Chuck, our one-year-old Lab, is chasing them and making just as much noise. It's at times like this that I find myself missing Bam more and more. His age caught up with him just after Brooklynn was born, and after watching him struggle for months, we made the painful decision to put him to sleep.

Chuck was Nate's idea, and even though I love having his crazy butt around, I still miss my beautiful beast.

"Ember?"

I look back up at Nate, forgetting what we had been talking

about, and give him a raised brow and secretive smirk.

"Why don't you let Kaylee play with her sisters without my makeup," I add in Quinnie's direction. "I need to show you something."

He still looks beyond confused, but with one more kiss, he places her on her feet where she joins her sisters and Chuck as they dance around the living room. I grab Nate's hand and pull him into the kitchen, giving us a moment of quiet so I can talk to him.

I walk around the island, using it as a shield between us and slide the little rectangular card toward him. He looks down, and I see it the second he registers what's written on the card.

"Oh, hell no!" He looks up, and I can see that he is about as far from happy as one could get. Not that I blame him.

"Now, listen to me, honey." He opens his mouth to complain, but I give him the same look that I give the girls when they're out of line. "We agreed you would take care of this. Our family is complete. It's time, big boy."

He places both his hands on the island and gives me a hard glare. "It is most certainly *not*! I'm not letting some jackass cut into my cock when I still have work to do with it."

I roll my eyes. "You're being unreasonable."

"Uh, no. I told you last week when you brought it up that I wasn't getting fixed. No fucking way. Not until I have my boy in your belly. You need to call and cancel this appointment." He picks up the card, and like the very presence of it offends him, he walks to the sink and shoves it down the disposal before turning the water on and flipping the switch. The whole time it's making its shredding noise, he looks at me as if he's won.

Oh, how wrong he is.

"Nate," I warn when he shuts everything off and stomps over to me. "Don't you dare."

He, of course, doesn't listen, and before I can get another word in edgewise, he has me over his shoulder—gently—as he walks into the madness where our girls are still laughing and playing. They stop instantly when we walk in, and I'm sure if I could see them, they would be standing there just waiting to see what crazy thing their daddy is doing now.

He places me on my feet, and I open my mouth to give him some attitude, but it comes out as a squeak when he spins me and I'm looking at the gray wall.

"Five minutes, Ember. Time-out for trying to keep my boy from me."

"Oh, Mommy is in trouble!" Quinnie laughs.

I hear Brooklynn snicker, but I just start to count as a huge, happy-as-hell smile pulls at my lips. I start counting out the minutes in my head, playing into Nate's craziness as I enjoy his grumbling behind me.

Over the years, with each birth of our children, achievement with the club, or with my artwork, our love has just continued to grow. We rarely fight, and when we do, it is usually always about when we will stop having children. I think, if Nate had his way, he would continue having them until I physically couldn't, but I knew it was time.

Especially now.

And since I love seeing him get all riled up, I figured this would be the funniest way to bring it up. And if everything goes as planned, I'm going to enjoy the benefits of provoking him later.

I hit the three-minute mark and turn my head to the side. I see the painting of *A Beautiful War* that Nate had bought all those years ago and my eyes mist. He made sure that was the focal point in our family room. Luckily, we have the space with our vaulted ceilings because it takes up the whole top half of that wall. I let my mind wander to the large photo canvas that is over our bed, my heart filling with love.

Nate surprised me a few weeks after our wedding with a canvas portrait I didn't even know was taken. It eerily looks just like the painting in our living room; only it's a picture of us on our wedding day.

The center being our hands, clasped together at our hips as we both look to the side and into each other's eyes. You can't see anything else but half our bodies as we hold hands and look at each other with so much love.

"Honey?" I call from my spot in the corner, having had enough, and I'm ready to knock my handsome husband down a few pegs.

"What?" he snaps.

I turn and look over at where he is petting Chuck with Kaylee hanging on his back.

"I don't need to cancel that appointment."

He stands and puts his hands on his hips. Kaylee giggles and I have to fight with my desire to look at the way his muscles always bulge when he does that.

"I don't need to cancel because I never made one. I picked

up an appointment card when I was leaving my gynecologist last week. She shares an office with the urologist."

"I'm not following." He looks so damn hot that I struggle not to rush into his arms and kiss him hungrily.

"The way I see it," I continue as if he hadn't spoken. "If you get your boy this time, we can make the appointment then. If not, we'll talk about you giving up on that boy and enjoying a house full of women."

His eyes widen, and he woodenly starts to walk over to me. Kaylee still laughing and squealing on his back as she continues to act like she's a monkey. When he's standing in front of me, he reaches out and I feel his knuckles brush against my belly before reaching up to take my face between his hands.

"My boy is in there?"

"Or girl, but yes." I smile through my tears. Even though this will be my fourth pregnancy, I'm still overcome with emotion when I think about how far we've come together as the proof of our love grows in my belly.

"God, I love you, woman."

I don't get a chance to tell him that I love him too because his mouth is instantly on mine. Our girls all start yelling and laughing at their parents as we kiss deeply, my tears mingling with his.

I sink into him and, not for the first time, I realize just how lucky I am to have the love of a man like Nate Reid. True to his word, he's never stopped making sure that he gave me the world. He thinks I give that to him, but standing there with his mouth on mine while our girls dance around happily, I know that will never be the case.

Eight months later, our world grew with even more love when our son, Elijah, was born and Nate got his boy.

The End

Thank Yous

To my family: Thank you for every ounce of support. I love you guys and your love for me keeps me going. You guys might be the only people that love me more than Felicia does. ☺

Felicia Lynn: HA, you thought there would be something here, didn't you? I dedicated the book to you – so you get nothing more! :P

To my amazing readers: I would be nothing without you all. Your support keeps me going every single step of the way.

To my amazing publicist, Danielle Sanchez: I'm so beyond lucky to have you in my life. Thank you for ALL that you have done and continue to do for me.

To the women behind making my books shine: Lauren Perry, Sommer Stein, Jenny Sims, Ellie McLove, and Stacey Blake – I would be lost without each and every one of you!

A special thanks to my beta reader and friend, Lara Feldstein. You've been with me through so many books and I can honestly say I value your opinion to the moon. You're incredible.

A special thank you to JM Walker. I love you, Jo-Anna. Thank you so much for all those 'pretties' and for loving my crew! You're the best.

Made in the USA
Middletown, DE
23 May 2016